TRUTH WARS

THE BATTLE
FOR THE HUMAN HEART

JOHN PASCAL

TRUTH WARS
September, 2018

ISBN: 13-978-0692177952
        10-0692177957
Copyright: John Pascal Books
Fourth edition

Bible quotations are from "The New International Version."
Copyright: 1984, Zondervan Corp.

ACKNOWLEDGEMENTS

The author expresses his gratitude to his proof readers and his
critique group in Temecula California hosted by Rebecca
Farnbach. Much inspiration, and factual information, was
derived from David Barton and his American Heritage Series.
The back cover painting is the creation of Doreen Terryberry.

This is a work of fiction and any resemblance to real persons
is coincidental. It is, however, based on real situations in the
university and the political scene, so parallels may seem
evident to the reader. One character, although brief, deserves
special mention. "Aimee West" was fired for essentially the
same charges as those leveled against the real Amy L. Wax,
but other events in the character's life are fictional. For real
world information, I refer the reader to Ms. Wax's opinion
letter in the Wall Street Journal: Friday, March 23, 2018. Also
of interest is the earlier report on her case in the same paper by
Heather Mac Donald.

A LIE TOLD OFTEN ENOUGH BECOMES THE TRUTH.

Vladimir Lenin, 1911

"Stand firm then with the belt of truth around your waist...
and take the sword of the Spirit which is the word of God.
Ep.6: 14-17

FORBIDDEN SPEECH

"This I gotta see, Lisa—a Christian conservative actually speaking at Berkard?"

"Yeah, they didn't schedule tests this time and you're going to listen from the front row, Emma." She slipped a lanyard over her friend's brown neck. "Presto, you're now a deputized reporter for the Berkard Capers."

"Fine, so long as I don't have to write anything. I don't even write home—hey, you using sunscreen? One hour in this sun and your freckles will be flashing like turn signals."

Lisa giggled. "No, but thanks for caring."

The Free Speech Rally was ready to begin on the lawn beside the wooded edge of a university campus. One might expect an outdoor wedding from the look of it. White folding chairs were arranged in rows facing a raised platform and a podium. Students and others walked in from an adjoining road on one side, and the campus on the other. Except for a few protest signs bobbing up and down, and one contingent wearing black, all seemed peaceful on this warm, spring Friday afternoon.

Emma plopped into a chair. "They're not gonna let her talk, you know. They'll shout her down like the last one."

"We'll see. Hayley's a TV personality. That should count for something."

"Counts for nothing. Ya think because I'm black I'd get a pass? One mention of God, or love of country and they'd chuck me in the can."

"Well, hang on for the ride." Lisa chuckled and took out her notepad. "Now hush. It's about to start."

The Chancellor strode to the podium dressed in a gray pin stripe suit and faced a crowd of three hundred students. He stood erect, his head held high, glancing occasionally at the faculty and guests seated behind him. He delivered a long speech extolling the tolerant virtues of Berkard University and concluded with these remarks:

"So as we move forward in this ever changing world, I appeal to those of you who will soon graduate. Let us work toward progress in global unity. Let us unite in a triumphant movement that discards the sexist, racist bigotries present in America since its founding." He paused and smiled, soaking in the scattered applause.

"When you leave Berkard University, I will count on you to persuade our legislators to forge a *new* constitution, one that will bring us into coexistence with the world community and put an end to sacrificing the rights of the many for the demands of the capitalistic few. It is my hope that you young people will live to see this country joining other nations and progressing boldly toward the collective good." Loud applause.

"But so that no one can accuse us of ignoring the right of stale voices from the past to be heard, we have invited Hayley Jones to be one of our speakers." Loud boos.

"Now, now, she'll only talk for ten minutes…" Boos. "But we *promise* a rebuttal afterward. Don't you want us to look fair and balanced on "The News Box?" He wagged his finger at a TV camera and the students laughed. "We only have our campus police on hand, so remember, you promised to be tolerant."

The chancellor gave no further introduction but returned to the seats behind him. Hayley came to the podium amid a crescendo of cat calls, boos and waving signs. She sported a pink and white dress and a defiant grin. "I love you too." She waved at the audience.

Hayley waited for the noise to subside a bit, but gave a nervous glance toward the people, garbed in black, who were slipping on masks and lining up along the surrounding trees with protest signs. They began to chant and wave signs that read: "No more hate" and "Fascist go home."

Hayley called out over the noise. "I'm guessing the News Box doesn't have many fans here, but you may want to see my show tonight. I just finished an interview with the Education Secretary. She has a new direction in mind for things like prosecuting sex abuse on campus." She glanced back at Stengel. His head was down and busy texting.

The chants became louder and those in black moved forward. "I planned to talk about free speech in college, but I think I'll use my ten minutes to talk about Thomas Jefferson instead. I had to walk around what's left of his statue on the ground over there. Your professors called him an atheist, but he said he was a follower of Jesus Christ and acted on his beliefs."

More Boos. She smiled broadly. "I'd like to show you that he and our Founders modeled America on God's laws and teachings."

Those in black continued to chant and move closer. "Racist, go home. Fascist, go home." A smattering of seated students joined in. "They called Jefferson a slave owner," she shouted. "True, but he was a champion of emancipation. He cried out to King George to end slavery because the king had made it illegal to set them free."

The protesters on one side moved forward and gathered on one side of the podium. Now they shouted, "Liar, liar, liar!"

Hayley looked on either each side of her for the police, but only two campus cops stood on either side of the platform.

She hollered, "If there's anyone out there who still loves America, raise your hand.

"Oh look, we have a few left." A tomato zinged past, crossing in front of her. "No thanks. I had lunch. Who among you knows the definition of fascism?"

No hands were raised. She threw up her arms, bouncing her blonde hair in the air. "Nobody? You're *shouting* it. Don't you think you should know that one?"

One tomato smashed against the podium with a thud, splashing her dress. "How about this? Who here knows that God still reigns?"

At this, the dark sea of protesters roared in anger, hurling fruit and stones, but only from one side. Obviously planned, the objects that missed sailed past the podium and fell on the grass beyond. The black-masked ones on the far side held back out of range, bouncing their signs and chanting.

Hayley dodged another tomato. "Can you guys please just listen for a minute? Jesus once said, 'He who has ears, let him hear.' Right now no one can hear."

She glanced at the Chancellor behind her. He was entranced with cloud formations. Those wearing the black began to chant, "No more hate. No more hate."

Suddenly a well aimed stone struck Hayley in the face. She cried out, "Oh, God," and retreated down the side steps toward the campus policemen.

Holding a bloody hand on her cheek, her expression pleaded with them for help. They answered her unspoken question with, "If we intervene, it may turn violent."

Hayley grasped an officer's sleeve. "Can't you call for backup?"

He pointed across the lawn to a car parked in the street with a man standing next to it. "Lady, your car's over there if you're going."

The black-robed mob began to spread out and were silent except for scattered laughter while she talked with the police. Hayley sprinted for the car, losing her pink pumps, but the attackers ran faster and surrounded her chanting, "No more fascism! No more hate!"

The "cluster of black" quickly contracted around Hayley. She was trapped. The students waved their own signs from their seats and chanted as well. The faculty stood up to watch. Only one man ran to the edge of the platform and shouted, "Stop! For the love of God, stop!"

The side lawn was covered with swirling black garments, shouted obscenities and flailing protest signs. Briefly, a whiff of blonde hair flew above the black, then it was gone. A woman's terrified scream broke through the din but was cut short. Silence.

Emma pounded on her cell phone, crying out, "Where are the police? My God, where are the *police*?"

Lisa stood up and shouted at the mob. "Hey, leave her alone!"

The mass of black robes became quiet. The red and black banners of communism and anarchy appeared above them, and they fled toward the street, flags flapping as they ran. Professor Dylan Coz and the two woman students were the only ones who rushed toward the scene as cars started up and the protesters roared away. All they could see was a pile of signs heaped on the lawn.

The campus police walked over as Dylan and the women began to furiously toss the signs aside. Beneath the pile, Hayley lay sprawled beside the bloody rock that had crushed her head. Emma screamed.

FRIDAY NIGHT TV NEWS

NEWS BOX, breaking report:

"Syndicated columnist and Box News contributor, Hayley Jones was killed today in a vicious stoning attack by members of Antifa staging a campaign they call 'Fascism No!'. We warn you, the scenes we are about to show are not for children.

Ms Jones was an invited speaker at a free speech rally at Berkard University and only uttered a few sentences before the increasingly bold Antifa organization ran toward her. They threw things at her including stones and knocked her down.

As you can see in this video, the attack was carried out with military precision while the campus police are seen standing to one side and taking no action. This next scene shows her body lying underneath their protest signs. Her face has been edited out for television.

We reported earlier that no outside police were requested at the rally since the University had received a pledge of non violence from the student body. Later we will have an anonymous interview with a campus policeman who told us that they were ordered to stand down. The city police were called after the incident but they have no suspect in custody at this time. Neither the police nor the university agreed to go on camera, citing the ongoing investigation.

We will postpone the airing of Hayley's interview with the Secretary of Education until tomorrow. Ms Jones leaves behind a husband and two children: a girl age twelve and a boy, age nine. She was our beloved colleague and everyone here at News Box is in mourning.

Stay tuned. After the break, we will bring you an interview with a former district attorney who will discuss the legal jeopardy of stand down orders."

RNN EVENING NEWS:

"A student protest at Berkard University turned violent this afternoon when the controversial right wing personality, Hayley Jones, shouted at students with speech they deemed hateful. Unfortunately, one threw a rock resulting in her demise. The student has not come forward and police are investigating. We go now to our reporter, Sam Watts, on campus with a comment from congresswoman Moxie Watver.

"Congresswoman, what is your take on this latest incident of cams violence?"

"Well, while I fully understand and sympathize with the cause of the protest, I will join the university in condemning violence even in response to the hateful speech and policies of this administration." She chuckles. "This one does look like David and Goliath, though, doesn't it?"

The camera view returns to the anchorman. "Ms Watver had to leave but promised more comments at a fundraising speech she will deliver tonight. Back to you.

"Thank you, Sam." It will be chilly tonight with clouds moving in. After the break, Julia will give you an update on our accurate five day weather forecast."

FRIDAY EVENING

Dylan Coz's wife was pruning bushes near the front door, expecting her husband to come home soon when his white Passat screeched to a halt in their driveway. She pocketed her shears after he slammed the car door and strode her way. His briefcase was under one arm, his face twisted in a frown.

"Dill, I heard." She opened her arms as he drew near. "It must have been awful."

His eyes narrowed to slits as they met hers. He walked past her. "Can't talk out here, Sally."

Sally followed him through the door. He dropped his case and turned to embrace her. Heaving sobs began from deep in his throat. "Oh, *God*, Sal. They just killed her with a *rock*. *Sob*. They were like a pack of animals on the hunt—we were animals too—only we were like *sheep*, just watching."

Sally stroked his hair while he spoke. "Come on in and sit. Tell me everything." She released him from the embrace. "I've made you some tea."

As Sally went into the kitchen, Dylan picked up his case and took a few slow steps to the center of the living room. He shook his fist in the air and hurled his briefcase at the couch. "Damn." It bounced back and landed on the floor scaring his basset hound who scooted away.

He plunked down on the sofa, head in hands, and cried out to his wife in the next room. "We did *nothing* Sal, nothing. Only two of us were yelling for them to stop--like these demons would even listen."

Sally rushed back from the kitchen holding a tea tray. "Here's a little comfort when you're ready." She put the service down on the coffee table, sat beside her husband and put her arm over his shoulder. "The news made it sound like an accident."

Dylan turned his rheumy eyes toward her and sniffed. She had a tissue at the ready and he blew his nose. "Accident, huh? You must have been watching RNN. The last time these thugs were at our university they were just chaotic and destructive. *This* time it was different. *This* was a planned assassination."

"Oh, Dill, how can you say that? Didn't the students just get carried away?"

"No way. They had two groups on either side of the podium and I doubt many of them were even students. One bunch threw rocks at her to drive her out into the open and the second group attacked her. Disgusting, cowardly. They all ran into nearby cars right after. Had to be planned."

"Well, gosh, what were they trying to accomplish?"

16

"You mean, what *have* they accomplished. This murder has shut down all open forums--all dialog. It's terrorism, Sal. No conservative or Christian speakers will be invited, much less allowed to speak."

"Ever?"

"Not until a secure environment with police protection is provided and there's no chance of that right now. I've talked with administration. They just want to retreat and avoid all such events, so whoever is behind Antifa has won." Dylan's face fell into his hands.

"Dill," her voice softened. "Did you actually *see* Mrs. Jones being killed?"

"All we could see were black uniforms swarming over her, but everyone heard her scream. I'll never get that out of my head, or--or seeing her smashed face."

"Ugh. Did you ever meet Ms Jones before?"

"I talked with her bef..." Dylan looked up at the ceiling and swallowed hard. "On the podium before she spoke, I was sitting next to her. We talked about her family mostly."

Sally put a cup in his hands. "Heard she had children."

"Two kids." He automatically sipped some tea. "She said she wanted to be back in time to see her daughter's first soccer practice."

"Oh, Dill, that's just *terrible*. You should take some time off."

"Way ahead of you, Honey."

His basset hound ventured back, placed his head on his thigh, and looked up with eyes that read, "What's the matter boss?"

Dylan rubbed behind his ears. "You're a good boy, Arthur. You did nothing wrong."

Turning back to his wife: "They gave me two weeks and covered my science and history classes."

"Oh, good. Should we go away somewhere?"

Dylan turned to his wife, held her shoulders and made eye contact. "Darling, if it's okay with you, I just want to be alone for a few days, maybe in our mountain cabin."

Sally reached for the hands on her shoulders and gave them a squeeze. She smiled a loving smile. "I understand. You take as long as you need, Sweetheart. Maybe this is a good time for you restart that Bible reading program. With the solitude up there, you could start to talk with God."

"Oh, Sal, that's something you do. I know God's out there; but if it makes you feel better, I promise to read and pray. How do you talk to someone you can't see, anyway?"

Sally took her hands away but gave his hair a tussle on the way. "That part is easy, Darling." Her eyes twinkled. "Just say hello, and expect an answer."

"Sure—look, Sal, are you really okay with my leaving for awhile?"

"Of course, and I understand. I think maybe I'll go on that Garden Tour Sunday afternoon. Besides, while you're there, I'll expect you to get to work and have the whole place all cleaned up and ready for our summer vacation."

Dylan gave a little chuckle. "Throw in some of that stew in the fridge and it's a deal."

They kissed.

SATURDAY

Lisa and Emma skirted around the men dismantling the stage used in yesterday's rally. She slipped her pale arm over her companion's shoulder. It bore an American flag tattoo floating in a sea of freckles. "You sure they're finished with the memorial?"

Emma returned a broad, gleaming, African-American smile. "Trust me, Miss Pigtails, they've been out here since dawn, and I saw that boy who likes you and some other guy come back before lunch."

"Good. I want to get this story out tomorrow."

"Shouldn't you have a camera? You might want to show a picture."

Lisa pulled a phone out of her jeans pocket. "Of course I will. This baby's got more pixels than your TV, but I want you in a shot too. You were the first to see that awful horror. I can't get it out of my mind—poor Hayley lying there--all that blood."

"Oh, God, yes." Emma grimaced and stuck out her tongue. "Yuck. I'll never get over this. Somebody has to pay."

Lisa glanced at the bag Emma was carrying. "When are you going to show me what's in there?"

"In a sec, but…" They looked into the ring of yellow barrier tape on the lawn ahead. "but I don't see anything in there."

Lisa took her arm off Emma's shoulder, gave it a tap, and pointed to one side. "There. It's on the edge of the clearing."

The small memorial stood in front of a wild, green bush on the edge of the woods. The students had erected a white, wooden cross bearing the stapled-on photo of Hayley Jones. Strings of flowers were draped over its cross bar. Behind it, they had placed one of the Antifa signs in the ground. It read, "No more hate."

Emma dropped to her knees and began to sob. Lisa began to gently rub the back of her neck, and cried out, "Oh God, this is just *awful.*"

Between sobs, Emma pulled out a pink pump from her bag and stood it up against the foot of the cross. Lisa stepped back and snapped her photos.

Emma, still kneeling by the cross, began to pray. "Oh, Lord, please forgive these people for their sins. Show us *Your* way to find peace in this land. Show us *Your* way to throw this hatred away." They both said, "Amen."

Lisa knelt down beside her. "Oh, God, Em." She began to cry too. "Do you think God will hear?"

Emma nodded and placed her hand on Lisa's shoulder. "Oh yes. He always hears, and He'll tell us where to find peace, too. Question is: will we listen?"

Visitors to the memorial early Sunday morning found the sign and the shoe missing. The cross was splashed with mud, the flowers trampled, and one cross beam hung broken.

However, by that afternoon, while the broken, muddy cross remained unrepaired; the memorial was surrounded with heaps of fresh flowers. Lisa came back and took another picture. The bush behind it was now in bloom. It bore pink, hibiscus-like flowers and had become beautiful.

SOLITUDE

Dylan's Passat "complained" about the deep potholes in the dirt road as it wound through the forest. The County had not yet done its yearly grading. He hung onto his phone through the bouncing.

"Hello, Sheriff? I wanted to call before I lose my signal. This is Mister Coz at 707 Lakeside. I'll be in my cabin for the next week."

"Certainly, Mister Coz. Good to know. We make the rounds there twice a day, but I think you'll have the lake to yourself."

"Fine by me. Just wanted you to know I'm not one of those squatters breaking in."

"Have a good time, Sir. I'll bet you'll catch the fish unawares."

"Hope so. I wouldn't want the tartar sauce to go to waste. Thanks, officer."

The fronts of the lake houses faced the perimeter road and all the back yards opened onto the mountain lake. Dylan found his place intact but there was one cracked window and numerous pine branches on the ground. *I just hope the electricity is still on.*

Squirrels and rabbits scattered as he pulled into his parking space and walked to the side of his cabin to turn on the electric main. Inside, it was musty and dusty, but he was glad to see the lights come on.

He unloaded his gear, put on clean sheets and sat on the edge of his bed feeling a melancholy numbness come over him. *Maybe this was a mistake. With nothing to distract me, all I'll do here is think about Hayley's dead body.*

When it was dark outside, Dylan took out one of the instant meals he had put in the freezer, but put it back when a wave of nausea hit him. He stepped out on the back porch and lifted up his hands to the starry sky.

"Okay, Lord, I'm here," he said out loud. "Help me with the anger I feel toward those murderers. Help me find the right next step for me in my life."

He didn't hear an answer but realized how exhausted he was with only a couple hours of sleep in two days. He took a few gulps of bottled water, flopped down on the bed and fell asleep.

At six in the morning, and unable to sleep any more, Dylan burst out of his mountain cabin still wearing yesterday's travel clothes. He strode to the edge of the lake in the day's early gray light and peered into the cool mist, gritting his teeth. Through the fog, the white wings of a barn owl swept above the water with noiseless strokes.

He threw his arms out and shouted into the dawn.

"God! Why did you let this happen! She was a righteous woman. Her family needs her—this nation needs her."

Tears of rage streaked his cheeks. Dylan sat down on the damp grass at the water's edge his breath coming in spasms. He stared at his jogging shoes, shook his head and whispered, "It's just not right—God, it's just not *right*."

"And, my colleagues actually said she had it coming," he remembered, *"One moment they said they deplored violence, the next day they're saying, 'Well, maybe her death will stop those liars.' Lies? Hayley was just a news anchor looking for the truth."*

Dylan sprang up, realizing his trousers were soaked. "Ahhh!" He took off, jogging on the public path that wound around the lake.

Partway around, he came to a small footbridge that spanned a brook. He paused there, gazed over the water, and screamed, "Why did they kill her? What kind of foul demon would do this? God, if you're really there, tell me *why*?"

Dylan stood there for awhile but only silence returned his call. He resumed his jog around the vacant lakeside cabins, trying to drain away his anger with exertion.

On the far side of the lake he came up upon a young man in knee high boots, standing in the shallows, casting out a fishing line. The fisherman had a dark beard, a plaid shirt and a floppy hat full of lures stuck in the sides.

Dylan jogged up to him and rested, hands on knees and panted, "Hey, I didn't think anyone else was here this early. Name's Dylan. Any luck?"

With that, the man reeled in his line, splashed out of the lake and held up two small trout from a basket that hung from his waist. "Two, so far." He handed them over. "Here, you take them. I'm angling for a big one I see nearby. Call me John."

"Hey, thanks, John. I'm here for a week or so. Maybe I'll try my luck fishing tomorrow, too. Is this a good spot?"

"Wherever the fish are is the perfect spot." John smiled but Dylan was startled by his penetrating eyes.

"Dylan, God doesn't stop murder because humans have dominion in this fallen world. He grieves beside you for this evil act."

"What?" Dylan's mouth fell open. "How did you...?"

"You were shouting pretty loudly, my friend."

Dylan's glance went skyward and he grinned. "Of course. Sorry—hope I didn't scare the fish."

"The one who killed her lives under a deception. So many do these days—worshiping man rather than his creator.

26

The evil one only succeeds when his deceptive accusations are believed by those he desires to control."

"You seem pretty wise for a young man. Are you a pastor?"

"I'm older than I look, Dylan."

"Then, maybe you have an idea about how we can fight these deceptions you're talking about. They're ruining our world."

John took a step forward, their faces now only inches apart. "I do. Every righteous person has a unique assignment." He placed his hand on Dylan's shoulder. "Yours will be to fight deception with truth and love. Despite the persecution you'll receive, your anger will be turned into joy."

"I—I—who *are* you?" Dylan took a few steps backward, suddenly feeling weak. "I better get going."

"It was nice to finally meet you." John held out his hand and touched his shoulder. "There, you'll feel stronger."

Confused, Dylan hastened away, but after a few strides, he stopped and turned back, another question on his mind. He searched the bank but John had disappeared.

He felt a tug on his hand and looked down at the two fish flapping on the line he held. At least they were real.

TV NEWS

BOX NEWS ALERT:

"This is Stephen Rogers, Box News, Washington. Tonight we welcome terrorism expert, Sebastian Karpinski, to our show. He is the author of the highly acclaimed book, 'New World Order.' Mister Karpinski, welcome. Let me start with your take on the 'Fascism-No!' organization. We have witnessed increased boldness from them recently, but Berkard last Friday was the first time their protests resulted in a death. They're really a terrorist organization. Don't you agree?"

"Absolutely right, Steve, but unlike many other terrorists, they are not sponsored by a country or religious ideology. The Antifa group began in Germany before World War Two promoting communism. They remained active in Europe, but now they're reorganized and funded by New York and European donors for their own political purposes."

"Really? And, who are they?"

He chuckles. "Well, Steve, I think you know the political party most friendly toward them, but I won't reveal the names of all the billionaires until my evidence goes from solid to incontrovertible."

"Sebastian, as a terror expert you've written a lot about Islamic terror. It puzzles me that these two groups don't even talk much about each other, much less fight."

"I assume they plan on dividing up the world later, but meanwhile they both work to destroy their common enemy."

"What's that? Democracy?"

"No, not really. While they will attack anyone who opposes them, of course, their mortal enemy is a Judeo-Christian based government with individual liberties run by the people themselves. They both wish to destroy those who worship the true God of Abraham, Isaac and Jacob. Christianity and truth are what terrorizes *them*."

"In other words, they're against everything America stands for, but with all due respect, I find it hard to believe that any political party would sponsor a rogue army like Antifa."

"The party benefits, but only their donors are directly involved. Far left radical ideology is gradually transforming the party and the media to their own liking. Basically their ultimate goal is to run a globalist, dictatorial government.

"I find it ironic--" Stephen shakes his head with a frown. "Antifas' ideology and methods are basically fascist, but they present themselves as *anti* fascist, altruistic socialists. Their favorite attack seems to be accusing others of what they are doing themselves."

"Exactly." He points at Sebastian. "Accuse them first even without evidence. Hughy Long, a Louisiana senator in the fifties, quipped that when fascism returns, it will be in the guise of *antifascism.* Socialism has always had such a good-sounding ring to it—like you must be cruel and selfish if you believe in anything else—and you're certainly a racist."

"Warm and fuzzy, right, Steve? I picture socialism as the ultimate psychedelic drug, its users floating on the sweet smelling vapors of pseudo altruism. In actual fact, these 'drug pushers' want a government that totally owns everything and them in charge of it all. The 'users' are seduced by an imagined utopia where most everything is free. I picture them hugging a big teddy bear with a red heart on it."

Steve snorts. "You're waxing poetic on us, but their methods aren't real cuddly."

"No. To put it simply, it comes down to a lust for power promoted to the human failing of greed."

"These so called drug pushers lie a lot, right?"

"No, not always, especially to their supporters."

"Really?" He gives Sebastian a stern glance. "Are you saying that you yourself believe in some of their message?"

"Oh, yes. I believe it when they say they intend to win by 'any means possible.' Their methods not only include this recent murder, but I predict we'll see personal attacks and intimidation directed at any and every opposing party or spokesperson, particularly if they have Christian affiliations."

"Sebastian, you're making this so called antifascist organization sound more like the Hitler youth corps."

"Their socialist message, really communism, is especially appealing to young people who are not taught truthful history. They're taught to think free market enterprise and America are evil ideas and socialism is a wonderful new concept. Instead, it's an old one that has failed every time. I've counted seventy countries in world history whose government has failed with a socialist type government."

"Wow." Stephen sits up straight. "So, it's not the cure for war and poverty?"

"They say so, don't they?" Sebastian shakes his head. "These elitists who want to rule the world try and sell the idea they're a 'Big Sugar Daddy' who will just keep writing out checks for everyone—a benevolent father—a Robin Hood who takes from the undeserving rich and gives it to the needy. They hold out free 'candy' but chains hang from their belts. Can you hear their violin music?"

"Are you implying that our youth are so gullible they're listening to some siren song?"

Sebastian laughs. "I think the Pied Piper played that same tune while he led the lemmings off the cliff."

THE CHANGE

Sally was upstairs when she heard her husband come in, whistling a tune and greeting their basset hound.

"Arthur!" he said. "I'm glad to see you too, you lazy old schumschkee."

She thumped down the stairs and giggled at Dylan who was kneeling down and playing kissy-face with Arthur on the floor.

She came up behind him. "Hey, big guy, miss me too?"

Her husband scrambled to his feet and gave her an embrace and a kiss. "Uh, huh. Maybe a little."

Sally pulled her head back and wiped her lips. "That was nice—a little dog slobbery, but nice. Thanks for the texts, but tell me first hand. How was life in the cabin?"

"Oh, wow. Kinda surprising, and wow."

"Wow?"

"Yeah. Let me get my grip in and get settled first."

That done, Dylan settled on the living room couch with the lemonade, chips and bean dip she brought in. Arthur became very attentive to this development. "You manage okay by yourself, Sal?"

Sally found a comfortable way to recline on the couch facing her husband. "Sure, let's see. Garden Tour on Sunday, then I went to Long Beach for a couple of days to visit Jim and Susan with our cute little grandson. I finished crocheting his baby cap for Christmas, by the way, but I discreetly left when my daughter in law began to grind her teeth."

Dylan chuckled. "Susie really does like you, though. So, no parties out with the girls--you know--watching the Chippendales do their thing?"

Sally laughed. "The party girls were in my Bible study group. That count for a party? Anyway, you're supposed to be telling me all about 'wow'."

Dylan put his drink down and made level eye contact. "First night, nothing interesting. I'll tell you about the 'wow' in a second, but I got a branch off the roof and you'll be glad to hear, I got the place all cleaned up."

"Oh, how's my garden?"

"I weeded that and threw some stones at the rabbits. I mostly paced around the lake shore, and I did do some Bible reading too. The lake community was deserted but beautiful— really peaceful. We should find a way to get back up there when it's off season."

"You mean that family of seven two cabins over weren't serenading you?

"Nope, and it didn't seem like the same place without their mother's screech-laugh."

Sally chuckled. "So, you didn't try praying?"

Dylan threw his head back and stared at the ceiling. "Sure I did. At first I cried out to God over the deserted lake asking Him how He could let this horrible thing happen, but it felt like I was talking to myself."

Dylan returned his gaze to Sally. "That first day and night I was skipping my microwave meals and feeling sorry for myself. I hollered out loud: 'God, if you're really there, just let me know, huh?' Boy, was I surprised when He answered."

Sally's eyes grew wide. "In words?"

"No, in person. I'm guessing an angel, maybe even Jesus himself."

Sally croaked: "*What?* That's more than a *wow*, Dill. White gown? Coming out of the sky?"

"Nope, just a fisherman in wading boots, but I could feel love and concern coming out of every pore. I could sense the authority he had with every word."

Sally jumped over to sit next to him and gave him a hug and a cheek kiss. "Yes, yes, and I love you too. Welcome to the disciples club. I'm sure it was Jesus. What did he say?"

"He said that it is *people* who do evil—people who don't know God's love."

"Right, Dill. He gave us dominion over the Earth and that leaves us free to choose between good and evil. Anything else?"

"He said something like, 'Speak only truth, son.' Right away I felt convicted of the lies I've been telling. He said that each of us is given a purpose on Earth—I guess he means a mission. Mine is to fight deception with truth and love."

"That's so cool. He's sending you out like an apostle, but--" His wife wrinkled her brow, puzzled. "What lies?"

"Yeah," Dylan blew out through his cheeks. "What I've been doing at the university is wrong. I haven't been confronting the world. I've been playing it safe and hiding the truth when I teach—following the narrative the university expects us to follow. God wants me to start telling my students how it *really* is, not give out someone else's propaganda even if it brings personal consequences."

Sally pulled back wide-eyed and cocked her head to one side. "And you'll stop doing what they tell you six months from now when you're tenured, right?"

Dylan shook his head. "That would have been the old me. Sally, what would you do if God spoke directly to you and told you to do something?"

She grinned. "Do it right away and not worry about consequences." She tossed her hands up. "Okay, I'm with you. I didn't anticipate this, but of *course* I'm with you, Darling."

He embraced her and they kissed. "I didn't expect this either, Sal, but I'm so at peace with it. I feel like there's a solid rock inside me. Thank you for understanding."

"Oh, no problem." Sally tousled his hair and chuckled. "But, it's a good thing our cabin is paid for. We may end up living there."

IMPOSSIBLE TRUTH

Tray in hand, Lisa searched the cafeteria, found who she was looking for, and zigzagged through the tables toward them. "Ah, there you two are."

Emma held up a finger at her while she spoke to her boyfriend. "Are you going to finish that chocolate cake?"

He slid it over to her with a grin. "C'est pour tu, mon amour."

Lisa placed her tray on the table opposite them and put her hands on her hips. "Sorry to disturb you lovebirds, but I need to talk to you about something."

Emma kept her eyes on him but gestured toward Lisa. "Wally, this is my friend Lisa Combes. Careful what you say to her 'cause it might show up in our newspaper." Glancing up, "And Lisa, this is Wally Kim, my genius, mostly Korean boyfriend."

Lisa shook his hand and sat down. "Mostly Korean or mostly genius?"

"Mostly Korean." His head slanted to one side. "You two are best friends. She didn't tell you about me?"

"I know a little about you: an IQ of one hundred ninety two, taking graduate courses in particle physics and auditing World Religions."

Wally leaned toward Emma. "You told her that?"

"No, only the genius part."

He leveled his gaze at Lisa who was munching hard on a hamburger. "So, you accessed the university's secure data file."

"We investigative reporters have our ways and never reveal our sources." She chuckled. "Hope you don't mind. One ninety two is pretty darn impressive."

"Could have been higher, but two of their questions were flawed. Anyway, how can we help you, Lisa?"

"Okay, here's the thing." She pushed her tray to the side and took out her phone. "There's a real mystery here. It's about the flowering shrub where Hayley's memorial was."

Emma said, "You mean the bush in the woods right behind it?"

"The memorial is all gone now. The Chancellor had the grounds keeper take it away."

Emma stuck out her tongue and grimaced. "Ah phooey. Nothing religious on Berkard grounds, right?"

"Probably. Might *offend* someone, you know, but the bush is still there."

Wally rested his chin on his hand. "What's so special about this rose bush, Lisa?"

"It's not an ordinary rose bush. I think it's a Rose of Sharon, and I'll explain why I need both Emma's Jesus freak mind and Wally's genius."

Lisa flipped through some pictures on her phone, and showed them one. "This is the first shot I took of the memorial. Notice the bush behind it is all green leaves." She flipped to the next one. "Now here is the defaced memorial, but with a blooming bush behind it."

Emma shrugged. "It's spring. So the blooms came out."

Wally took the phone, enlarged the photo with two fingers and squinted. "It's a different shrub."

"Right on, Mister 'one-ninety-two.' The first one has different leaves and no buds."

Wally handed the phone back. "The first plant is the common, wild 'coyote bush.' The second one is the pink variety of Rose of Sharon Althea. I assume you are puzzled by the fact that the twigs and leaves around the shrub show no sign of having been disturbed so no one dug up the old one. Possibly the trunks were grafted together."

Lisa giggled. "Oh, Wally, you are so *good*. I inspected the ground around the base up close. Not a mark on it, and no sign of the trunk being grafted on. How can that be?"

"That's easy, Lisa. It's not possible—at least not from any known human endeavor. You do have a fascinating mystery indeed."

Lisa turned to Emma with a grin. "So, now we turn to our biblical scholar."

Emma's eyes sparkled. "Oh, yes, I see now. Our Lord did this. Um, let's see. Some think this bush, which is rare in Israel and only seen in one valley, represents Jesus. Others like to think it represents His bride." She got up with a start. "Let's go check it out right now."

The three walked briskly toward the site. When they got close, Emma sprinted the rest of the way and stood staring at the bush, arms opened in prayer. Wally knelt in front of it and inspected the ground around the base. Lisa snapped a photo.

Wally stood up and stated flatly, "The soil here is untouched."

Lisa grinned. "So you would say it's a miracle, Wally?"

He gestured to Emma. "That's her department."

Emma didn't look at them. She was kneeling palms upraised. "Oh, dear Lord, thank you for this miraculous sign, and such a beautiful one, too. Hayley is with you, isn't she?

We pray we may never forget that You are always here with us, even when we suffer."

Lisa said. "You bet, and I'm the one who'll make sure the whole world knows."

Emma stood up quickly, tears streaming down her cheeks. "No, Lisa, you mustn't print a *word* of this."

"Don't kid me. This is the best story, like *ever*--the Berkard Miracle story, and my exclusive, too. Every paper in the world will want it."

"Lisa, don't you see? The atheists here at Berkard would only rip it out. For now at least, this story is just for believers." She glanced at her boyfriend. "And you keep the secret too, okay?"

Wally shrugged. "Hey, no problem. Talking about miracles would keep me out of graduate school." He put his arm around Emma's shoulders and handed her a tissue. "So if God did this, what do you think He's up to?"

"My opinion? I think this Rose of Sharon represents Hayley's faith in Christ. Jesus is the bridegroom. In that role he would naturally present His bride with flowers." Emma slapped her hand to her mouth and started to sob again. "This is just so beautiful, guys."

Lisa cupped one of the hibiscus-like blooms in her hand. "It's a really pretty flower, isn't it? I notice it's the same color as Hayley's dress." She looked at Emma and pursed her lips. "Would a lightning bolt kill me if I plucked one?"

Emma laughed, picked one herself and stuck it in Wally's shirt pocket. "Course not. Let's each wear one and watch our friends scratch their heads."

HIDING TRUTH

Congressman Bernard Luchow leaned back in his desk chair, took a final puff on his cigar and looked up at the man standing in front of him. "I can absolutely give you the building contract, Stanley. I only need to hang it on an education bill that has bipartisan support, but first, you need to hit me with your sweetener."

"Four hundred thousand and giving your speech credit for settling our union dispute."

Bernard puffed out his cheeks in thought and snuffed his cigar in an ash tray. "This project is worth thirty five million, Stanley. My tax exempt charity is planning to rebuild some homes in Haiti. Maybe half a mil would do it."

Stanley gazed out the window overlooking Oakland and the bay beyond. He chuckled. "Your charity mainly pays for speaker fees for your friends, fundraiser events, and money laundering."

The congressman slowly lifted his head, pursed his lips and gave his chest a pound. "I 'represent' that." He chuckled.

"Okay, Stanley, I could throw in the access road from the school to Interstate Four—no extra charge."

"And, what building held by your charity do we have to buy at such an exorbitant price?"

"The Steelcase warehouse complex, or the Miller Condominium. Your choice."

"Deal. We'll be watching on C-Span. Hope you…"

A buzzer went off and Luchow's secretary spoke from the desk speaker. "Sorry to disturb you, Sir, but Chancellor Stengel is on the line again. He says he *really* has to talk with you."

"Tell him to hold another minute." Bernard turned to the contractor. "I guess we're done for now?"

Stanley nodded and slipped out.

Bernard's gaze turned to an attractive young woman sitting in the corner of his office, punching her tablet. "Monica, have you been learning how deals are made?"

She looked up and grimaced. "Yeah, but is that *legal*?"

"Of course, but if I need to, I'll find a judge who'll make it so."

She shook her head and giggled. "Wow."

"Look, my Dear, this call I have to take is private. How about your doing some real 'interny' stuff like asking Scotty to review the voting demographics?"

44

Monica got up with a slump face. "Okay, but that's real boring, you know."

"Sure, but I'll make it up to you." He stood up with a sly smile. "I'll start by meeting you in the downstairs lounge at noon. We'll do lunch."

Monica's look became quizzical. "And that's a start? A start of what?"

"Well," his eyebrows went up. "We can talk about a congressional trip with a stopover in Bali two months from now."

"Oh, goodie. That's *real?*"

"Absolutely."

Monica returned a big smile. "Later," she said, and opening the door, she blew him a kiss on the way out.

Bernard sat on the edge of his chair and punched line two. "Is this Chancellor Stengel?"

"*Yah, look Bernie, we have a big problem here.*"

"First, Henry, are you on the special line we installed?"

"*I am. Look, no one said anything about a killing.*"

"That decision was made in the field. I didn't know beforehand, but most of the media and the investigation are all covered. You have nothing to worry about."

"*Bernie, you don't control all the media and we have student journalists trying to be heroes.*"

"Aw, I know you can control the on campus situation. This sort of thing dies down and gets forgotten in a week without media coverage. Besides, there's an extra benefit from her extinction. No other Christian conservatives will ever bother you about speaking."

"The News Box is hounding me for an interview and the local police are investigating—I mean really investigating."

"D__m Box. Henry, I understand your upset, but you know the drill: no comment due to an ongoing investigation. The local police are a bit more delicate, but give me a few days. I'll handle it."

"I'm not giving any interviews and, so far, the police haven't asked for a deposition."

"Look, the media will follow any story we give them like a dog after a squirrel. This morning, a black man was shot by police during a robbery in Francisco. We're planning a big anti-police demonstration. That's their squirrel and the other story dies."

"So, I'm going to be on tranquilizers for awhile, right? If it gets out that I helped Antifa, I'll send you a postcard from Belize."

"You worry too much, Henry. Here's something to make you feel better. The bill with Berkard's perimeter road and outdoor theater got out of committee today."

EARLY TRUTH

Dylan smiled and nodded as his students filed in and flopped down on the curve-around writing chairs of the lecture room. When it seemed to him everyone had arrived, he got up and walked to the front of his desk. "Hello, everyone and welcome to the summer session course on Early American history."

He gestured to one woman who was seated in the far back of the room. "Let's all move up front. It looks like we are only going to be a dozen or so in this class, so we'll form a half circle up here. It's summer and the air conditioner doesn't work very well, so we'll be informal and on a first name basis."

The woman who had been called forward carried two notebooks. She sported a grin and two outward-flying pigtails. Dylan pointed at her. "I know you from somewhere."

She grimaced. "Lisa Combes, reporter for the Berkard Capers. I interviewed you about the Hayley Jones murder."

"Oh, right. Ghastly thing, but the general papers never called it a murder."

"You did. So did I, and I'm still trying to find out about the police investigation."

"Well, I hope they nail that creep, Lisa." He swept his glance around at the students. "Okay, folks, my first question for you is how many had American History in high school?"

Three hands went up. "In my opinion, every hand should have been up. In this course we will cover early history through the Civil War. You should have your basic text already, and the books on the reference list are in the library.

"Here's my second question. When did someone from the Western world first come face to face with an American Indian?"

Dylan pointed at the raised hands. "Columbus," said one. "That Americus guy," said another.

"The answer is not certain, but probably some fishermen in what is now known as Holland in 60 BC. Cornelius Nepos, a Roman historian, described an event in which two men in a small boat landed there half dead. They spoke no European language but still were able to explain they had been carried by a great storm over the "Atl," an American Indian word for water.

"The men were described as Asian looking with darker skin, but no one knew where they had come from. Perhaps, in truth, the Indians discovered Europe first.

"Next question. How long ago did the first European set foot on the North American continent?"

Lisa's hand went up half way and Dylan gave her an expectant look over his glasses. She said, "I know Columbus only landed in the Bahamas and Jamaica. Does that count?"

"Even if it did, it would have been way late."

Lisa's eyes popped open. "Ooh, ooh. I remember. It was those Vikings, right?"

"Very good. They made several voyages around one thousand AD, but we all know this continent was already full of people. Next question: Where and when did *they* come?"

A dark hand went up and Dylan nodded toward him. "Just so you know, I'm part Choctaw. I'm told my ancestors migrated here twelve thousand years ago from northern Asia."

"Yes, well established truth. However, there is anthropological evidence of earlier migrations, including Caucasians, possibly related to the Ainu of today. This is a fascinating subject, but without written history, one that may only be solved by anthropology. For our purposes, it is important to know that when the Europeans came here they found a wide variety of cultures and over two hundred languages."

A woman with straight brown hair and lowered eyebrows was recognized. "I'm Susan. But who do *you* think was first, Mister Coz?"

He grinned. "I don't know. In searching for the truth, opinion doesn't matter, but when there is factual evidence, one may come up with a theory, or at least, a more informed opinion."

She grinned back. "Okay, can you give us one of those things."

Dylan looked at the ceiling for a moment. "All right, an *opinion*. The American Indians don't look Caucasian, Black or Chinese. They are closest to the Polynesians and that's why Columbus first thought he was in the Indies. My guess is that since there were several migrations they all inter married."

"But, but…"

"We're out of time. This Thursday we will talk about the early colonies and your assignment is to read pages six to eighteen in our text. I promise to add in some truth you won't find there."

DISCOVERING TRUTH

Police detective Ryan strode over to his friend Matthew's desk, papers in hand, excitement on his breath. "Matt, look. I've had a breakthrough on the Berkard case."

"What?" He scowled. "You're supposed to be on the Albertson robbery. Sean, you *know* that case will be closed next Monday."

"And that's weird, too, isn't it. Ever had a closure date a week ahead?"

Matt pursed his lips and shook his head. "Nooo. It's closed right *now*—accidental death. It's just a little too soon for the announcement. Look, is this about those text messages on Chancellor Stengel's phone?"

"It wasn't, but they're more significant now. Remember, the Chancellor left his phone on the podium in the excitement and a student on cleanup duty found it. He saw Stengel's message, "Start the melody?" and the response: "Strike up the band.""

"And you, of course, think it's a secret code, huh?"

"Well," Sean grinned, "The response came from a phone belonging to Reinhardt Corporation, and there was no music at the rally."

"Reinhardt is a big contributor to the university and, I'm sure, to the music department."

"Hold that thought. The video showed nine new black SUVs escaping the scene with the Antifa perps. I checked the local rental agencies. Three of them each rented three cars like those. Can you guess the renter?"

"Reinhardt, right? Okay, that sounds suspicious, but if that's all you got, detective, the DA won't be impressed."

Sean sat in the interrogation chair beside Matt's desk. He sighed and turned around the picture of Matt's family to look at it. "You ever look at the murder rock?"

"Just pictures, and only the victim's blood was on it. Drop the 'murder' word, Sean. I'm your friend and I got your back. You must know that both the chief and the mayor want this to go away."

Sean turned the photo around to face his friend. "You know, you wife looks a lot like Mrs. Jones."

"Stop it, Sean."

"That rock was twelve pounds and was selected to have a hand hold."

"Okay, that's it. You're getting obsessed."

Matthew was startled by the hard stare facing him. Sean spoke in a level, even tone.

"Promise me this is just between us, okay?"

"Sure. What gives?"

"This morning we found positive DNA matches from under Hayley's finger nails."

"What?" Matthew's hand slapped the desk. "You're *serious*?"

"Like a heart attack, buddy. Scott Hutchins did the detective work. There's DNA from two men and a woman. Two are yet to be identified, but we nailed one guy. He's being brought in for questioning this afternoon. Want to join me?"

"No, send me a tape, but what did you tell our pick up officers?"

Sean grinned. "Why, that he's a witness to the Albertson robbery, of course."

ALTERED TRUTH

Lisa found the door ajar and Professor Edward Stark writing on his desk. He rolled his eyes up at her through large round glasses. "Get the door, will you, and have a seat."

She complied and sat stiffly upright in the chair opposite his desk. "Yes, Sir, you asked to see me?"

Stark gestured with two fingers at a glass jar on his desk. "Jellybean?"

"No thank you."

He held up two sheets of paper and read, "Lisa Combes, A+ in my sophomore English class, and the other one is an A in the Journalism elective." He grinned at her. "Now you are the editor of our school paper. You deserved it and I recommended you."

"Thank you, Sir, and you have been our faculty advisor all year. Is this about my op-ed? Uh, were you the one who cancelled my article on the murder?"

Stark took a deep breath. Showing no emotion, he studied Lisa's inquisitive face. "I particularly liked two of the articles you submitted in your *sophomore* year. Do you remember the ones on environmental protection, and more funds for urban grade school education?"

"Yes, Sir. Of course."

"Still passionate about those ideas?"

"Oh, yes. I feel it is my mission to bring out the *truth*, and I'm going to submit an update on that last one. Sixty five percent of our eighth graders are below reading level, and one in five who graduate high school are functionally illiterate. Can you believe that? More money hasn't helped, but alternative schools are doing so much better and the reasons should lead us to chan..."

"Hold it." A wry smile began to form on Stark's lips but it never quite got there. His head twitched twice in sort of a nod. "Truth," he rasped.

"Right. I mean, what's a newspaper for, anyway?"

"We didn't cancel the story about the fatality at the rally, just postponed it. Don't call it a murder unless it is proven. You can run a story on the *incident* next week, but no picture of that cross and I'll have to check it first. Understood?"

"Yes, I guess. I could just say there's a homicide investigation, but why not run the story when it's current?"

"Students would be frightened if you called it a murder. It's unproven, and many would be offended by the display of a religious symbol on public property."

"But Sir, I'm not comfortable with just telling a part truth. Isn't it obvious there was a murder?"

"No." His palm slapped the desk. "Check with the police for what *they* are calling it. If you're looking for truth, I think you'll find that there is no homicide investigation."

"Really? There was no announcement."

"Really." A brief smile flickered over his lips then faded. "There's another thing. Two months ago you began a column called 'Church Corner.' We feel that has to be changed. Only Christians gather at a church so it is offensive to others. Perhaps call it 'Interfaith Corner.'"

"No problem there, Sir, but the column is just about giving students a chance to tell others where they worship and why."

"We know of a student who would like to explain why Islam is the only true religion. He feels persecuted and intimidated by your title."

"So, I'll change the title. In the interest of fairness, I'll run a companion article explaining why Christianity is the only true faith."

"No, you won't," he snapped. "Column's for persecuted minority faiths or non faiths."

"Really? We never thought of that. Persecuted minority, huh. Well..." Lisa gave him a doe-eyed grin. "Judaism, then?"

"Ms Combes, I'm making your editor position a shared one. Aboud Ali will be joining your staff as co-editor."

Lisa jumped to her feet. "What! *Aboud*? He's just the most leftist radical on campus. Don't you remember him leading a march in town, hurling obscenities at Christians and running off students protesting at the abortion clinic?"

Stark looked at Lisa as though she were a little child who didn't understand. "Ms. Combes, we all know that every voice must be heard."

She stamped her foot. "All voices. Right. Just not Christian ones?"

"I think we're done here—any *other* questions?"

"Yeah. We 'all know', huh—I got it."

REVEALING TRUTH

Dylan pulled up a chair in the center of the half circle of students. "All right class, you should have read through chapter three. Has anyone looked through any of the five supplemental books?" No hands were raised. "My instructors manual said not to assign more than five so that's why I pulled The Communist Manifesto and replaced it with the Bible."

Tittering and shaking heads went around the circle. Lisa's hand went up. "Sir, there isn't a copy of that in our library."

Dylan grinned. "Not true, but I'm glad you looked. Their copy is in the sealed historical books section. You can sign in and read it inside that room."

One student tossed his hand up. "Sir, no one goes in there."

"You're right." He grinned. "So I thought I would donate a dozen free copies." He looked at Lisa. "Perhaps we could stash them in your office at the school paper?"

She laughed. "Okay, but wrap them in brown paper and I'll try to find a safe place. I hope you don't want me to keep track of them all."

"Nah, no records required. In fact, no one is allowed to return them, and here's another gift for everyone." He got up and handed a stack of pamphlets to the woman on the far end. "Please pass these down the row. All of you now have your own copy of America's Declaration of Independence and The Constitution—required reading."

Dylan went to the white board. "We'll start today by listing the reasons settlers came from Europe to make a new life here. Raise your hand when you think of one."

He pointed at one man who's hand was up. "Everyone share your first name. I want to remember who you are."

"I'm Dave. They came for adventure, 'cause everything was new."

Dylan wrote it on the board and pointed to a hand on the far edge of the circle.

"Susan. Their countries sent them to search for gold and wealth, right?"

"Yes, good one Susan. We're talking back in the sixteenth and early seventeenth century here. Anyone else?"

"Tom. They were poor and starving and wanted a better life."

"That came later. Tilly?"

59

"Maybe 'cause they like to sail. I like sailing. If anyone has a sail boat, maybe we could..."

"All right, Tilly. Jim?"

"Because *someone* had to start the NFL."

The students laughed. "That came a *lot* later, Jim. Anybody else?" Dylan saw no hands raised, then one popped up right in front.

"I'm Betty. Spain, France and England: they all wanted new land to claim as their own. France claimed middle America and Canada, too."

"Right on, Betty."

"Weren't some prisoners sent here from England?" Dave asked.

"That was mostly Australia, but there was one colony in Georgia. Come on, people, another reason was mentioned in the text...Lisa."

"Spain wanted more than conquest of land. They wanted to spread Catholicism all over the New World. They put missions in Florida, Central America and all up the California coast."

"Very good." Dylan put his marker down and returned to the front. "So, for the first few hundred years the European countries fought each other for conquest. Even the Netherlands and Sweden had opposing claims. The European kings saw great possibilities in wealth from their colonies and sent mining prospectors in hopes of discovering gold and jewels. Of course they also wanted to start farms to raise crops for their empires. Not much luck finding gems and gold in Virginia, huh?

"All the countries had an established religion and the protestant reformation was only a hundred years old. But, Lisa, the first English settlers had some ideas of their own as well. Do you know where did they first make landfall?"

Lisa looked down and flapped her pigtails side to side before she tapped the book on her desk. "Roanoke Island. The settlement was commissioned by Sir Walter Raleigh, but it failed."

"Yes, landfall in 1585, Lisa. The colonists all disappeared, probably captured by the Indians. So how about the first *successful* colony? Betty?"

"I think that would be Jamestown Virginia, on an island up the Chesapeake Bay."

Dylan grinned at his students. "Yes, 1609. Your text isn't wrong, but it leaves out the fun part. The voyage was organized by an Anglican priest to bring the gospel to people who hadn't heard the 'good news.' He sent Robert Hunt to be the chaplain, and when they were offshore, Hunt organized a landing party on what is now known as Cape Henry."

He opened his hands. "Anyone care to guess *why* they landed on this little point on the beach?" He pointed at one student. "Jim, redeem yourself."

"Sure. Obviously the ocean beach was no place for a town, but it was at the mouth of the river. If it were me, I'd set up a cannon to guard the settlement upriver."

Dylan nodded. "A plausible idea, Jim. Good, but that isn't why."

No hands were up. "Chaplain Hunt had everyone on board wait for three days praying for their personal examination and repentance. Finally, they launched a landing party on the point and set up a large wooden cross. They had a prayer service consecrating this entire continent to the glory of God. "Hunt read this interpretation of Matthew 15: 13: 'All planting which our Heavenly Father has not planted with you will be rooted up.' That means if you don't dedicate the land you're settling on to God, He will root it out."

The students sat motionless, their mouths either gaping or showing gritted teeth. Dylan added, "I'd guess Pastor Hunt was thinking about the destruction of the earlier colony and wanted to start this one right. There's a National Monument and a stone cross there today, complete with people suing to have the cross removed. What do you think?"

After an awkward silence, one student ventured a slight elevation of his hand at the wrist. Dylan smiled and nodded at him. "Dave?"

"I think you just got into big trouble, Sir."

SEEKING

Two detectives hurried down the corridor at their headquarters. Scott glanced at Sean. "I thought the Berkard case was closed, but now you've arrested a suspect. Really?"

"Yeah. Why do you think we're heading for Interrogation? I need you behind the glass while I question him."

"He must be our one DNA match." Scott put his hand out and stopped him. "Wait, if he's a suspect, you shouldn't talk to him without a public defender."

"This guy called a lawyer right away—and one showed up in less than an hour. He's in there with him."

"So, he's rich?"

"He's a street cleaner, slash garbage man." Sean had the sly look of knowing a secret. "This attorney is from the same firm Reinhardt uses."

Scott nodded. "Ahh, now I see." They resumed walking. "Good work finding our positive match."

"Thanks. Lucky he had one on file—petty larceny, age nineteen. His employer doesn't know about it."

"There's a bit of leverage, huh?"

Sean opened the door to the one way mirror room. "All right, keep an eye on us and make sure the recorder is working, okay?"

Scott looked through the window and studied the men seated at the table. The suspect was a Mediterranean type in coveralls. His black T-Shirt bore the image of a raised fist. "So, the Chief knows about this? He reopened the case, right?"

Sean grinned. "I thought I'd mention it to him when I get some results he can't deny."

Scott laughed. "I love it."

Sean entered the interrogation room with slow, casual strides. He put a clipboard on the table and smiled at the men. The suspect returned a wide eyed apprehensive stare while his lawyer, clad in an impeccable grey, pin-striped Armani suit, studied Sean with a steely squint. "Hello, I'm Detective Sean Ryan. Don't get up."

The lips above the suit spoke through clenched teeth. "I trust we can make this quick. I have another appointment. The charges of suspicion of murder against my client are patently ridiculous and unless you show me some clear evidence I demand his immediate release."

Sean gave the attorney a polite smile but addressed the suspect. "For the record, you are Paco Gutierrez, 1225 Rivera Street, apartment 334, Oakland, here for questioning."

Paco nodded. "Yes."

Sean turned toward the chilly, iron stare, "and you are Paco's counselor. Please state your name for the record."

"Charles Lucent, Attorney at law."

Sean gave the suspect an expectant look. "All right Paco. Please tell us about the incident at Berkard University from your point of view."

Lucent promptly interjected. "He wasn't there. Give us evidence of why you think he was."

Sean grinned at Lucent. "Counselor, Paco is not on trial here. I suggest you let him answer as he pleases." He turned his grin toward the wide eyes now darting glances around the room. "Paco?"

The suspect looked at his lawyer. "I wasn't there?" His head quickly swiveled back to Sean. "You have proof that I was?"

"I have certain proof, Paco, and I'll show that to you in a moment. Meanwhile, tell us what happened."

"You couldn't have proof!" He sat straight up. "I know there were cameras, but our masks covered everyth..." He clutched his leg, having just been kicked. "Ow."

Sean scowled. "Counselor!"

"Paco, I can tell you that the evidence we have places you in direct contact with Mrs. Jones."

Paco slid his chair away from Lucent but looked at him while he rubbed his leg. "They're trying to frame me for the murderer, but see, I'm not the one who killed…"

"That's enough." Lucent shot up. "Don't answer anything more until they show us this so called proof. I'm sure they are bluffing. Remember, you said you only saw it on television."

Everyone was quiet for a few moments, glances darting between each other. Sean sighed. "All right. Paco's DNA was recovered from Hayley's fingernails."

More silence, this time broken by Lucent. "Really. Why didn't you say so in the first place?" He strode toward the door. "I'm withdrawing from this case. Do the right thing, officer." He slammed the door as he left.

Paco slid his chair back against the wall and was breathing heavily. Sean held up a hand and spoke in an even tone. "Take it easy, Paco. No one is going to frame you for something you didn't do." He slid a paper over to him. "Right now you don't have an attorney. These are the Miranda rights you saw earlier. If you want to get another lawyer before telling us more, just say so."

Determination spread across his face and Paco scuffed his chair back to the table. "No, I want to tell you everything.

Reggie killed her. He must have gotten carried away. It wasn't supposed to be that way."

"Okay, thank you, but start at the beginning. Why were you with all those Antifa?"

"Well, they have rallies that get us all worked up about the fascists taking over this country. Reggie's our leader. Then they pick out people they want out on the street. We get a hundred bucks for an action."

"An action?"

"Yeah, an action--you know where we go and bust up stuff."

"And Berkard was an action. Was there a plan going in?"

"Sure. Reggie told one group to chase the fascist pig off the stage by throwing things and the rest of us would grab her in the open, knock her down and maybe bloody her nose. He didn't say anything about killing."

"Uh huh. That 'pig' you mentioned was Hayley Jones, correct?"

"Yeah, right."

"Okay, how do you know it was Reggie who killed her?"

"He was talking to us all the time. He's got a red band at the top of his mask."

"Did he have the rock?"

"Oh yeah. He had it with him. She was a fighter—scratched us up pretty good, but we knocked the pig down."

Paco looked at the table for a moment nodding his head. "Sorry—well someone held one of her arms and I sat on her legs. Reggie's girlfriend fought with her and sat on her chest. He called her Sharon, Charon or something like that."

"Did you see him hit Mrs. Jones with the rock? You only knew it was him by his voice, right?"

"It was Reggie, all right. First he shouted what he thought of fascists and spit on her. She got a hand free from Sharon for a second and scratched off his mask so, yeah, I saw his face. Then he smashed her—surprised the heck out of me."

Sean sat back, shaking his head. "Whoa, ugly. Was she still conscious?"

"Yeah, still making noise and struggling. Someone said 'That's enough, Reggie', but Charon said to hit her again."

Did you ever hear Reggie's last name?"

"No, but I heard one of his friends tell him, 'Don't worry. They'd never do anything to a Luchow.' No idea what guy said it, though."

Sean stood up. "Thank you for being cooperative, Paco. We're not going to press charges against you, and you can go. I just need you to stay in town and answer your phone when we call. Are you okay with that?"

69

"Sure, Boss."

"You might consider staying with a relative for awhile. The prosecutor will likely give you immunity, but you'll be called as a witness."

REPORTING TRUTH

"They really gonna let us inside?"

"Of course Emma." Lisa pushed through the revolving door at the News Box Studio. "They invited me, remember?"

"You ever been in a TV studio?"

Inside the lobby, Lisa adjusted their lanyards to show their press credentials. "Nope."

The man at the reception desk looked them over, with a scowl, studied the badges, and checked his clipboard with a totally bland expression. His monotone voice told them, "An escort will be out for you shortly."

Lisa was trying for eye contact. "Will he be an android too?"

Emma elbowed her. "Lisa!"

Finally, he cracked a smile. "We're working on the female model, Ms Combes, but we just can't get them to behave."

Lisa laughed. "Well, maybe she's perfect and you don't know it."

He grinned and gestured for them to be seated. Emma was not amused, and whispered through clenched teeth, "You almost got us chucked out, Ms Sassypants. I want to see this place."

Shortly a young woman in a purple dress came out, spoke with the receptionist and approached them. "Hello, I'm Rebecca Fern. I work for the Hammer Time Show. You must be Ms Combes and Jackson, correct?"

"Yes, I'm Lisa and this is Emma Jackson."

"Great. Follow me." She escorted them onto an elevator. "We're going to a production room in the basement first. Would you like to see a studio after?"

Emma raised two fists. "Oh, yeah, man."

Rebecca chuckled. They went through a large room stuffed with electronic equipment, monitors and busy workers. The women staggered behind, necks swiveling as they went.

Finally, they went through a door into a smaller room with a large TV monitor on the wall and Rebecca sat them down in front of it. "Our video of Hayley's attack is under court order not to be released to the public until the investigation is complete, but they did not impound it."

Lisa nodded "I understand, and I'm grateful for the chance to look at it. As I mentioned, I'm writing an article I hope will be accepted by the Oakland Flame."

"Sure. We're all reporters here, Lisa, but you guys are witnesses as well. After you've looked at our recording, I'll tape an interview with you if you don't mind. We may not run it, but that's up to Mister Hammer."

"Oh, glad to," Lisa beamed. "Now what I want to focus in on would be Stengel's activity, the campus police response and what was being said at the time. If possible, I would also like to interview the camera man who took the shots."

"You really are a reporter, aren't you?" Rebecca chuckled. "Welcome to the business."

AMERICAN TRUTH

Dylan Coz paced in front of his white board and a pull-down map of colonial North America. "Okay, so various colonies are coming here and you read about the Pilgrims and the Mayflower since our last class." He squinted at his students. "At least I hope you have."

After a little student tittering, Dylan asked, "So, what does the book say about why they came?"

A pretty woman with straight blonde hair and a wiggly torso put her hand up. Dylan nodded. "Yes, Tilly?"

"It said they were treated real rough in England so they moved to the Netherlands for awhile, then got together for a trip here. They were the first colony in New England."

"Very good, Tilly. Treated rough or persecuted, but for what?"

"It says for religion, but I thought England was Christian."

"Ah, there's where the text leaves you guessing, doesn't it? The British kings had an *established* religion, The Church of England. After the Protestant Reformation many

74

countries, including England, punished those not conforming to State established religion.

"The so called reformed Christians adhered to the word of God spoken in the Bible, and they avoided the added rules made up by men."

Dylan strode over to Jim and handed him a Bible. "Read us Matthew fifteen, nine."

"It's okay to read this aloud?"

"I'll take the heat, Jim. Go ahead." Jim began fumbling through the pages. "While he's looking, ask yourselves that same question. The pilgrims suffered and even died so that you and I could open the Bible like Jim is doing and read it without fear. That fear is creeping back into this Country and we'll talk about why later in this course."

Jim said "Aha," then read: "They worship me in vain: their teachings are but rules taught by men."

Dylan took the Bible back and smiled at his class. "Wanting to make the rules has been man's problem since Satan whispered lies to Eve in the Garden of Eden, but the Massachusetts Bay Colony did some controlling of its own. They required a religious test to be in their government. Then what happened?" He opened his hands at the class."

Lisa raised her hand. "Roger Williams disagreed and founded the Providence Colony. Also a Mrs. Hutchinson had a

Bible study group and championed the idea that people could read and understand it for themselves."

"Excellent. She founded a colony near Providence as well, but it was Williams who first coined the phrase 'separation of church and state'. Just as the king wanted to control the church, he felt it was equally wrong for the church to control the government. Who knows what a church controlled government would be called?"

Puzzled looks. "It's called a theocracy. An example of that today would be Iran." He pointed to a raised hand. "Betty?"

"But, Mister Coz, my pastor said Americans formed a Christian government."

"Great question, Betty. No, our present government was never *run* by religious leaders requiring Christianity for all citizens. We have no religious test to live here. However, we took our *laws* and moral principles from God's word. We'll get into that more deeply when we study our constitution." A black man had raised his hand. "Jevon?"

"But that separation thing--that's why you can't talk about God in school, isn't it? It's illegal, right?"

"No, and ignoring God is far more dangerous, Jevon."

SCORNED TRUTH

Sean Ryan hastened to the Chief's door, a folder under one arm, rapped twice on the door frame and went in. "Hey, thanks for calling, Chief. I was just about to call you anyway. I'm excited about the latest developments in the Jones case and I want to bring you up to date."

The Chief looked up with a bland expression. "Uh huh. Is that the complete folder?"

"Oh, right." Sean put it on the desk in front of him. "Chief, we've had a big breakthrough. We don't have the killer pinned down, but we located an eye witness with DNA. He's actually an unwitting party in the murder."

"You're a good detective, Ryan. I can see you have made some progress here. Can the witness positively identify the person he feels was the attacker?"

"He called him Reggie, but does not actually know who he is. I have an idea, though and we'll start working on that next."

"Sean, I asked you to work on the drug deals going down on at Cortland and King street. What have you done there?"

"Uh, the activity on that corner is at dusk. I'm setting up a sting, but look Chief, I think we'll pin down the Jones murderer this week. I was going to ask you for another field agent to help."

"Well, here's the thing." The Chief picked up the Jones file and set it on a table behind him. "This Berkard incident has been taken over by the FBI. They are sending a runner to pick up all the data we have."

Sean stared intently at his boss. He responded in a soft croak: "What? This is a *local* murder—not their jurisdiction."

"Sorry, I know you've put a good bit of energy into this. The Bureau said Antifa operates in many states so they're claiming soverenty. Anyway we're out of it now."

Sean leaned forward, hands on the desk. "Will there be a meeting with the agents?"

"Don't know. Meanwhile, they just want all the files. Look, I'll give you an extra man for field work. You can use him in the drug sting."

Sean stood upright and coughed. "I get it. Someone high up is looking down on us and doesn't want the facts in this case to get out."

"Not for us to reason why, Ryan. Maybe there's a national security issue. I understand you're upset. Look, take an extra hour for lunch, but there's plenty more work to do when you get back." He answered his desk phone, offered Sean a thin-lipped grin, and gave him a 'go away,' back of hand motion.

Sean headed for the front door to get a breath of fresh air. As he stomped through the waiting room mumbling to himself and shaking his head, a young woman in a pink jeans bounced up from a chair. "Oh, you are Detective Ryan, right?"

"And you are?"

Lisa held up the badge hanging from her neck. "Lisa Combes, reporter."

"Really? Excuse me, but you look like a fifteen year old in pigtails."

"That's harsh, Sir. I'm twenty one, but could I ask you just a few questions on the Jones murder case?"

"Sorry, I'm upset right now…" Sean blew out through his cheeks. He paused for a moment, looked into her bright, expectant eyes and his expression softened. "Sure, come on. I was just stepping out on the front porch to get some air."

Sean opened the door for her and gestured toward the low concrete wall on the side of the entrance porch. "I notice you referred to it as a murder. Our official report calls it 'The Berkard Incident'."

Sean hefted himself up and sat on the wall. Lisa gave him a furrowed-brow look. "I was in the audience the day it happened. Sir, I can tell you're really upset. Should I come back another time?"

A half smile flickered over his face. "No stay. Maybe I need to talk." He gestured to one side. "Pull up a piece of concrete."

Lisa giggled, bounced up on the wall beside him and pulled a notebook out of her purse. "Okay, Detective, let's start with why you looked like you had a case of acute indigestion when you walked in."

"Humph. Here's a scoop for you. Two minutes ago our department turned the whole case over to the FBI. I was about to crack it and now I'm reassigned."

"Wow, thank you---I mean thanks for the scoop. But, bummer. I see why you're upset." She put the tip of a finger in her teeth and made eye contact. "You'll still get to work with them, right?"

"Nah, it's been pulled. The Chief, the mayor: they want nothing to do with it."

Lisa studied Sean's face, waiting for more. She began swinging her legs, bouncing red sneakers off the wall. "My investigative reporter instincts just got a smelly whiff of cover-up coming my way."

Sean chuckled. "You're a smart young lady."

"How about a clue as to what was about to crack open the case."

"You know I can't talk about the details of an ongoing investigation."

Lisa knocked him back with a big, sparkly grin. "Then it's so *fortunate* there is no investigation in your department." She batted her eyelashes.

He laughed. "Zing. You got me."

"Hey, maybe I could do some more investigating for you if you pointed me in the right direction."

Sean silently watched people coming and going out the front door. Without looking at her he spoke softly. "If I give you something, you'd have to promise not to publish until I say it's okay."

Lisa's head was bobbing up and down as he turned to her. "Yes, Sir. Absolutely, Sir. You have my word."

"Do you know of a Reginald Luchow?"

"Oh, sure, a far left agitator and Congressman Bernard Luchow's son. He's led protests all over and even one on our campus last—my God. He's the *murderer*?"

Sean raised his index finger at her. "Not saying, but if he's got a girlfriend named Charon, and I can check both their DNAs, then probably. Yes."

Lisa was open mouthed and open eyed. She clutched her notebook to her chest. "You'd let me get that for you? Really?"

"Officially, we didn't even talk. Our department would deny any such knowledge, and besides, it could be really dangerous, Lisa."

"Oh, Sir, you gotta know. I think I was born for this kinda thing."

MIRACULOUS TRUTH

History class was in a good mood and everyone was busy conversing and laughing when Dylan came in. He waved at them and pulled a chair into his spot in the center of his "teaching circle." "Hello, everyone. I expect you're all experts on early colonial history right?"

Jevon Patrick, the black, male student who challenged him earlier, finger-pointed at his teacher. "You gonna tell us more about history that isn't so?"

"Nope. I'm going to tell you important historical truths you won't find in your textbooks."

"Then tell us why all those nice Christians had slaves, huh?"

"Ooh." Dylan's expression became compassionate. He gave him full eye contact, and his voice became measured. "Next week we'll talk about the kings who *demanded* slaves on colonial plantations and the struggle our Christians settlers had to finally free them. That story?"

Jevon sat back with a defiant look and tossed his head to one side. Dylan added, "I won't sugarcoat anything, Jevon.

There are some bad guys on our side, but there's a lot of truth lost under a smelly heap of propaganda."

Dylan had a small table sitting in front of his chair and he opened the text book on it. "You all should have read through section six. The cities in America grew quickly from northern European immigration, and even as early as 1640, Boston had sixteen thousand people.

"Virginia and the Carolinas had a good climate for growing tobacco, rice and indigo but these crops were labor intensive. British companies set up plantations and in the early 1700s, the slave trade flourished with boats coming from Africa through the West Indies."

"Yeah, see," Jevon said without raising his hand. "And them Christians said it was fine because it was in the Bible."

"Some did and were wrong to do so. The Bible also mentions infant sacrifice to pagan gods, but that doesn't mean it endorses the practice." Dylan studied Jevon's sulk. "Speaking of the Bible, who knows where the largest population of slaves came from in the Old Testament?"

A woman's hand went up as far as her cheek. "Uh, Ethiopia, I think."

"Nope. Not the largest. Remember, I said the Old Testament."

He smiled at one student whose hand was waving. "You, with the bouncy pigtails."

Lisa giggled. "The Jews from Israel. They were brought to Egypt."

"Bingo. They peaked out at almost a half million of them and God used Moses to free them all. So the big story about slavery in the Bible is emancipation and, as the number of American Judeo-Christians grew, so did the desire to free those locked in slavery in this country."

He smiled at Jevon. "More about this later, okay?"

"America's thirteen colonies continued to enlarge and prosper and France and England fought for control of the Ohio Valley and lands to the west. In 1755 British generals Braddock and Gage attacked first. Who knows what happened?" He nodded at Jim.

"It was a surprise ambush. The French and their Indian friends wiped us out."

"Yes, that was the start of the French and Indian War. Seven hundred and fourteen killed and twenty six were officers because they were singled out. The British later brought in their naval fleet and full army to bear and won the war. Good thing, too, or we'd only have a coastline country today."

Dylan glanced around at his students. "Who knows an important man who survived that first ambush?"

Several hands waved. "Susan?"

"George Washington."

"He sure did." Dylan grinned. "Who would like to hear a true but politically incorrect story about his survival?"

Eyes rolled, teeth bared. "Colonel George was in the thick of battle and two horses were shot from under him. When they completed their retreat, Washington's coat had four bullet holes right through it, but he was completely untouched."

The student's faces turned to a mixture of wonder and unbelief. "The incident was confirmed by independent records of Colonial, British and the French military. Later the Indian Chief who had led his men came to see Colonel Washington. He had fired two shots at him at close range and now wanted to see the man 'protected by the Great Spirit'.

"Washington wrote a close friend that God, in His divine providence, had protected him. Later we'll describe other battle stories where divine providence continued to play a role in our securing independence."

Jim bolted upright, turned, and headed for the door. "Bullshit," he said.

RISKY TRUTH

Emma skipped and jogged along the path to Berkard's rose garden and found Lisa standing on a bench and waving to her. Emma put her hands on her hips when she got there. "Just what have you been up to, girl? Never seen you so excited."

Lisa looked all around and slid down to sit on the bench. "You'll see."

"Uh oh, I know that look on your face, and it's a dangerous one. What's up?"

Lisa giggled and put a finger to her lips. "Ever wanted to play spy for *real*, Emma?"

"Uh, my feet are shouting 'turn and run' before it's too late."

"Seriously, we have a real chance to help catch Hayley's murderer."

Emma bit her finger. "Oh, shoot. There's that *other* look of yours--your Dad's Master Sergeant look--the 'Jump out of the foxhole and lets get go em' look."

Lisa laughed. "You know me too well, don't you? Here's the thing. The detective in charge of the investigation wants me to try and get a DNA sample from two suspects."

"And the police isn't getting it for themselves because…"

"Because they transferred the case to the FBI and Detective Ryan can't act officially. Besides, he knows the FBI won't follow through on it."

"Are you sure?"

"Absolutely. Some people at the top are up to big time whitewashing. You've seen the reports. None of them ever use the murder word."

"Yeah, that part I agree with. Okay, who are the suspects we're going after?"

Lisa swiveled her neck around for a perimeter check. "The son of Congressman Bernard Luchow and his girlfriend."

Emma's legs began a rapid running in place. Lisa laughed and gave her a swat. "Not to worry. I have a plan."

"Oh, good. Like your plan to get us dates at the frat house by pretending we were taking a survey?"

Lisa bit her lip and nodded. "Ouch, ya got me. Listen, that's how we learn, but this is really important. Don't you think we have to at least *try*?"

A little eye-rolling. "All right, what's this plan of yours? Just don't let it be: we're taking a survey of murder suspects and we'd like a blood sample, please."

Lisa put her arm on Emma's shoulders and bent her over. She spoke in a loud whisper. "Reggie Luchow organizes leftist rallies to fire up his supporters. He's got one next week at the Adolfo Hotel. It's a fund raising dinner for donors and Moxie Watver is speaking."

"Lemmie guess. You sold your car so we could buy thousand dollar tickets."

"Oh phoo." Lisa gave her shoulder a little swat. "I pulled a favor from a liberal friend. He thinks I'm now open to his ideas and want to earn some money. Half right. Anyway, we're bussing tables that night."

"Not bad, girl. So, we're getting paid by the people we're spying on. Okay, that gets us close to the target, but what do we have to do to get the DNA? If you think I'm gonna sleep with Reggie, forget it."

"Oh, God." Lisa convulsed in silent laughter. "You're bad. No, *any* bodily secretion will do, even hair follicles. They just need something with cells."

"I assume you have a plan for that, too?"

"Yup. We'll be creative and spontaneous."

"Yup. Now I have a spontaneous vision of jail time."

CHALLENGED TRUTH

The only thing new under the sun is the history
you don't know. Harry S. Truman, 1949

Dylan sat on the edge of his desk facing his class. "We've been learning about prerevolutionary times for the past few weeks. Before we move on, I'll start by asking if you have any questions—anything at all."

No one moved for a few moments and then Jevon, his expression a deep scowl, flicked his hand outward.

Dylan cocked his head to one side. "Was that a spider on your hand, Jevon, or do you have a question?"

"So, the world was *always* a white supremacist place, right?" Two students gasped.

"Ahh," Dylan grinned. "Here's another 'stump the chump' question from your Sociology class. I guess I'll have to come up with a 'history class' answer. Jevon, do you know who Genghis Kahn was?"

"Yeah, a tough Chinese guy who kicked butt all over the place."

Dylan raised a finger and pursed his lips. "Kahn was a Mongol and might have called you a racist for describing him that way."

A student chorus: "Ooooh."

"Mister Kahn conquered and controlled the largest land empire in history. Should we call that yellow supremacy? Of course, there was an extensive Persian Empire. Let's call that tan supremacy. But to be fair, the Nubians conquered the Egyptian Empire around 700 BC. That would be black supremacy, huh?"

Jevon gave a thumbs up.

Dylan grinned. "Yes, and colonial America was part of the far flung British Empire. White guys to be sure, but the motivation of human empire building is not racism, just human greed for money and power. Which one of these empires is still around and ruling the world? Anyone?"

Jim's hand was up. "Not a one."

"Right. Are you back with us for good, Jim?"

"Yeah. Tilly said I make the class fun for her."

Dylan chuckled. "Thanks, Tilly. Okay, do you remember Pastor Robert Hunt's quote about the fate of lands not planted by God? Can anyone name a country beside ours that was dedicated to God?"

Tilly and Lisa's hands went up together. "We owe you one. Tilly?"

"Israel."

"Right, and how long since it was founded? Lisa."

"Uhh, I guess about four thousand years ago and still bouncing around."

Dylan laughed. "Sure is. Israel's size varied, and sometimes the residents got exiled, but it was never a true empire. Okay, but how about any *recent* empires, say in the last few hundred years? Go ahead, Jevon?"

"You're gonna say us and, we're an evil empire."

"Are we? What countries did we conquer, plant our flag and claim for the United States?"

"We fought a lot of wars and killed a lot of people."

"But, Jevon, we've *liberated* countries. After World War Two we restored Europe and…"

"I know. We got Alaska."

"We *bought* Alaska as well as Louisiana and Manhattan. Good capitalistic investments, huh?"

Jevon slouched back with a frown and grumbled, "We conquered the Indians and planted our flag."

"Ahh." Dylan sat back against his desk. "There's a good, *colonial* point, Jevon. Let's take a moment. The British Empire did most of the conquering and killing, but I admit we were not blameless either.

"In our favor, America has shown some repentance. We allowed the Indians to retain some land and keep their culture while giving them citizenship as well. Jefferson promoted a law sending out missionaries to teach them the gospel—taxpayer expense. That was the opposite of separation of church and state, wasn't it?" Jevon shrugged.

"Okay people, the empires I was looking for were the Communist Empire and the short lived Nazi conquest. Think a minute. How were these different from the older 'charge in and conquer' empires?"

After a moment, Jim's hand went up. "I think they tried to convince their people that they had an idea that was better than anyone else and worth fighting for."

Dylan pointed a finger at him. "Very *good,* Jim. With more widespread education, cultures have become more sophisticated today. Leaders now need to convince their population on why the world should be transformed so they'll have a reason to go out and fight. They need to instill their *ideology*, but neither the socialist republic called the USSR nor the Nazis survived, did they?"

Jevon sat up. "Yeah, but we're fascists like the Nazis."

"Glad you brought that up, Jevon. One of the last things Hayley Jones said to all of us before she was murdered was to look up the definition of fascism. Susan, I see a cell phone on your desk. Could you look that up for us?"

In a moment, Susan held out her phone at arms length, cleared her throat and read, "a prevailing style of dress—

oops." The class laughed and she removed a pair of glasses from her purse.

She giggled and punched the word into her phone. "Sorry. *Fascism*: A political philosophy or regime that exalts nation over the individual and stands on an autocratic government and a dictatorial leader who exerts force and suppression to maintain control and keep the population in regimented social and economic order."

Tilly was wiggling around and frowning.

Dylan gestured to her. "Tilly, something to add?"

"Uh, huh. Why does everybody have to be so mean?"

Some tittered, but Dylan gave her a sympathetic nod. "That's actually a profoundly important question, Tilly. The Bible says we live in a fallen world and we tend toward wickedness, but we're not without hope. Please note, by the way, that America's founding principals put the *individual* over the state."

He turned to Betty. "I'm not going to get into that future hope of ours or proselytize in this class, but here's a woman who has the answer. Show them your purse."

Betty got up with a grin and displayed the side of her purse which read, "John 3-16."

"The line after that is the world saver. Talk to Betty after class if you're interested."

Dylan let out a sigh. "Well, back to history. Susan, fire up that phone again and give us the definition of socialism."

"Socialism. A society where all property and production of goods is owned by the State and given to the people as the government sees fit."

Dylan opened his hands. "I think it was Lenin who said the ultimate goal of socialism is communism. Fascism and socialism share the idea of complete state control. Today, one slow and sneaky way of nationalizing property is to regulate it. Jim, you have a way of putting things in a nutshell. What is similar about these two systems?"

Jim was grinning and nodding. "Bad guys rule your lives." Someone's notebook hit the floor.

"Couldn't have said it better, but the *differences* are harder to express. Lisa, I see your hand up. You want to try?"

"Fascism is easy. The idea is to convince your nation that you're better than everyone else and people like yourself should be in control of the world. With socialism I guess the pitch is you don't have to work hard and Big Brother government will take care of everything for you."

"Uh, huh. In general that's the propaganda, at least. What they have in common is State control, but every politician tells it with their own twist, don't they? We'll talk about our American system next time, why it's different, and why it has survived so long, but first I have to sidestep and mention a large movement that seeks to take down our 'by-the-people' government. Anyone heard of Fabian Socialism?"

He glanced around, but no hands were up. "In the late 1880s, an influential group of elite Englishmen founded the Fabian Society and the London School of Economics. They were known, at first, as the Fabian Socialists and they believed they could design a utopian society where all mankind would live in peace and altruism. Their views are diametrically opposed to the providential view dear to Americans for over two hundred years.

"The Fabians are atheists and believe that man will build this utopia. Their strategy is one of gradual conquest, the technique used by the Roman general, Fabius Maximus. Their mascot is the snapping turtle—slow to move but quick to be mean."

Tilly sounded out a "raspberry," pouted and said, "There, you see?" Some laughed.

Lisa raised her hand and she got the nod. "But everyone would laugh at the idea of a utopia today. Did the society die out?"

"Nope. They know better than to use the word utopia in public, but the Fabian Socialists are stronger than ever. Sidney Webb and other society members came here in 1888 to actively train and recruit. This led to the American Economic

Association, the Rand School Of Social Science, and the Intercollegiate Socialist Society—yes, Susan?"

"I know that one. The Chancellor and lots of faculty go to their meetings. Are they on other campuses, too?"

"Sure are. For over a hundred years they have been active in spreading their dogma at the Ivy League schools such as Columbia and the University of Pennsylvania. Most large universities have chapters today. You might have seen their coat of arms--a wolf in sheep's clothing."

"Seriously?" Lisa asked.

"Seriously." Dylan allowed widespread mumbling and stirring in his students before he continued. "To bring it close to home, who knows who Margaret Sanger was? Betty?"

"She founded Planned Parenthood."

"Yes. That was 1916, and she championed eugenics. The Fabian Society fervently believed that eugenics was necessary for their utopian society and the so called 'deplorables' should not be allowed to breed. As an upper crust member of the Fabians, Sanger summarized her vision this way: 'I look forward to seeing humanity free someday of the tyranny of Christianity and Capitalism.' Who knows what the Fabian Socialists are called today?"

Tom called out, "Global Socialists?"

"Good to hear from you, Tom. If you're thinking worldwide perhaps, but in America they work gradually in 'sheep's clothing' to achieve their goal. They call themselves the Progressives, but they're actually a group of billionaires working to first destroy, and then take over a transformed America."

The students sat stunned. "If global socialism is the ultimate end point goal, why is that different from socialism in just one country, like what they have in Venezuela?"

One hand was up, and it was in a fist. Dylan chuckled. "I hesitate to ask, but yes, Jim?"

"Bad guys ruin *everyone's* life." There were strains of laughter, groans and head shaking.

Dylan finger pointed at him. "That nails it, Jim. Okay, everyone: the American Revolution next week."

CAPTURED TRUTH

Emma and Lisa looked each other up and down, adjusting their black aprons and brown, short sleeve shirts. They were alone in the Adolfo's ladies bath room. Emma pulled a Rose of Sharon bloom from her purse and pinned to her headband. "That's for luck."

Lisa peered at herself in the mirror and patted at her hair with a frown. "So, tell me, why'd you insist I change my style?"

"Sorry, Sister, but tiny pigtails are fifth grade, not Radical Progressive."

"I must look like a bowling ball from the back. You got our plan down?"

"Sure, we'll pray first, then we just do our job for twenty minutes while we check them out. I didn't see anyone looking like that picture of Charon out there."

"She's at a different table next to Reginald." Lisa peeked out the door into the noisy room. "He's just finished addressing everyone and giving introductions. Don't know why they're not together, but it might make it easier for us."

She turned and made eye contact with Emma. "Sure you're up to this?"

"Terrified."

Lisa giggled "Good, we're together on that. Just keep looking for the right moment to do your thing. After that, we're simply bus girls again. Anything else you'd like to say?"

"Yeah, if they kill me, tell Mom I love her."

The two students moved out onto the large ballroom floor, smiling and filling water glasses as they walked between the round dinner tables.

A woman held a microphone on one side of the room and shouted to the crowd. "You can see the enemy trying to stop us, but they will never win, my comrades. We have the schools, the media, and the entertainment industry in our pocket now, and the government is giving way. They are the mountains society rests on."

"Most voters already believe our enemies are racist bigots. We have the economy near collapse from debt and the religious nuts are cowering in their churches making frightened concessions."

Their overweight lady boss hustled over to them. "Where *were* you two? We're picking up the hors d'oeurve plates right now. Fill any empty wine glasses. Don't expect the *waiters* to do everything. Get on it."

Lisa nodded vigorously with a "Yes, M'am."

When she left, Emma whispered, "They'll make her a military commander when they take over the world."

"So not gonna happen. Who are all those women giving Charon hugs?"

"Beats me, but it's gonna be hard to get close to her."

Emma did her best to elbow her way closer to Charon's table but without success, and the speaker was distracting her concentration.

The message droned on: "So, people, character assassinations, lies and deceptions are your best weapons toward defeating those in power. Once we collapse the economy people will beg us to save the country."

She laughed and raised her fist. The audience copied the move. "Our ultimate global victory justifies *any* means you need to bring to bear, and remember, you'll always have back up. Any questions?"

A man called out, "What'll we do if Americans begin to revolt?"

"We'll have taken their guns away before that." She pointed. "You, in the back."

"How about the News Box. What should we do about them?"

"We're handling that. Our donors are buying out the parent company as we speak."

Another man yelled, "What do you say to the reporters?"

"Most are on our side, but if you have no answer, tell them that the other guy is a racist, homophobic, misogynist xenophobe."

"What's a zen-probe?"

"Just say it, and if you're talking about a white man, add white supremacist, Nazi."

A woman wearing enormous round eyeglasses had her hand up. "But what do we say we are *for*?"

The speaker squinted and pointed at the audience. "Listen up. You tell em we want to *restore* American values. We're for human decency, income equality, open borders and an end to capitalist greed and the enslavement of the American worker. We promise free health care, free college and equal pay for everyone." She gave a thumbs up. "Got it?" Widespread applause.

As she concluded her remarks with a final exhortation, Charon got up and headed toward an exit. She was tall and buxom, but her face was stern and masculine. Emma followed at a distance, entered the ladies room behind her, and went into a stall to peek over the door. Charon was heaping makeup over the scratch scars on her cheeks and muttering profanities.

Another woman came in. Charon turned and greeted her. "Well, hello, beautiful."

The woman grinned and drew close. "That speech was a real call to action, huh?"

Charon pulled her into an embrace. "And, here's some action, too." She kissed her.

Emma swallowed hard but thought this might be her only chance. She walked boldly out of her stall and strode toward them. "I won't tell if I can have one too."

Charon laughed, grabbed her, bent her backward and planted a big one on her lips. Emma feigned a struggle but deftly reached behind her ear, singled out a few hairs between her fingers and jerked away. "Wow, you sure do that great."

Charon chuckled. Emma faked a laugh while she slipped the catch of hair into her apron pocket. "Thanks, that was a great tip."

"Join us after, young one. Maybe I can double it. What's your name?"

"Cerise." She nodded, grinned, and scooted for the door. "See you later."

Outside, she spit into a tissue and wiped her lips. "Ick."

Meanwhile Lisa continued to work the tables, pouring wine and water, replenishing butter and rolls, but she kept her eye on Reginald, waiting for the right moment. That came when the slender blond at his side tousled his hair, got up and excused herself.

Reginald downed the last gulp of his red wine and began looking around. Lisa took a bottle from the service cart and moved next to him. She pretended to stumble, spilling a little near him. With one hand she grabbed for the glass and broke it on the table. With the other she simultaneously jabbed the side of his hand with a small medical lancet. "Oh gosh," She dabbed at the wine with his napkin. "So *sorry*, sir."

"D---d fool!"

"Oh, my gosh, your bleeding." She patted the drop of blood she had drawn with his napkin. "I'll get you a new…"

Reginald grabbed her wrist, slamming it down amid the glass fragments and pinned her to the table. "Just a dammed minute, you."

"Sir?" She gasped in terror and pain. "Wha-What's the matter?"

He pointed to a tattooed American flag showing just below her sleeve. "You one of them *patriots* thinking you could sneak in here?"

Lisa was caught. She couldn't move her hand off the table and still clutched the lancet in her fist. "I, uh," she coughed. "You see, I keep my *Workers Party* flag in a more private place where only my good friends get to see it. This is just so no one will suspect."

Reginald's angry scowl, only inches from her face, began to slowly melt into a smirk and his grip relaxed.

"You're showing a *deception,* huh?" Now a wry smile. "I see. Very good."

Lisa forced an anxious grin while she quickly pocketed the napkin and the little jabber. "You don't miss a *thing*, do you? I'll get you a new glass and fresh napkin, sir." With only a slight tremble, she poured him a full glass of Cabernet.

Reginald held up a finger for her to wait. She could feel her pulse in her throat. He handed her his card. "Perhaps I could see that *better* flag of yours sometime?"

Lisa looked straight into his leering grin, took a fresh napkin off the cart, and carefully laid it beside him with a sweet smile. "Why, I'd be honored, sir."

The women finished up their bussing, forcing their minds to detach from the fiery exhortations pouring out of the speakers. Moxie Watver was the loudest of them all, exhorting everyone to harass and terrify the opposition in every public place.

Afterward, in the change room with the other buss girls, they only dared to nod at each other. The shuttle took them to Emma's car in the parking lot but she held up a hand to Lisa. "Let's talk later. I just want out of here."

Finally, they pulled into a space back at the dormitory and Emma ventured, "I think my heart's out of my throat now. I forgot I had a campaign sticker on my bumper. Didn't dare drive and talk to you at the same time." Her head fell back on the car seat.

"But you got a sample, right?"

Emma put her keys in her purse, pulled out a plastic bag with the hairs inside and handed it to Lisa. "Oh, yeah, and I saw you get yours, too."

Lisa held up two shaking fists next to her cheeks. Her voice squeaked. "We *did it*, Emma, and we're still both alive."

They did a double fist bump with gritted teeth and stared at each other with wide eyes for a moment before they screamed and shook their hands in the air.

Emma was laughing as she got out of the car. "Okay, Sister, but that's the *last* time I pretend to be a double agent. You looked like you got *caught* back there."

"I thought so, too. Listen, not a *word* to anyone, not even your mother or BFF."

Emma stopped walking and turned to her. "No problem. I like living, but tell me why Reginald grabbed your arm."

"He saw the flag on it and thought I was a spy. I told him I keep my Worker's flag in a more *private* place."

Emma giggled. "But, that's a lie."

"No. it's not. I have a book of flags and they're in the privacy of my dorm room." She put her arm over Emma's shoulders as they walked toward the dorm. "Look, I just want to say how proud I am of you. There's no other friend who'd have helped me out like this."

"Yeah, well," she gave Lisa a swat in the ribs. "Just don't kiss me."

DECLARATIONS

As Dylan got more and more into his message, he began pacing in front his class. "The American Patriots became increasingly impatient with King George's autocratic rule which extended to every facet of their lives—Tom: cell phone off, please."

"So what were they to do? Americans had a providential world view, not the secular one foisted upon them by their dictator, the king. Beginning with the first American settlers, the Bible was taught in all schools for two hundred seventy years, but that ended in the nineteen fifties."

Still pacing, he raised his hands. "Their local, biblically based laws were—Tilly, longer skirt next time, okay?—were often cancelled by the king.

"And, Jevon, they did protest slavery, too. Thomas Jefferson wrote numerous letters to the King complaining about it. According to British law, if anyone freed a slave the former owner would be put in jail. Yes, Betty?"

"Then why didn't they free all the slaves when America got its independence?"

"The founders tried. It lost by one vote. Remember the plantation owners were sent by the king specifically to grow crops with cheap manpower. Also, many state laws in the South still forbade emancipation. Slaves who fought in the revolution were awarded freedom but it took the Civil War to finally and completely free us from this curse."

Jevon shook his head, scowling. "Doesn't change the fact that millions of blacks were enslaved by racists right here."

"West Africa exported about four million to this country. At least the owners here provided housing for their families, clothing, some spending money and sometimes even land for workers to grow their own crops. Those Africans spread out over America and now they have over forty million descendants, all fully American citizens." Dylan smiled at Jevon. "Some even go to college."

"Still doesn't make it right. We should get reparation money."

"From who? Perhaps from England? They imposed it on us. In America, descendants of slave *owners* are a small fraction of our total population. Should they or every American be liable for something that ended one hundred and fifty years ago? Thousands of white men died to free the slaves. What is fair, Jevon?"

"Everyone in America should pay up. The country is rich and keeping slaves was wrong."

"How about a law allocating forty million dollars for reparations? Would that satisfy you?"

"It would be a start."

"But, every black person would only get one dollar. What sounds like a fair amount to you?"

"Ten thousand should do it."

Dylan chuckled. "I'm going to need a calculator, but I think that would cost four hundred billion. About seventy million families and businesses pay taxes. Eliminate black families and, just for a rough estimate, let's say that's sixty million tax payers."

He pointed to Betty. "Please calculate the tax increase per family."

After a moment, she slapped her head. "It's all sixes, but I get six thousand, six hundred sixty six per family."

"Whoa, all those sixes sound evil, but it's unlikely that a tax increase like that would pass congress.

"Look, I agree with you that slavery was evil, Jevon, but compare the fates of our four million to the *fourteen* million sold to Muslim countries. Want to know why they don't have descendants there?"

"Cause they let em go?"

"Sadly, no. Their slaves were castrated, kept in cells and worked to death."

Dylan paused and took a deep breath. The students sat quietly with scowls on their faces. Jim pouted and raised his hand with his index finger upward. Dylan bared his teeth. "Uh, oh. What is it Jim?"

Jim turned to Jevon. "Look, Pal, we've been buds a long time, but just so you know: no way am I giving you six grand."

When the laughter died down, Lisa raised her hand. "Sir, did you really say *public* schools actually taught the Bible?"

"Did everyone hear the question?" Dylan searched the faces trained on him. "Teaching the Bible and morality was actually *required* in school. The first schools were private but it continued into public schools too. As I said, this was for two hundred and seventy years. That is before, during and after the Constitution."

Jevon let out a guffaw. "Yeah, well it's been *unconstitutional* since before we were born."

"We're jumping a few weeks ahead of our course schedule, but this is important. Does anyone know who wrote that famous first amendment?"

Dylan noted the blank stares. "It was written by a man named Fisher Ames. He noted that many books are read in schools and commented, 'should not the Bible regain the place it once held as a school book?' Does that sound like he meant to take the Bible *out* of our schools?"

"Also, Gouverneur Morris, an active member of the Constitutional Convention who helped create its final language had this to say: 'Religion is the only solid basis of good morals; therefore education should teach the precepts of religion and the duties of man toward God.'"

Tilly wiggled her upraised arm and her torso. "But everybody says there's separation of church and state."

"They do, don't they. We're almost out of time, but for the next class I'm assigning you to find that famous clause in our Constitution. And, by the way, if you *really* want to get serious about the Constitution, I recommend taking Aimee West's course as an elective. She lays it on straight. My job is to give you the historical motives behind the scenes."

Lisa's phone, hidden under a book, began to vibrate. Dylan stepped toward her, index finger raised. The bell went off and the students rushed for the door except for Lisa, trapped by his stare. "Lisa, you know I asked for those to be turned off."

"I'm sorry, but I'm waiting for a *real* important text—uh, school paper business."

Dylan grinned. "Well, class is over. Check it."

She looked at her phone, jumped up with a screech, eyes wild with excitement. Dylan said, "Good news?"

"Oh, yes, Sir. Wait until you see the weekend paper."

Her text read: *Two bull's eyes. No names in your article, please. Good work.*

PUBLISHED TRUTH

THE OAKLAND FLAME, weekend edition
ANTIFA INVESTIGATION:

In the past few months, new information has come to light regarding the death of TV personality, Hayley Jones, who died on April 14th at Berkard University.

Initially, local police released a statement indicating that she was killed accidentally by a stone thrown during an Antifa riot. However, their records show that her demise came about from a large rock too heavy to have been thrown any distance.

Television footage revealed that the attack was orchestrated and apparently preplanned. While it is true that a stone did indeed strike Ms. Jones at the podium, that stone caused no significant harm. Despite this, no public statement of correction has been released, and they continue to refer to it as a "matter," not a murder.

Oakland police were required to turn their investigation over to the FBI and refer all further inquires to them. Our sources indicate that at least some funding of the

Antifa operation came through an organization that heavily supports a California congressman. The FBI will not comment on anything under investigation, and continue to label it "The Berkard Matter."

However, a reliable inside source claims with absolute certainty that three individuals have been identified as participating in the murder, one of whom is an eye witness and has been questioned.

What is unknown is the reason the FBI has not issued any statements. Political reasons are suspect. We will continue to press for justice, and we will continue to refer to their "matter" as "The Berkard Murder."

Lisa Combes, reporter at large.

Lisa presented herself to the Chancellor's secretary. "Hello, m'am, I presume he wants to speak to me about our paper?"

The secretary did not answer but said, "Go right in. He's expecting you."

Chancellor Stengel sat at his desk signing papers and did not look up when Lisa walked in and stood before him. After a minute, she politely coughed.

His expression morphed into annoyance and his eyes rolled up at her. "Ah, yes, Ms. Combes. I was talking with Professor Stark this morning."

"About my newspaper, right?" She flashed a happy grin. "Did you notice we're doing two editorials now? And, how about the new color process for the front page picture? Really sharp, huh?"

Stengel leaned back and glared. "First of all, young lady, it was never *your* newspaper, and second, you never informed Stark that you also have a job at an outside paper."

"Isn't that great?" She clasped her hands. "I didn't want to boast. Professor Janeway, you know she teaches Journalism, was so happy about it. On my test she wrote: "nice work, cub reporter," and added a gold star. That was kinda second grade, but I really apprec…"

"Stop."

"Sorry."

"If you are working for an outside paper I'll have to remove you from ours, and was it really necessary to reprint it in the Caper? As your last duty, you will do a retraction and an apology. Everyone knows that The Oakland Flame is a lying, right-wing trash heap."

"But, Sir, I'm just a freelance. I'm not on their regular payroll and no one ever said I couldn't write for outside newspapers. The English Department encourag…"

"Enough." Stengel waved his hand. "You want one last chance to stay on our paper?"

"Oh, yes sir, *please.*"

"Then tell me who your sources are for the information in your article."

Lisa straightened up, her mouth agape. "Chancellor, you *know* I can't reveal my sources."

"Then I assume they're fabrications. I'm considering having you expelled."

"Oh, my God. But sir I…"

He brushed her away with the back of his hand. "You're fired. Go pack up your office at the paper and get out of here. You're wasting my time."

WHAT IS TRUTH?

Dylan Coz walked into his classroom early to get set up but found the desk chairs were already arranged in his preferred semi-circle. Lisa sat in the end chair, bent over on the writing arm, head buried in her arms. She was crying. Her former pigtails had been transformed into a single braid behind her head.

Dylan put his briefcase on the desk, took a tissue from a box, quietly walked over and sat beside her. "Anything I can help with, Lisa?"

Startled, she sat up and stared at him through bloodshot eyes. "Nah."

"He extended the tissue. "Cheeks are kinda wet."

Lisa took it and blew her nose loudly. "Thanks."

"I'm sorry." Other students began to come in. "Can we talk after class?"

She nodded.

He went behind his desk and unpacked the briefcase. Tilly arrived in an overly demure olive dress. Jim entered in a Rams shirt and gave her back a little tickle as he passed behind her. Jevon had earphones on, twitching to a rap song. The seat beside Lisa remained empty.

Dylan stood in front of his desk. "Hello, everyone." He hoisted himself up to sit on the edge. "Before we have fun talking about all those battles that followed the Independence Proclamation we'll discuss the declaration itself. Yes, Betty?"

"You said to quote the place in the Constitution that says Church and the State are separate."

"Oh, yes. Quite right. Read that to us."

She tittered. "Those words aren't in there, but people say it's the First Amendment."

"Exactly true, Betty. I see you have it open. Read aloud the first phrase about religion."

"Congress shall pass no law respecting an establishment of religion."

Dylan pointed to a burly student with dark, curly hair. "Zeke, you've been quiet lately. What do you think that phrase means?"

"Well. it's…" He scowled but then his eyes grew wide. "Oh, yeah. The colonists hated having a state *sponsored* religion telling them what to do. They thought that line would prevent the government from ever messing with their religion again."

"Brilliant." Dylan gave him a grin and a thumbs up. "I'm nominating you for a Supreme Court Justice. Yes, the phrase is meant to protect religion from *Congress*. Clearly, it was to block a State sponsored denomination from wiping out religious freedom. They never expected they'd also have to protect the faithful from proclamations by the mayor of Oakland or whoever's running Berkard University."

Betty added, "Next it says no one can interfere with the free exercise thereof."

"Exactly. That part *does* tell Congress and our Chancellor to not object to a scripture quote at a graduation speech, even if someone is offended by the idea of God being real."

Jim boomed, "So, the Supreme Court flipped the law on its behind and gave the middle finger to Christianity. Too late. They've ruled, so it's *true now*."

Silence prevailed for a while. All eyes trained on their professor to see his response. He shook his head and smiled. "Colorfully put, Jim. You guys, are we ever going to get back to history? Okay, *truth* is important to history—and everything else as well, so lets go there."

Dylan jumped off his desk and went to the white board. "Listen up. Phones off. I don't want to hear any Google answers, just your *opinions*. There is no right or wrong here. Every opinion counts. *"*

He wrote "TRUTH" at the top. "Pontius Pilate threw this question out at Jesus' trial: 'What is truth?' Let's try and answer him." He turned his back to them. "Shout out your definitions, but one at a time."

- Truth is what ever "the man" says it is.
- When it feels *right*, that's truth.
- Truth is whatever you want it to be.
- If the song makes you cry, it's truth.
- Jesus is the truth, the way and the life. Without turning around, Dylan said, "Thanks, Betty." She tittered.
- It's what science proves.
- If it makes them happy, it's true for them.
- Truth is just relative.
- Keep repeating a lie and it becomes truth.
- If your ideas sound better than theirs, it's truth.
- In accordance with facts and reality.

"Okay, who googled?" He turned around to see Susan tittering, and pointed a finger at her. "Let me make my point another way. Show of hands. How many here believe in *absolute* truth?"

Glancing around, "Four. Who votes for truth being relative? Nine." He chuckled. "And somebody voted for both."

"Well, here's the thing. Philosophers define truth as 'that which exists independent of all thoughts concerning it.' They're talking about absolute truth, aren't they? Our Founders believed in absolute biblical truth. Yes, Tilly?"

"But still, how do you know truth really *exists*?"

"The answer might lie outside of human knowledge but it wouldn't change the fact. For instance: is there an earthlike planet on the other side of the universe? The answer has to be yes or no, but it will likely never be known. More often people ask if there is a God or not. The answer can't be settled by someone's *opinion*, but never the less, it has to be either yes or no. Jevon?"

"Yeah, well, what about fact checkers. They tell you what is true or not."

"They can be helpful by uncovering what is false. Unfortunately, some are sponsored by biased organizations with a specific ideology in mind. Susan?"

"I still don't see how any of this tells us whether Supreme Court decisions are right or not."

"Good point. With human writings, the purpose and context of the writer must be taken into account to discern the intent of his true meaning. A court can ignore that and create what is, in effect, a new law, at least temporarily. SCOTUS declares *opinions,* not absolute truth. Their rulings can be reversed by Congress or another court." He pointed at Jim whose hand was raised.

"So, now I'm getting that the Constitution actually *guarantees* religious expressions in school? It's the complete opposite of what's happening."

"Right on, Jim, but truth has a resilient way of shining through eventually. We can have unlimited falsities but there's still only one truth."

He smiled and opened his hands toward the class. "I've heard you guys like the idea of being rebels. Okay, next time we'll talk about that rebellious document called the Declaration of Independence."

PAINFUL TRUTH

Lisa remained in her end seat writing in a notepad while the other students filed out. Susan and Betty remained and sat behind her, hands on her shoulders. Dylan pulled one of the chairs around and sat down facing her.

She looked up and shrugged. "Here's an absolute truth for you, Professor Coz: Stengel fired me from the school paper."

Dylan jerked his head up, his brow in deep furrows. "Can't be, Lisa. You're a great writer. Wait, was it because of your murder story and the FBI's response?"

"Probably--yeah. He said it was because I wrote for an outside paper, but yeah, it was the murder story."

She turned around, thanked her friends, and asked them to wait for her outside. "You were right there with Emma and myself when the murder happened. Can I tell you something you can't reveal to *anyone*? I'd like your opinion."

"I guess so."

"Sorry, not good enough. This is dangerous information—seriously."

Dylan blew out through his cheeks. "All right, I promise. No one."

"Okay, an Oakland police detective has DNA evidence on Hayley's killers and an eye witness besides. Someone in that stratosphere at the top pulled a blanket over the investigation and he had to give all his information to the FBI."

"Well, that's probably all right, Lisa." He opened his hands. "They have all kinds of resources to find the killers and Antifa operates in many states."

"My reporter instinct tells me the move was just to keep the investigation in dishonest hands. They never worked *with* local police, and besides, this detective was able to identify the murderers even though he's not supposed to be on the case any longer."

"He'd have to check his DNA sample against actual people."

"And they're very well connected people. He sent Emma and me, posed as bus girls to a party they attended, and we snuck out the DNA proof the detective needed."

"Wow, that was gutsy. Now I understand the story you wrote."

"My question is this, Mr. Coz: should I tell a lawyer? Should I drop out of school or transfer? Frankly, I'm afraid of these people."

Dylan leaned back in thought. "Where do your parents live?"

"New Mexico, at least for another month or so. Think I should drop out and go there?"

"Nah" he grinned. "You're too tough a girl to back down and they would implicate themselves if they went after you directly. Besides, I doubt they'd see a college student as a real threat. More likely types like these would pressure you by doing something to scare your folks."

She grinned back. "My Dad's a sergeant in the Marines and so is my brother. He's at Camp Pendleton."

"Oh good. Normally, I'd say tell your parents, but in this case I'd wait and see. I'll bet your parents don't scare easily."

Lisa glanced over at Emma who had come in and was standing by the door. She waved her over. "I was just telling Mr. Coz what we've been up to."

Emma came up to them with books in her arms. "We're gonna be late for English Lit, girl." Smiling at Dylan, "But I'm glad we can talk to *someone.*"

"You're brave ladies." He got up. "I don't know what I can do to help get Hayley's killer but If I think of something, I'll let you know. One thing though: can you prove those samples are actually from the people being accused?"

Emma put her books down and pulled a phone from her purse. "Wanna see my party pictures?"

Dylan checked them out. "This guy is famous for something—a congressman's son, right?"

"Yeah, he led the attack gang and killed Hayley."

Dylan's hand slapped his forehead. "Maybe you girls are in over your head." Worry showed on his face. "But it sure would be good to bring these creeps to justice. Got a next step in mind?"

Lisa raised her index fingers in the air. "I'd like to do another article if the Oakland Flame hasn't fired me too."

"I dunno." Dylan scrunched his face. "I think we need more advice—someone who's streetwise and knows more about criminals than I do."

Emma's face brightened. "I know just the man. He's old and wise, been in the Black Panthers back in the day, worked for a congress woman, then got a new life in Jesus. He got a college degree in the Army and runs a counseling service for people in distress."

"Perfect," Dylan shrugged. "Go talk to him if you can."

"And, *and* he's the best banjo player in the state. He's in town doing a concert at a small venue in town. I could get you both in tomorrow night and you'd get dinner besides."

Lisa said, "Done deal for me, Sister."

Dylan said, "No kidding. Sally's away at a convention so I could join you. What time?"

Emma scribbled on a piece of paper. "Six o clock. Here's the address. Just tell them at the door you're with Emma Jackson."

He pocketed the paper. "Sounds like fun, too. How come you know this fascinating guy?"

Emma chuckled. "He's my grandfather."

PROTECTION

Sergeant Ryan caught Scott outside of headquarters as they were walking in. "Hutch, hold on a minute. I need to talk to you about an assignment."

Scott gave him a quick finger point. "Sure Boss, I'll see you in your office in just a sec."

"No, no," He gestured to one side. "Let's talk right here."

Eyebrows up. "You want to talk business in the open?"

"Yep. I've done some of my best work on our front porch."

They ambled to one side. Scott peered through squinted eyes. "Uh, oh, this is about something you don't want anyone to overhear, right?"

Sean grinned. "And what a smart detective nose you have. That's why I like working with you."

"Please don't let this be something the Chief will fire me for."

"Relax, nothing like that. Besides, you'd just be following orders. How are you doing on pinning down the times and places for the drug deals?"

"Just about ready. I've established a pattern but I'll need another week or so to check reliability. Eight to nine PM has to be locked in on my schedule, otherwise I can adjust my time for something else. What's up?"

Sean waited for some people to pass and lowered his voice. "This is about those Berkard women who got our DNA samples."

"Oh, right, and Ms Combes published an article about it—pretty gutsy of her—a little crazy, but gutsy. No one's challenged what she said so far as I know."

"The other media are ignoring it, but it's not them I'm worried about."

Scott studied his face for a moment before he replied through gritted teeth. "You think the Reinhardt boys are gonna take her out?"

"No, no, probably not." Sean glanced from side to side. "But if more comes to light, who knows? Look, what I want you to do is keep an eye on her for awhile. Stay out of sight but find out if the bad guys are trailing her. Lisa's risked a lot for us. We owe her a little protection at least."

Scott tilted his gaze skyward and blew out through his cheeks. "Oh, great. Just when I promised myself to avoid all women, now I'll spend every day following a crazy one."

BATTLE TRUTH

"Okay, you guys," Dylan chuckled as he greeted his class. "We're a full day behind after chasing down these side roads. Still, there are three battles I want to briefly tell you about before we get to the Constitution—two in Boston and one on Long Island.

"Thirty years before our revolution, in 1746, King Louis the 15th sent an armada of 73 ships, 800 cannons and 13,000 troops to take back Nova Scotia from the British, burn Boston to the ground and ravage New England.

"Immediately on hearing this, Massachusetts Governor, William Shirley, declared a day of fasting and prayer. They prayed for deliverance.

"Historian, Catherine Drinker wrote that the sky was clear and sunny on the morning of October 16th when people assembled in the Old South Meeting House in Boston.

"Reverend Thomas Prince presided and prayed: 'Deliver us from our enemy, Lord. Send thy tempest upon the waters to the east. Raise thy right hand. Scatter the ships of our tormentors and drive them hence. Sink their proud frigates beneath the power of thy hands.'

"Immediately, the church was in shadow and a violent wind shrieked around the walls and all by itself, the steeple bell tolled two strange, uneven notes. Thomas Prince raised his arms extolling that the bell rang for the death of their enemies. 'Thine be the glory, Lord, amen and amen.'

"A violent storm came up scattering and drowning the French fleet. Only a few made it back to France. If any of you like to read Longfellow's poetry, he wrote one about this salvation."

"Two decades later, the American Revolution had started and George Washington was training his troops near British occupied Boston. His Colonel, Henry Knox, was sent to Fort Ticonderoga in upstate New York to bring back fifty nine cannons to help drive the British out of Boston.

"Your text merely states that Washington placed cannons on Dorchester Heights and British General Howe, realizing he could not take Boston, sailed away. Wow, what an understatement.

"In December, 1775, Knox loaded the Ticonderoga cannons on flat bottom boats and started the trek to Boston, rowing them in freezing weather to the southern end of Lake George. He tried sliding them down thin ice on the Hudson

River. Then he had to make sleds and get eighty oxen to drag them through the snow toward Boston.

"Historian Victor Brooks called this dragging of heavy cannons 300 miles in winter 'one of the most stupendous feats of logistics ever recorded.'"

"Then, in the dead of night, they had to quietly move the cannons up to Dorchester Heights overlooking Boston Harbor—or the 'hah bah,' as they say it. To make it look even more impressive, they painted some logs to look like cannons. Anyway, when General Howe looked up the next morning he remarked: 'The rebels did more in one night than my whole army would have done in one month.'

"Never-the-less, on March 7th, 1776, General Howe prepared three thousand troops ready to unload from his ships and storm the heights. General Washington unleashed his counter plan. Who can guess what that was?"

Jim was recognized. "He fired every cannon and started a landslide."

"Nope." Dylan pointed at Betty's raised hand.

"I'll bet he prayed, too."

"Right on, Betty. Yes, he declared a day of fasting, humiliation and prayer asking for divine favor and protection.

"As Howe was about to attack, a violent wind and snowstorm erupted. Howe pulled back. The next day he wrote Washington that if the British were allowed to leave Boston peacefully, they would not burn it down. Not a single life was lost and we took Boston."

"Okay, Guys, isn't the real story more fun?" He pointed to a raised hand. "Yes, Susan?"

"Do you really think God answered their prayers?"

Dylan grinned. "Tell you what—ask me again after you hear one more real battle story. This one is the Battle of Brooklyn Heights, the first big battle after we had declared our independence. Your text simply says that Washington sent 19,000 troops to defend New York that summer but were outnumbered and outflanked by the British so they retreated to New Jersey.

"Your handout, however, has references to the battle strategy and the details make interesting reading, but even these accounts leave out some crucial points.

Dylan surveyed his students and was pleased to note their rapt attention. "On August 28th, 1776, General Howe had surrounded Washington's army in Brooklyn Heights. Probably still fuming about the humiliation in Boston, he was determined to put an end to this revolution in America.

The British had 130 ships to prevent escape by sea. I think we had less than a dozen ships in our little navy. The battle raged on with our backs to the water and we were about to suffer total defeat. The Revolutionary War would have *ended* right then and we'd be British subjects today. Any comments?"

Dylan chuckled as he pointed to Jim who's arm was waving. "Another battle plan, Jim?"

"No, but if Howe had won, today would be the last day of this course."

The class laughed. "Ah, so true, Jim, but who has any idea what Washington did?" He pointed to a raised hand. "Betty?"

She grinned. "I'll bet he prayed again."

"Right on, Betty. And a Nor'easter storm came in, sinking the British carts and cannons in mud. This was followed by an unusual deep fog, so Washington was able to evacuate all his troops by sea, undetected by the huge British navy.

"Some look at this battle as a defeat, but Washington's escape made our ultimate triumph possible. Notable victories against the British superior forces followed. We won the battle of Saratoga in October 1777 when the generals got their signals crossed and we took six thousand prisoners."

"Washington prayed before each battle. The final major defeat for the British was at Yorktown in 1781. General Cornwallis thought he had a perfect plan, but with the help of the French navy they surrendered and our independence assured."

Susan and Betty released three words in song: "God bless America."

Jim called out, "You're not really saying God saved America, are you?"

"Well," Dylan chuckled. "I guess we could at least say George Washington's prayers were answered."

FOUNDER'S TRUTH

Dylan greeted his students the next class day. "All right, now you know my weakness—discussing battles, particularly miraculous ones, but now it's time to study our government's foundation. Once we were free, it was time for America to set up its government."

"The Constitution is our set of fundamental laws and the Declaration of Independence, the mission statement that preceded and lead toward them. We need to ask ourselves why our Constitution is the longest lasting one in history and still going strong. The first place to begin is the second paragraph of the Declaration. Jevon, I like your reading voice. Read the first few lines aloud for us, all right?"

Jevon pointed to himself. "You want me?" Dylan nodded at him with a grin.

"Ahem. We hold these truths to be self evident, that all men are created equal, that they are endowed by their Creator with certain unalienable Rights, that among these are Life, Liberty and the pursuit of Happiness."

"Okay, pause there, Jevon. That beautiful sentence, that statement of *truth,* changed the world forever. No nation, with the exception of Israel, has founded itself on God's principals. Who would like to explain what it means? Betty?"

"It means that God created each of us and we are equal in His sight."

"Very good, but what else?" He pistol-pointed. "Emma?"

She raised a finger in the air. "It also declares that our rights come from God, not from men."

"Jim, you look like you have something to add?"

"No, but we're not supposed to say that now."

"You mean we aren't allowed to mention God? Some *man* said that, right? But, how about *this* man? President John Kennedy said: 'The rights of man come not from the generosity of the State but from the hand of God.' Perhaps they have a different platform today, but he was a Democrat, and I believe there are people alive today who heard him say it. Jevon, next phrase, please."

"That to secure these rights, governments are instituted among men deriving their just powers from the consent of the governed."

Dylan spread his arms to the class and smiled. "There you have it—American exceptionalism in a nutshell. We declare that 'we the people' shall govern ourselves to protect the rights given to us by God. Yes, Susan?"

"Ms. Thorn, our Sociology professor made a big point of the fact that God isn't mentioned in the Constitution."

"I'm glad you brought that up. I'm going to make the case to you that, not only is God's *law* written into the constitution, but its unique success is *based* on that fact.

"The Declaration enumerates twenty seven grievances they saw as violating God's law and the Constitution was written to correct all of them. So, why do you think our rebellious colonists thought they could take on the greatest empire in the world? That's in the last sentence. They had a 'firm reliance on the protection of divine Providence'" He pointed at a raised hand. "Yes, Betty?"

"You're saying they were not afraid to take on the British Empire because they knew God would protect them?"

"Yes, that is *just* what the declaration says." Dylan scanned the students and opened his hands. "Why do you think that might be? The answer to *why* was because of what had been going on in the previous few decades. Here's a hint. It begins with, 'The Great'. Anyone?"

He straightened up and waited for a few moments. "I only hear crickets. This was the period of The Great Awakening. It peaked around 1740. Betty, it looks like you just thought of something."

"Our pastor said that the religious revival of that time was started by Pastors Jonathan Edwards and Whitfield."

"Sorry, your pastor is wrong." Betty pouted.

Dylan gave them a stern look. This was the first major revival in America, and there were others later. I think they were somewhat like Pentecost. God *personally* came and dwelt among and within His people. Only *God Himself* can bring about a Revival where thousands are suddenly aware of His presence. The men you mentioned, and others, were inspired to preach about it, even anointed, but the reassuring belief of divine protection mentioned in the Declaration came from God Himself."

Lisa had her hand raised and got the nod. "Okay, but how do you go from believing in God's protection to knowing he'll back your revolution?"

Dylan began to pace in front of them. "Very good, Lisa. Exactly the question George Washington and his friends asked themselves."

He tapped his head. "So they wouldn't decide all on their own, they prayed to God for the answer. Wrestling with that decision inspired George to make up a flag that flew on our naval ships, our first American flag. It was a spruce tree with the inscription 'Appeal to Heaven'."

He stopped and faced the students. "I presume God answered them and said something like. 'I will be with you and deliver them into your hands.' At least we know they faced the start of the Revolution confident of God's protection. Yes, Wally?"

"An actual *voice* of God?"

"There's no record, but I think it's likely."

"But maybe what they really heard was a stored personality matrix in their bicameral minds."

Dylan laughed loudly and so did others. He waved a finger at the audience. "Wally is asking, in polite scientific terms, if they were insane."

Returning his gaze to Wally, "My answer would be that there are millions of *sane* people who hear words from God—words that were proven to impart knowledge and prophesy beyond their own human capability. I'll refer you to Pastor Wong for further discussion on that one, okay Wally?"

He cleared his throat. "Anyway, our Founders felt God was with them when they declared independence and the evidence confirms it. Remember the miraculous wins in battle? Later, when they wrote the Constitution, they based our laws on His teaching."

Susan called out, "But Ms. Thorn said 'I challenge *anyone* to find scripture verses in the Constitution.' She went on about how man has risen up above primitive superstitions."

"Wow." Dylan grinned. "Our most common sin: only man exists and he knows everything. I won't get backed into theology again, but it will be fun to take her challenge.

First off, a study of all available quotes from our founding fathers shows that the Bible was the most frequently referenced, and one scholar referenced six hundred thirteen civic lessons taught in the Bible. Yes, Betty?"

"But isn't she right that the Constitution itself has no quotes?"

"*Exact* quotes, no, but the meaning interpreted for our times is clearly there." Dylan took out a little notebook from his shirt pocket and put his thumb on a spot. Leviticus 19: 34 admonishes its people to treat the aliens living among them as though they were native born. Okay folks, go to Article one, section eight, third paragraph. Betty, you read that one."

"To regulate commerce with foreign nations, among several states and with the Indian Tribes. To establish uniform rules of naturalization…"

"Wait, this one's even clearer: Deuteronomy 17: 6. 'No one should be put to death on the testimony of only one witness.' Okay, now turn to Article three, section three where punishment by death for treason is described. The second sentence reads, 'No person shall be convicted of Treason unless on the testimony of two witnesses.' Get the idea?"

Jevon waved his hand. "But those might be laws from anywhere."

"Perhaps, if there were only two, but our Constitution is full of them. I'll give you a handout next time with cross references. Most founders gave verbal tribute to divine inspiration for the Constitution they created, especially Ben Franklin, Alexander Hamilton, George Washington, James Madison, and James Wilson. Remember, all of them had experienced The Great Awakening."

Jim blurted out, "But the Supreme Court took religion out, didn't they?"

Dylan tossed his head back and chuckled. "So, now you have a few unelected men who have just recently tried to change the purpose, spirit and soul of our nation. Earlier Supreme Court precedents disagree with them as well, but this was a political decision, and recent judges tossed out the precedents."

He thumbed through his notepad. "Ah, here it is. In 1833, Supreme Court Justice Joseph Story wrote: 'One of the beautiful boasts of our municipal jurisprudence is that Christianity is part of the Common Law. There never has been a period in which the Common Law did not recognize Christianity, its light and its foundations.' This opinion was reaffirmed by the Court and our Presidents on multiple occasions until the sixties."

Betty and Emma were grinning, but the rest of the students looked like a gun had just gone off.

"I'll leave you with the words of John Adams. 'It cannot be emphasized too often or too strongly that this great nation was founded, not by religionists, but by Christians; not on religions, but on the gospel of Jesus Christ.' There's a quote worth memorizing."

The class was hushed. "All right, next time, your assignment is chapters twenty three and twenty four. I want to compliment you guys on your mid terms. As a class you got an A minus average—best I've seen at this university since I've been here. See you next week, and God bless you all."

Dylan walked the campus path toward the parking lot, briefcase in hand. A man sitting, on a bench, got up as he passed by and walked beside him. "Excuse me," he said. "Professor Coz, I don't know if you remember me. I'm Professor Watkins, Physics department."

"Sure I do. Sam, right?" Dylan smiled. "We talked over lunch a few months back. How's that old dog of yours doing—a Collie, I think you said?"

"Shepherd mix, named Bosco—sadly he passed away a few weeks ago."

"Ahaaa." He shook his head. "Sorry to hear it, Sam. They're like family, aren't they?"

"Yes, look I'm glad I caught you. I want you to know something. It may appear that all your colleagues are against you, but I'm not. In fact, I admire your courage."

Dylan stopped walking and faced him. "Against me? What are you talking about?"

"The word's out you're talking about God in class." Sam produced a thin-lipped smile. "Here at Berkard, they burn people at the stake for that."

"Why should they care? Anyway, I think I only quoted our Founding Fathers in my history class."

"Yeah, well, they do care. I think God and truth are the new hate speech. Anyway some of the faculty met to censure you, but I want you to know that you're not alone. We may be a silent minority, but you do have friends here."

"Thanks, Sam. It means a lot to me to hear that. Maybe the silent minority could throw a few silent prayers my way, huh?"

"Oh, yeah. We're already doing that." Sam nodded enthusiastically. "And I'm gonna talk to them about not being so silent, too. Besides the obvious, anything specific you'd like us to pray for?"

"Sure," Dylan chuckled. "Pray that you won't have to bury my charred remains next to Bosco."

BANJO TRUTH

Dylan's Garmin announced: "You have arrived at your destination." From the street, a cross in a display window hinted the venue would be a church. A sign in the alley next to it read "sorry, lot full." He felt he was lucky to find a spot on the street only a block away.

A small brass plate beside the doorpost read, "Calvary Covenant." Below it a tacked-on, handwritten note announced, "CC Jackson, tonight"

He mumbled to himself, "She said a music concert, but I guessed right: it's Emma's church."

Inside, past the foyer, he found one large room, well lit and crowded with long tables facing the stage. Dylan had begun to savor the fried chicken aroma when a Hawaiian-looking woman hustled over to greet him.

He shook her extended hand. "Hi, I'm with Emma Jackson." She smiled and pointed to the Jacksons reserved table up front.

"There you go. Enjoy."

Dylan spotted Lisa working on some chicken wings. Emma startled Dylan with a welcome hug from behind. She pointed to one side of the room. "We don't serve the main course until the break, but please help yourself to juice, and appetizers. I'm so glad you could come, Professor."

"Glad to be here. Other than food, how is this different from your church service?"

"There's lots more music, not all of it Christian, and the pastor only talks for ten minutes—at least that's what he said. Look, they're getting ready to start."

Dylan poked his carrot stick in the dip and checked out the band. Five people, five different races. That made him grin.

The singer/ announcer wore a sixties style dress, long auburn hair and called out in melodic tones. "Welcome everyone. Are you ready to shout out to the Lord?"

The audience responded with a chorus of yeas. "For those who don't know me, I'm Irma, and we're gonna have some fun tonight." She gestured toward the keyboard manned by a Polynesian man. "Let me introduce Saroyan on the keys, and here's Running Deer on base." Applause.

"And, hold on," She gestured to one side. "Our wild man on drums, Chang Xi." More applause and a drum roll. "And, as advertised, here's our one and only *CC Jackson!*" Applause, cheers, and a "badda badda BOOM" on the drum.

CC was an elderly black man with a huge smile and a gray afro that said he didn't care if that style had passed. CC strummed a few "hello notes" on a guitar. Dylan leaned toward the students. "Thought you said he played the banjo?"

Emma said, "Our guitarist, Sanjay, isn't here so I guess he's filling in. Not to worry. Banjo is coming."

Traditional worship music began the program with "How Great is Our God?" and others, but when CC reached behind him and switched to the banjo, the crowd whistled, cheered, then fell silent.

With a little keyboard intro, CC belted out "Roll in My Sweet Baby's Arms," his deep raspy voice sounding like it was the fifties all over again. Between measures, CC would spin off some electrifying riffs for his appreciative audience.

The band switched back to two worship songs with Irma's crystal soprano voice, then CC let loose with "Old Salty Dog Blues." Dylan leaned in to Emma. "Wow, I got goose bumps on that one. Your grandpa's the best I've ever heard. Does he have a CD?" She grinned and held up two fingers.

Pastor Wong came on stage for a short message "complaining" that no one could follow that last number. He invited everyone to dig into the chicken and chili while he talked about the wonderful blessings the Lord bestows.

He concluded with, "It looks like most everyone here is familiar except a few. If there's anyone who hasn't accepted Jesus, you'll see two prayer team couples by the door when the concert is over. Uh, you don't get dessert unless you see them first." Chuckles. "Only kidding of course." He walked off waving. "Enjoy the rest of our show."

And what a show it was. CC saved his best for last, flooring everyone with "Dueling Banjos" and getting a standing ovation.

Right afterward, CC came off the stage and did a quick waddle toward their table and embraced Emma. "And how is my little munchkey tonight?"

"Oh, Gran-pop-pop, you were just *great*."

He chuckled. "Well, gimmie another twenty years and I'll learn how to really play that thing." He pointed to Lisa and Dylan. "So who did you lure into my clutches this time?"

"You met my friend Lisa once before, and this is Mister Coz, one of our professors."

CC came around to their side of the table, fist bumped with Lisa and shook Dylan's hand. "Coz. That sounds like a saxophone player I know."

"Hi. I'm Dylan. The only thing I play is the CD."

As they sat down, Emma said, "We're hoping you can give Lisa some advice."

"Honey, you know that's what I do for a living—but here at church I have a special private office." The "office" was the corner of the room with folding chairs facing each other.

CC sat opposite them and reached for Dylan and Lisa's hands. "First, if ya don't mind, I like to start with prayer."

CC ignored Dylan's "Oh, no, I'm all right," and bent his head down giving thanks for blessings and asking for the help of the Holy Spirit.

"Yes, yes, I see." His voice became low and smooth. "These two are father and daughter."

Lisa's eyes popped open, her head shaking, but he went on. "Not what you're thinking--you are a *spiritual* family, fighting a common evil. "This one." He raised Dylan's hand, "Is fully with You, but he will need Your wisdom in the trials ahead, Lord."

"But, this one," he said raising Lisa's "bounces around between faith and disbelief, between trust and doubt. Sometimes she is courageous, sometimes fearful, but she always returns to seek you, my Lord." He dropped their hands and sat upright.

Lisa stared at his wide grin. "Whoa," She said.

Emma stood behind him, hands resting on his shoulders. "Did I mention that granddad is a prophet?"

CC asked, "So, what's the problem you two think you need me for?"

Dylan said, "Look, I'm fine. I'm just here to help any way I can."

"Really?" CC's expression waxed to compassion. "You are about to be severely tested, young man, but tell me what brought you to see me."

They all took turns relating the story of Hayley's murder and the investigation. When they were done, CC let out a big breath. "So, you are dealing with evil people in high places. Remember this: your battle is not carnal but mighty through God to pull down the strongholds and principalities of darkness. Well, that's not an exact quote, but you get the idea, and the idea is to seek God and pray."

Emma wiggled his shoulder. "But we *are* praying, grandpa. Can't you think of something else?"

CC smiled at his grand daughter. "I think I see why the Lord sent Lisa to me. Emma, do you remember what your Uncle Will does?"

"Uh, he's in the government doing something, isn't he?"

"My son is with the Los Angeles office of the FBI."

Lisa let out a squeak. "Wow, so maybe he can tell us what's *really* going on."

"Maybe yes, maybe no, but if I do get anything out of him, you can't print his name, or anyone he might mention as a source.

He leveled his gaze on Lisa. "This bright-eyed cub reporter does understand that, right?"

"Oh, absolutely. We protect our anonymous sources like a tiger."

"Good, but with these guys at the top, you can be sure your phone and internet are flowing right into their hands. You do know that, don't you?"

"Uh, I guess you're right. I'll be careful."

CC squinted and nodded. "Got to be, Honey. Emma will tell you if I learn anything but then I'll give it to you in person right here in church on Sunday."

Lisa smiled. "Now why did I think you'd get me to become a church goer?" He raised a finger. "Not only that, but we're about to offer you the salvation prayer. Remember what Pastor Wong said: you won't get any of my wife's peach pie without it."

CONSEQUENCES

Dylan saw the Chancellor's door was ajar and peeked in. "Good morning, Henry. I got your Email. You said you wanted to see me. Is this a good time?"

Chancellor Stengel looked up from his desk with a scowl. "No, but this won't take much time, Coz."

Dylan approached his desk with a grin. "What's up?"

"How *dare* you become a radical after all these years."

"Henry, I'm no radical. You should know that."

Stengel grabbed two papers on the edge of his desk, stood up and waved them at Dylan. "I'm looking at two letters about you that came this morning--one signed by five students and one signed by six of your colleagues. Have you become a proselytizing Jesus freak, Coz?"

"I've never tried to convert anyone at Berkard, in or out of class, but I admit to being a Christian. If that's now illegal, I missed the memo."

Stengel rose up, leaning forward on his knuckles. After a pause he squinted at Dylan. "Don't toy with me, Coz. They sent me recordings. You've been quoting Scripture verses in class—even handing out Bibles to your students. You know the speech code here at Berkard. Do you need another copy?"

"Sir, I've *only* quoted what our Founding Fathers said. I can't help it if some of *their* words are scriptural. It's all in the context of our history. The bibles are for literary reference."

"Did you or did you *not* get the latest teachers guide to your course?"

"Of course I did."

"Does it mention God or the Bible in any way?"

"No, the closest thing is noting that some came here for religious freedom."

"And why can't you just leave it at that?"

"Because our Founding Fathers were passionate, born again Christians who founded our country and all its laws on the word of God."

Stengel threw the papers to the side. "Not *anymore*, they're not. Do you know how offended some of your students are?"

Dylan nodded, his tone even. "Henry, many people have been offended by God for millennia. Others fall on their knees and worship him—their choice, but I only mention God's word in class as it pertains to history. It's vital for them to unders…"

"Enough! And don't 'Henry' me. You're being put on leave of absence for the rest of the summer session. I've arranged for another to finish your course."

"But—*what?*"

"Look, most of your colleagues wanted you fired. I'm doing you a favor, Coz. You can return in the fall and teach your Astronomy course. That should be safe, at least, but we'll have to convene the full council to decide if you can ever teach history again."

"Whoa, I'm stunned." He opened his hands. "So, I'm off campus until September?"

"You are. Take time to think about what you've done. Think about your career, your retirement. You can plead your case to the Council this fall, but I can tell you this: If you open your mouth and flaunt any more scripture verses to our students, you'll be fired."

The next day, the circle of history students began to worry about their professor. He'd never been late before. His desk was clear of the usual clutter, save for an empty cardboard box. A woman came in the side door wearing a gray business suit and a frown. She didn't make eye contact with the students but dropped her briefcase beside the desk and went to the white board behind it.

She wrote: "Ms. Thorn," turned around, faced the class ands began in a monotone: "I'm Ms. Thorn and I will be teaching the remainder of this class. Mister Coz was called away on administrative leave. Put those chairs back in order."

The students sat, open mouthed and in disbelief. Stephen, the "silent" one who sat at one end, grinned and volunteered to speak for the first time. He raised a fist, grinned, and exclaimed. "Yeah!"

Ms. Thorn smiled back at him. "I see from the teaching notes you were studying our deeply flawed Constitution. We'll correct some teaching errors first. Then we will examine the history of American slavery in the south, and how industrialization in the north led to the evil of capitalism and the conscription of labor. For extra credit, we will discuss the coming new revolution which will correct the sins of our past."

She studied the students for their reaction and pointed to one woman. "You there, what's your name?"

"Lisa Combes, m'am."

"Tell us why you are crying, Lisa."

"I'm crying for my country, m'am."

Thorn stiffened up. "And well you should. There are many evils needing correction, don't you think?"

She went to a smaller white board covered by a roll up shade. "I'll put your daily reading and reference books over here."

She rolled up the shade, shrieked "Ahhh," and searched for the eraser. Not finding one she began to vigorously erase the words with her sleeve.

The board read: "Woe to those who call evil good and good evil. Woe to those who are wise in their own eyes and clever in their own sight. Isaiah 5, 20-21"

HOME

Dylan Coz quietly unlocked the front door of his house at two PM, headed for the living room and put his briefcase beside the sofa. He kicked off his shoes, gave a big sigh and stretched out on the couch.

Sally's voice called down from the upstairs. "If that's not my husband down there I'm coming down with the shotgun."

He shouted back, "It's me but you can bring the gun and finish me off if you like."

She clumped down the stairs and found Dylan, with stocking feet on the arm of the sofa, and a towel over his head. After giving his toes a quick squeeze, she bent down, lifted the corner of the towel and gave him a kiss on the cheek. "They cancel your class, Darling?"

"Nope, Stengel cancelled *me*, Sweetheart."

"What?" Sally knelt on the floor beside him and pulled his arm into her lap. "They can't do that—not without cause and one of those faculty meetings."

"Right. Stengel has a letter from some of my colleagues, but it's not like I'm fired." He tossed the towel aside and turned to his wife. "They put me on administrative leave until the fall semester."

"I think I can guess why," She pulled his hand to her chest. "But, do tell me about your cardinal offense."

"I told my class the truth about our founding father's passion for this country, their deep faith, and backed it up with their actual words."

Sally's brow furrowed. "I'm missing something here."

"Our American heroes were quite vocal about their Christianity and the fact that our laws are based on biblical principals."

"Oh, God." She stood up, walked in a small circle and threw up her hands. "Has it really gotten this far? The academics hate God *that* much? They want to rewrite Him out of *history*?"

"Oh, they do, yes." Dylan stood up beside her. "I'm sure the next step will be teaching that Man created the universe and only their elite few should rule the world."

"Yeah, well that's what they believe, isn't it? So, there's no good news here, is there?"

"Yes there is." He embraced his wife, drawing her close. "We get to go to our lake cabin three weeks early, and it's all cleaned up."

She chuckled and rested her head against his chest. "You've been different since you got yourself born again. You're all calm about this, huh?"

"Peace that passes understanding." He nuzzled the top of her head. "Anyway, I'll have plenty of time to prepare for the astronomy course. At least I'm still scheduled to teach that. Combined with Earth Science, it will be a large group in the main lecture hall."

"Well, that's good, and it's your favorite subject." Sally gave him a kiss and stepped away. "I hate to be the gloom and doomer, but why not apply to some Christian colleges next week while you wait for the fish to bite?"

He chuckled. "Maybe I will, but despite everything, I do love teaching at Berkard. Say, did I tell you what happened to my student, Lisa Combes?"

"She's the journalism major who wrote the story about Mrs. Jones?"

"Right, well first, she was fired from the school paper allegedly because she also writes for the Oakland Flame."

"And, of course, that's not the real reason, is it?"

"No, I think she knows something about who actually murdered Hayley Jones. I can't say more, but it probably involves someone in the elite Progressive circle, and they're trying to cover it up."

"You really think she's solved the case?"

"Don't know, but she might know who *did* solve it."

"Dil," She shook her head. "She's just a college student. How could she get access to special knowledge like that?"

"I'm not sure, but it's clear she did. Anyway, Stengel said she could stay on at the paper, but only if she told him her sources."

Sally covered her mouth. "Good Lord, that girl's in trouble."

TRUTH QUEST

Lisa walked into the lobby of her dorm and found Hall Monitor, Lynn, talking energetically with two campus policemen. As soon as she saw Lisa she called out, "There she is now."

"What's the matter, Lynn?"

"Two men were in your room. We thought they were maintenance. They had badges and everything, but the police don't know them."

The officers smiled. "I'm Sergeant, Susan Coleman, and this is officer Ann Roger. We would like you to take us to your room and report anything that might have been stolen."

"Sure. How long ago were they here?"

"Judging from the call in, they only left twenty minutes ago." Susan looked at Lynn who nodded in affirmation.

On the way up the elevator Lisa turned to the officers. "They must have known I was in a class. You should have a surveillance video, right?"

"Lobby and stairwells. We'll check it with you on the way out."

Lisa gasped when she opened the door. All her drawers were open and their contents on the floor. Her computer lay sideways on top of her desk. "Well, ladies, you don't have to be a detective to see they were after me and not my roommate."

The officers stood by the doorway. "Take your time, Miss."

She began to put her things away and held up a sock with a ten dollar bill sticking out. She recovered a credit card on the floor. "So what does this tell you about the break-in?"

"You're sure there's nothing missing?"

"Nothing, but I'll bet they copied my hard drive. I'm a journalist and I've printed some unpopular stories lately."

"Good. We're glad no harm was done. Before we go, we'll check the video recordings."

Lisa laughed. "You really think they won't be erased?"

"We'll check anyway." The officers turned to leave. "Have a good day, Miss."

Lisa locked the door, pulled her desk chair into the closet and reached up under the ceiling tile. She smiled as she retrieved her flash drive and slipped it into the inner liner of her purse.

She picked up her computer to return it to its place on the floor and discovered her book had been placed under it: Flags of the Nations, Past and Present. The page with the Communist flag had been torn out. Time for a better hiding place, she thought.

Lisa jogged straight to the bus stop and went down town. Alone on the street, Lisa felt vulnerable. She hastened to the elevator at the Oakland Flame and only began to relax as she walked through the copy editors at work on the third floor. Some glanced up and gave her a wave and a smile.

The door to the corner cubicle-office was ajar and bore the name: "Vera Sloan, Asst. Editor." Lisa knocked on the frame.

"Well hi there." Vera came from behind her desk and gave her a quick hug. "How's our favorite new reporter?"

The strain showed on her face. "In need of friends and prayers, Vera."

"Our specialty, Darlin." She motioned to the little sofa bench on the side wall. "Here, sit. You've obviously stumbled on something big."

"You mean because my article pushed against the FBI?"

"That and the two death threats our Editor in Chief got. Both said to drop the Berkard story."

"You think I should?"

Vera laughed. "Course not. If you're going to work here, and I really hope you do, these angry threats only mean we're onto something important. Anything new with you?"

"Someone ransacked my dorm room today and I was fired as editor of the college newspaper by our chancellor."

"Oh." She gritted her teeth. "Sorry. Did your Dean say why?"

"Not really, but he did say I could stay on if I revealed my sources."

Vera let out a chirp and covered her mouth. "Wow, you could win a lawsuit over that one, but let's put that on hold. What it really means is you've poked a hornet's nest, one with big important hornets. Did they find anything in your room?"

"No. What they were looking for is in my purse." Lisa watched Vera's eyes grow wide. "I'm at the point where I have to trust someone, and I hope it's you."

Vera got up, closed the door to her office and sat down next to Lisa. "Are you a Christian?"

"Sure am."

"Well, next to God, we reporters support each other, especially when we have the same worldview. Whatever you trust me with will stay with me. Not even the Chief will know if you say so."

For a few moments Lisa's expression implored her editor. "Okay, I'll tell you what I know. First, do you have a safe place for my flash drive?"

"I have a safe in the foot well of my desk covered by a wooden panel."

"Sounds good." Lisa reached in her purse and handed her the drive. "I did not make a copy. All my sources and their updates are on that, but I might as well just tell you before you look at it."

Vera leaned forward, her expression intent. Lisa went on: "The short story is that Detective Sean Ryan of the Oakland police has interviewed an eye witness to the murder who identified the killers. There was DNA evidence too, but the FBI took over and local police had to back off.

"Detective Ryan is really angry about this and asked if I would volunteer to get confirming DNA from the subjects. One of them is a VIP."

"Oh, my God. That's *way* too dangerous. I hope you're not going to try."

"Too late. See, I'm crazy, I guess. A friend of mine and I went to a party where the suspects were and we got the samples. They confirm the killer's identity, Vera."

"Ahh." Vera put her hands on Lisa's shoulders and lowered her head to touch the top of hers. "Good *Lord*, Lisa, you're the bravest girl I know."

"Thanks. In the anxiety department, it even beat out a dirt bike motor cross.

"Oh, gosh." Vera sat back and covered her mouth with a laugh. "So, the FBI should know all this. I'm almost afraid to ask who the murderers are."

"They're congressman Luchow's son Reginald and a lesbian accomplice named Charon. Funding for Antifa likely came through the Reinhardt Corporation, but I'm not sure what I should do about this, as a reporter I mean."

Vera blew out a breath through her cheeks. "Wow, I had no idea this was *that* huge. At this stage we should not be naming names in print, but our sources can trace money from Reinhardt for you. The regular media won't touch this with a ten foot pole, but maybe we can do teaser stories to push the FBI into a statement. If it makes you feel any better, I don't think the bad guys will touch you directly, especially since they don't know what info you have hidden away."

"Good, then I'll send you a short article to pressure the FBI. Right now I have to find an encrypted phone to call my Dad about something he says is important."

"Sure, use mine." She got up and headed for the door. "It's got the latest scramble program. I've got an errand to do anyway."

Lisa took to the couch and punched in her dad's number at the Marine base.

"Hi, dad. First I want to apologize. I won't be coming home on summer break. I have to work on an important story. Remember, I sent you a copy of my first article in the Oakland Flame? I'm calling from their office now."

"Ahh, you're so the career girl already. I'm expecting a transfer about that time anyway. I'm hoping for Pendleton where your brother is, but tell me, how's my little Darlin?"

"Getting into trouble as usual, Dad, and I'm working on something that may go national. So, what's *your* important thing?"

"Nothing except the base commander told me this morning that I should ask you to drop your investigation."

"Oh, my God." Lisa bounced off the sofa. "And where do you think he heard about what I'm working on?"

Dad laughed. "Well he certainly hasn't read your stuff. He only reads the Stars and Stripes. Obviously this came from higher up."

"Whoa, I'll say. Dad, to use your expression: you know you're over the target when the flak gets heavy."

"Yeah, and I know not to bother asking you to drop the story, but are you taking the bus and walking all around downtown Oakland by yourself?"

"Without a car, of course I am."

"Look, your old man is worried about you. We were going to get you a car for your graduation, but I think you need it now. Get whatever you want up to fifteen grand."

"Wha-hoo!" Lisa did a bounce and spin. "Gee, thanks, Dad. You know I love you."

"Lisa, just be careful. I didn't tell Mom about the threat, alright? If I get some time after the move, we'll see if we can visit. Okay, I gotta go. We love you Punkin."

Back out on the sidewalk, Lisa noticed a green sedan she had seen before parked nearby. A good looking man sat behind the wheel, watching her. She stepped over to the car and confronted the driver. "Hello, officer. Have I done something wrong?"

He laughed. "I'm Officer Scott Hutchins, Lisa. Sergeant Ryan asked me to keep an eye on you for your protection. Am I really so obvious?"

"Like a pink bow on a hippo, sir. Your only cover is you look more like a movie star."

Scott laughed. "You investigative reporters are just too observant. All right, smarty, what should I have done to be less noticeable? Keep more distance?"

Lisa bent closer, staring into his blue eyes. She smiled. "If you'd worn a Hawaiian shirt and drove a red Mustang, I'd have never noticed. Meanwhile you've embarrassed me in front of my workplace."

"I'll pass on the suggestion to my sergeant. And, how can I make up for your, uh, embarrassment?"

Lisa put a finger between her lips and donned a puzzled look. "Hmmm. Well, you could save me a bus ticket and drive me to the Appleby's near the campus. Then you could continue to *carefully* watch after me while I'm eating lunch alone at the counter."

Scott laughed heartily. "Just don't call this a lunch date."

"Course not." She scowled. "Between us, we're only two professionals discussing strategy."

"Good, just so there's an understanding."

"But between my *friends*, there will be a whole story about us on Pinterest."

He snort-laughed. "Just get in the car, you…"

SUMMER INTERLUDE

During the break before the fall classes nothing scary happened, but:

- The national media hinted about possible Conservative scandals, and interviewed people who said they were deeply distressed about: guns, global warming, those "hating" Christians, income inequality, Russian collusion, and bigoted white people in general.

- Dylan worked hard on preparing for his course on Astronomy and Earth Science. Sally fawned over him a bit too much both at home and at their lake house, but Dylan stood up under all the shoulder massages and chocolate cookies like a man.

- Emma and Wally got engaged, or rather "engaged to be engaged." She wasn't sure she could marry someone who was still unsure about God, but he did start attending Calvary Covenant with her.

- The Berkard Capers, now under new management, announced a six part series to begin this fall called "Islam, Persecuted and Misunderstood." The series will explain that if everyone accepted Islam it would bring about world peace and a greener planet.

- CC Jackson reported to Lisa that his son discovered what the FBI is doing with the murder investigation. The file is managed by their "Sensitive Matter Team" and marked "Berkard Affair- TS-IIO" which basically means "incoming information only." No one sees it except need-to-know agents with top secret clearance.

- Lisa did an article for the Oakland Flame about the world's climate. She interviewed several of the two thousand *nongovernment* sponsored scientists who know that man's activities have little to do with global temperatures. She also bought a used Harley Street Glide motorcycle to outrun the bad guys. It is pink and sports a yellow daisy on the front fender.

- In the interest of tolerance, Berkard opened a "free speech" booth in a remote part of the campus where "radical" students can talk about offending subjects. Wally calculated that the "free speech" zone covered exactly 0.0015% of the campus. Hecklers invited.

TRUTH BYTES

Lisa's cell rang in her dorm room. "Hello?"

"Officer Hutchins, m'am. Do you have a moment?"

"Hold on, I'll go look around and see if I can find a 'm'am' anywhere around here."

He chuckled. "All right, I guess that was a bit formal. Ms. Combes, then? Look, I heard about your room being ransacked. Our concern is for your computer. If you could walk it over to your campus computer lab, I'll meet you there in half an hour and check it out."

"Oh, gosh, you're right. I'll bet they put some spyware on it."

"Is now a good time? You're free?"

"Yeah, sure. Fall classes don't start for two days and I'm almost finished reading 'The Battle of the Bulge.' I'll be there."

Lisa arrived at the lab, her computer tucked under one arm. Scott was chatting with a professor as she put her machine down on a table. "Hi. You know each other?"

"Hello, Lisa. Professor Tyndale and I were in the same Masters program. He went on to teach 'Comp-Si,' as you know."

Tyndale nodded at Lisa. "I leave you in good hands." He grinned and walked away.

Scott said, "The University helps our department by letting us share some advanced equipment." He moved her computer to a test bench, slipped it out of its case and began hooking it up. "So, that book you're reading—is it about dieting or the military?"

She giggled. "Military. I'm a Marine brat and I like espionage stories and strategy--that sort of thing. You know computers, huh?"

"Yeah—you might say." He plugged a piece of equipment into her unit. "I almost went the same route as Tyndale, but police work is more fun."

"As for me, I'm a 'compu-klutz.' Vera, she's my editor, wants me to take a basic course this year." She stood next to Scott watching the complex of numbers and icons flitting across his monitor. "Oooh," she said.

Scott worked silently for awhile, his fingers flying around the keyboard. "All right, milady, the good news is they didn't put in an audio bug, but there's a tracking cookie reporting to another IP address."

"So you took that out, huh?"

"Nope. It's still there."

"What?"

"We don't want them to know it was deleted, so I installed an on-off switch for you." He pointed to a screen icon. "Leave it on when you're looking up generals in the Revolutionary War, but switch it off if you're looking up Reinhardt or asking about the FBI."

Lisa leaned forward to peer at the screen, one hand on his shoulder. "That's so cool. Thanks."

"Oh, you're welcome." He patted the hand and gave it a squeeze.

She withdrew the hand and blushed a little. "I had no idea something like that was even possible. Great. That's one less worry"

"Glad to help." Their eyes locked as both smiled broadly. "But, one more thing. Text me if you're heading out to the bus stop so I'll know when you're leaving campus, okay?"

"Sure, I'll text you, but you'll never catch me on my new Harley."

Chuckling, he looked at her and crossed his eyes. "Now *I'm* the one who's worried."

CREATION TRUTH

Astronomy 101 registered more than expected and the students filled Berkard's largest auditorium. Dylan surveyed the incoming crowd and was pleased to see that Emma and Wally were there with Lisa. He also recognized three faculty members slipping into back row seats. Not only was that unusual, but they taught Political Science, Middle Eastern Culture, and Sociology.

Dylan called out: "Welcome to Astronomy 101. The recommended text is 'Astronomy: The Cosmic Journey.' As you know, Professor Wycliffe is unavailable this semester so you'll have to put up with a mere Associate Professor. However, I've put a lot of effort into this preparation and I hope you won't be disappointed.

"In the interest of full disclosure, I've been known to make reference to a Creator on occasion, so raise your hands if any of you my find mentioning God offensive."

Three hands went up. "Only three out of a hundred ninety four? Okay, feel free to either drop this course or stay and tough it out. You might like the Poly-Sci course that's in the next time slot called "Our President: impeach or prosecute," but it's only one credit. If you stay however, I promise there will be no exam questions of a religious nature."

Of the three, one dropped his head, one gave Dylan the finger, and the third one walked out. "All right then, lets begin, and what better place than the beginning. As he walked over to the big screen, he sang the Sound of Music line, 'The best place to begin is the beginning. It's the very best place to start'."

His first visual went up behind him showing a cone of light starting on the upper left corner and widening out to the lower right. Stars were shown in the middle and galaxies to the right. "I plagiarized this picture from Discover Magazine from three months ago, so please don't tell on me."

"Here's what we know about our beginnings." He wiggled his laser pointer on the bright tip of the cone. "The best evidence to date reveals that our three dimensional universe was created roughly fourteen billion years ago from a four dimensional universe that still surrounds us. Perhaps it was a collapsing 4D black hole. We can't see the four dimensional stuff, but call it dark matter and energy. It comprises about 95% of our universe and its gravitational pull keeps us from crashing back into a black hole.

"At the point of our creation, about a thousand different types of sub atomic particles, energies and constants

177

were formed. Because each one of them affects the value of all the others, there's an unbelievable number of possible combinations, about ten to the five hundredth power."

Dylan paused to see if there was any reaction in the students. "Here comes the exciting part. Most of these combinations would *not* form a stable universe and only about five of them are compatible with a universe capable of supporting life."

Dylan grinned at them while a subtitle appeared at the bottom of the screen reading: "In the beginning, God created the heavens and the earth. Genesis 1:1."

"So, the chances of us living in a life-giving universe are about the same as winning a billion to one lottery a billion times in a row. If you can choose to believe that, then you believe we're really, really lucky. Another alternative is *someone* picked out and arranged our sub atomics." The boy who'd raised his middle finger, and one professor walked out.

Dylan stretched his arms out to those leaving. "A third alternative would be to walk away from truth."

He pointed to the starry part of the picture. "After the age of sub atomics, atoms formed, mostly hydrogen which coalesced by gravity into the first stars. These were massive short-lived stars. The heat and pressure within them resulted in atomic fusion and the formation of the heavier elements. When they became novas and exploded, the building blocks of our solar system, these heavier elements, were strewn around the expanding universe."

He moved his pointer from the stars to the galaxies.

"Gravity brought the swirling debris together again, heavier stuff in the middle, surrounded by dust which began to clump together forming smaller, secondary stars and early planets. Unlike our solar system, most stars are binary."

His next visual showed a black ball surrounded by thousands of particles. "This is the stage of the proto sun. At first, the Earth and the other planets being formed around it were in the dark since our forming sun has yet to be ignited." A caption appeared on screen: "The earth was empty. Darkness was over the surface of the deep, and the Spirit of God was hovering over the waters. Genesis1:2."

"Our solar system continued to form from countless collisions between the rocks and material falling in toward the sun to be. Density, temperature and pressure kept increasing until finally nuclear fusion occurred, and our sun ignited in a blaze of glory."

The visual changed to a blazing sun surrounded by planets and heavy debris. The caption read: "And God said, 'Let there be light.' And there was light. God saw that the light was good. Genesis 1:3."

"At this point in our history, about four billion years ago, Earth was hit by a large impactor about a third its size.

We wouldn't be the same without this precise glancing blow. It tore off a chunk of crust that formed the moon and put it into orbit. This chunk off our Earth was just large enough so that our moon appears to be the same size as the sun, allowing for perfect eclipses."

A hand was waving from the front row. Dylan paused and pointed at him. "If you're getting biblical on us, what about the creation in seven days?"

"I promised the Chancellor I'd stay out of theology." He grinned. "But since you *asked*, Gods thoughts and ways are not like ours. He gave us a hint about that when He said: His days are *like* a thousand years. That is an expression, not referring to an exact thousand but to a very long time. Living forever, I'll bet He sees time differently from us."

The student nodded and Dylan went on. "Wait, there's more to this impact. It caused the Earth to spin causing night and day, tilted its axis to give us seasons and made our orbit elliptical so that we have recurring climate changes."

The caption now read: "and He separated the light from the darkness. God called the light 'day' and the darkness He called 'night'. Genesis 1:4."

"After all this slam-bang activity, our poor, battered Earth was all lava and volcanoes, but after a few million years it cooled down. The lighter granite rock floated in clumps over the heavy, dark basalt and clustered to form the continents.

There was gradual cooling until it was cool enough for liquid water. The vapor in the atmosphere condensed and it rained. It rained a lot. Our oceans were born at that time."

A steamy, smoky ocean and rocky mountains appeared on screen with the caption: "Let the water under the sky be gathered in one place and let dry ground appear. Genesis 1:9"

"Next I offer you a humble apology from the scientific community. We have no idea of how life began here. Oh, sure, there are lots of theories like lightning working on organic precursors, or compounds brought together in ice crystals, but we haven't found a real 'smoking gun', so to speak."

The visual changed to one of lush primitive vegetation. "We do know that plants were first, presumably from single celled organisms in the sea, and then they migrated to the land." The caption appeared: "Let the land produce vegetation. Genesis 1:11"

"By this time, the oceans were full, our weather patterns emerged and there were breaks in the clouds. If those ancient ferns had eyes, they would have seen our familiar blue sky by day and stars at night." The caption read: "Let there be lights in the sky to separate day from night and let them serve as signs to mark seasons, days and years. Genesis 1: 14"

"Somewhere, somehow the animal kingdom began in the ocean as well. No one knows how, but there are those who have the yucky idea they arose from fungi." An image of dinosaurs and birds filled the screen. "A few million years is pretty short geologically speaking, but in this short time, life became hugely varied and complex." He grinned. "Some say it's all by lots of lucky, chance mutations."

"After the sea creatures appeared, I guess they noticed all the tasty vegetation on the land and staged an invasion. Those dinosaurs you all loved as kids have survived as the birds of today. The DNA of Tyrannosaurus Rex is very close to the chicken, but I guess a big chicken wouldn't make a scary movie." The students laughed. Dylan added the caption: "Let the water teem with living creatures, and let the birds fly above the earth across the expanse of sky. Genesis 1: 20"

"Finally, at least for the purposes of Earth Science, mammals took over the land when the original dinosaurs became extinct." The scene changed to a farm with cows and horses, but to one side was a tree with a raccoon staring back at the audience with a look of curiosity.

"Scientists still cling to a nineteenth century theory called evolution to explain all the enormous variety of life." This caption came on: "God made the wild animals according to their kinds, the livestock according to their kinds and all the creatures that move along the ground according to their kinds. And God saw that it was good. Genesis 1: 25."

"The truth is, we don't have a good scientific theory for the vast complexity of life on our world. Each living organism is intricately made, from the workings of every protein inside, to the interdependent organs, and to the 'finished' organism. We know a lot about how a body works but precious little about where it came from and why."

The screen shifted to an image of their textbook cover and Dylan spread out his arms to the students. "So, this is just a brief introduction folks. This first week you will be reading about primitive discoveries in astronomy. We will have fun uncovering the mechanics of our universe and, here's an incentive: the top twenty grades on the midterm will earn a trip to an observatory. See you next Monday."

Dylan picked up his briefcase and turned toward the door. Wally stood up and began to applaud. It spread around the audience, but there were some countering boos as well. Dylan said "Thank you," waved and went to the side door. Just outside, a campus policeman handed him an envelope.

The letter inside was signed by the Chancellor and read: "The emergency meeting of the faculty oversight committee has recommended to the Chancellor that Dylan Coz be terminated immediately on the basis of outrageous proselytizing. Chancellor Stengel concurs and has so ordered. Mister Coz may appeal to the full faculty at its next meeting should he so desire."

HOME

Dylan got home, parked in the driveway and walked around to the back yard. Sally spotted him from the kitchen window as he knelt in prayer on the edge of the patio. Shortly, she stood behind him, gently rubbing his shoulder.

He responded to her unspoken question. "They fired me, Sal."

"What!? But you made tenure at the start of this term."

"It's all right, Darling." He got up and embraced her. "I don't think I can teach there any more, I mean I don't want to."

"What? You're *tenured,* right?"

"Actually, no. There's a clause in the contract that says the first tenure year is dependent upon a majority vote of the University Board. Who knew? I could appeal or sue them, but I think I'll apply to some Christian colleges instead."

They turned to go inside. Sally threw up her hands. "You started talking about *God,* didn't you?"

"Stengel said not to *talk* about scripture. I didn't—not a word. Well, I answered one question, but I just put up a few screen shots, and they were completely appropriate ones, I might add."

Sally moved the patio slider to one side and his dog, Arthur, came out, hastening toward his master's scratching fingers. Dylan sat down on the patio sofa to give him a better massage. Sally sat beside him and sighed, "Let's stay out here awhile, huh?"

"Sure." He picked Arthur up so he could be partly on his lap. "At least I have you two for loyal friends—and there's a few on the faculty, too. The main thing that's going to bother me is the fact that I had quite a few students who were really getting my message. I'll miss them. I'll miss not knowing what's happening to them."

Sally nodded. "What really bothers *me* is that our whole country is headed for that fiery lake." She sighed. "What do you think we should do?"

"I've got a four-month severance. After that, if I don't have a job, we may be living in our little cabin."

"Oh, I see," Sally chuckled. "We'll be growing our own food and cutting firewood for heat."

"And you'll be scaling the fish." He grinned at her. "No, really, I'll get a job doing something."

Her face showed a sudden recognition. "I almost forgot, and now I understand. One of your students called. She said her name is Lisa, and she wants to come here with some friends about four. I said okay, but I'd call back if you're not here before then."

"Sure, I guess—probably just want to express their sympathy."

Sally shooed the dog to the ground and she nuzzled against her husband. She took his hands in hers. "Let's pray."

When four o'clock came, a pink motorcycle roared into the driveway carrying two young women, one black, one white, scarves flying. Emma jumped off the rear seat. "Whoo-we, you got a sweet ride, Sister."

They were giggling as they approached the house but stopped abruptly when Sally opened the door holding back a barking basset hound. "Hello, I heard you coming." Dylan told me about you—Lisa and Emma, right?"

Lisa raised her hands. "Guilty as charged. Hope the noise didn't startle you."

Sally reached for their hands as they approached the front door. "I'm Sally Coz, of course. Come on…"

Lisa was petting the dog but Emma turned around. "Wait, there's one more coming in my car."

An ancient Chevy Nova pulled into the driveway trailing blue smoke with the scent of burning oil. A young Asian man got out wearing large round glasses and a big grin. Sally said, "Emma, why didn't you drive your own car?"

"You're kidding." She pouted and pointed at Lisa. "And let my boyfriend put his arms around *this* one? No way."

Lisa chuckled and gestured to the approaching man. "Sally, this is Wally Kim. Wally: Sally Coz."

He shook Sally's hand and slipped his other hand around Emma's waist. As they went in, he whispered, "You're missing on one cylinder you know."

"My car or me?" He gave her a little pinch to hear her giggle.

Dylan came in from the next room to greet them. "If you guys came to cheer me up, it's working. Come on in the living room and have some snacks." Arthur rubbed against the ladies bringing them to their knees for his abundant dog kisses.

As they settled in, Emma said, "First, we said four o'clock because my granddad has some more FBI info. He said to come by the church at six, but changed it to seven. You could come too, if you like."

"Thanks, but you can tell me later. Was that all?"

Sally interrupted. "Seven is better, so now I can insist you all stay for dinner. I made a big pot of stew so it's no trouble at all."

The three looked from one to another. Lisa said, "Sure, we'll stay. Uh, Mister Coz, CC told us this info shouldn't get passed around by phone or Email."

187

"Oh, all right, I'll come with you. Maybe CC will play us some more banjo magic, huh?"

Emma chuckled. "Grandpa won't need much prodding to do that."

Lisa leaned forward making eye contact with Dylan. "But, here's what is on our mind, Mister Coz: there's eight of us who would like to finish those courses you started. We could even pay you something. We just want to find out the truth about early America, the universe and how God fits in. You don't have to say right now, but think about it, okay?"

Dylan's body relaxed. He took a deep breath and looked from one hopeful face to the next. Sally was biting her lip and on the verge of tears. "Guys, you just made my day. It would be my absolute pleasure. No charge. Do you have a meeting place in mind?"

Emma shook her hands in front of her face then clasped them together. "I was going to ask Grandpa and our pastor if we could use their side room. Oh, thank you so, so much, Mister Coz."

After dinner, they all hustled to the little downtown church. The doors were open and CC Jackson was rehearsing a banjo number on the stage. He didn't stop but winked at them as they moved into in the front row.

When he finished, they applauded. CC turned off the amp and pulled a folding chair around to face them. "Thanks for coming. My son has pulled out some interesting stuff. Just remember, you can't name him if you're gonna talk about it, okay?"

Lisa reassured him. "He's my confidential source and, as a journalist, I will *never* reveal him, or you either, for that matter." She glanced at the others. "And you guys better be cool with that too, right?" They nodded.

"Good. My son says the FBI has its own internal information system about things like this, and he tells me that there are a lot of rank and file agents pissed—I mean really bothered by the secrecy going on regarding the Berkard file."

Lisa raised a finger. "But how would they know what's in the file?"

"The information isn't secret until it gets in there. The big news is that three billionaires, Anton Boros from America, and two others in Europe are funding Antifa and other disruptive operations. West coast money is laundered through Reinhardt and some by way of Congressman Bernard Luchow with the help of his son, Reginald. He's the one who pays for the protests and fires up their people."

Lisa asked, "Did he say what their motive is?"

"Well, their affiliates also own many media outlets. The big picture is these elitists intend to first destroy the

American system and render Judeo-Christians impotent and, they hope, gunless. With the financial crisis they'll produce, and the resultant rioting, taking us over should be easy. They'd pretend to be our saviors and run the world. They have even picked out a name. Their new order will be called 'The United Socialist Republics'."

Dylan chuckled. "And my colleagues ridiculed me when I suggested that."

Lisa slapped her knee. "Yeah, well, someone will have to *prove* it, won't they?"

Emma pointed at him. "Uh, Granddad…"

CC threw up his hands. "Hey, don't look at *me*."

Emma laughed. "No, not that. I wonder if we could use the meeting room here one night a week. Mister Coz is going to teach again."

"Oh, sure. Any night but Thursday when we rehearse. Ask Pastor Wong so he thinks it's his decision."

DESPISED TRUTH

BERKARD CAPERS:

"PINK POSIES EXPOSED,"

A report by Mohammed Barsi

"Are you annoyed by seeing more and more of those pink flowers on Fridays? They seem to be everywhere: pinned in headbands, worn as corsages and attached to backpacks. Men are sticking them in lapels. I even saw one tacked on the back seat of a motorcycle.

"What do they mean? Is it a secret society, or just a way of saying TGIF? Our eavesdropping super reporters at the Capers have the answer but I'm afraid you won't like it. Now *we* know! It's a Christian cult honoring white supremacy and hatred of the oppressed.

They deceive one another, claiming the flowers 'miraculously' appear on some bush as an act from the god of their cult. However, one of our reporters, Steve, saw Emma Jackson going into a flower shop early one Friday morning. So much for their 'miracle,' right?"

"What are they planning? Whatever it is, it can't be good. Interception of their texts and emails shows them talking about bringing campus speakers, petitioning Planned Parenthood, restarting the University Chapel services and restoring marriage, whatever that means.

"I have personally seen a text message about some students meeting in secret with a former professor who was fired for teaching seditious, inflammatory ideas.

"They are planning something, folks. I'm sure of it. Maybe we should act first?"

The next Friday it began: name calling, backpacks trashed, and purposeful tripping. The Friday after that, it escalated to tire slashing, splashing passerbys with catsup, dirty water and even urine. One male student challenged his attacker, but two others were waiting nearby and they all beat him severely. A female student asked a boy why he had doused her with foul smelling stuff. Receiving no answer, she began to pray for him. He threw the canister at her and ran.

Finally, those who wore the Rose of Sharon decided it was time to act together. They met every Saturday morning in an off campus church and began their spiritual warfare, crying out to God to forgive, enlighten and save those who persecuted them.

TRUTH FOR LUNCH

Dylan carried his tray into the Faculty Lunch Room and pretended to ignore the angry scowls. He knew better than to sit next to someone, but landing one chair over from Myrna Clark seemed safe. She was a Biology professor and had been a long time friend.

He risked a "Hi, Myrna," spoken to the back of her turned-away-head as he sat down. She addressed the man next to her, "Excuse me, I'm going for some coffee." She never returned.

Dylan shook his head, grinning. *At least now I've got plenty of elbow room for a change.* He propped up his phone, punched in the current news and mixed his mashed potatoes into the meatloaf gravy.

A younger man with curly, black hair and an impish look on his face plunked his tray down right opposite Dylan. "Hello," he said tilting his head and making eye contact. "I'm Drew Sims, Astrophysics. I'm new here, but they told me you'd never darken Berkard's doors again."

Dylan smiled at him. "Hi, well I get to darken for two more days until I clean my computer and pack up."

"Oh, right. Anyway, I met you once at an Astronomy convention a few years ago, but I just transferred here this year.

"Yes, I remember." Dylan finger pointed. "You were the one asking the presenter all those questions he couldn't answer."

He nodded. "Yup, well the 'funest' place to explore is in the land of what no one knows. Say, it's a bummer you got fired. I asked around and they basically said you'd turned into a gospel preacher."

"Really?" Dylan chuckled. "Not quite. I put a few bible quotes on the screen while I was teaching Astronomy and I told my class that America became what it is because the Founders believed in God and biblical principals."

"That's it?" Drew's forehead furrowed. "I thought everyone knew that—course I went to a Christian college."

"I might be teaching at your Alma Mater soon myself." He tilted his head. "But, say—fair warning. Just being seen with me might lose you some friends around here."

Chewing, Drew mulled the flavor of the meatloaf. "Good thing life isn't a personality contest. Being new here, I got to ask a lot of questions. Just so you know--you're not alone in your beliefs."

"Yeah, well, I haven't seen any smiles lately. Stengel told me the faculty sent a unanimous vote of no confidence to the Board."

"And that is a lie, Dylan. The faculty vote was nine to seven."

"Really?" Dylan looked incredulous. "How in the world could you find that out?"

"Ah, well, that's my forte." He grinned. "I'm good at finding answers to tough questions. My insatiable curiosity needs daily feeding. By the way, those seven signatures were twice normal size. 'Course I can't reveal who told me that."

"And I won't push you, but it's good to hear. However, if you want to stay here, it's better if you don't discuss God with anyone, especially the students."

Drew laughed. "Don't forget race, gender preference or capitalism."

"Fortunately, there's the 'anti free speech' code they have written out for beginners." Dylan looked up at a man approaching them. "Uh, oh. I think I've already gotten you in trouble."

A slender, frowning professor stood behind Drew and placed one hand on the back of his chair. He wore an ancient tweed jacket with holes in it and tiny round glasses. "Ahem, Professor Sims, I know you are new here, but you should know you're talking to a convicted felon."

Drew turned and looked up at him. "Ah, Professor Weinrich--Geology and Anthropology, correct?"

"Yes, and as one of your mentors, I suggest you move your seat."

"But, sir," Drew said, his expression now one of childlike innocence, "I thought it was visiting hours."

Weinrich stepped forward and turned so he backed into the table and faced Drew directly. His voice became a growl deeper than one would expect from his slender frame. "I hope Coz hasn't polluted you already. His game is poisoning young minds to believe in a God and telling them how He created the universe."

Drew feigned total amazement. "Wow! Coz knows *how* God did it? Astrophysics is just finding hints of *what* He did, and Genesis tells us *why* He did, but *how*? Coz must be a genius."

Weinrich let out an expletive and strode away. Drew spoke to his disappearing back. "I'm sorry, sir, but if this guy really knows *how* God made all things, I gotta hear it."

"Drew," Dylan spoke through his convulsing laughter. "I think we're gonna be friends."

VERITAS VOS LIBERABIT

"THE TRUTH SHALL MAKE YOU FREE."

Classes were over by four on Fridays so those who wished to hear more of Dylan's teaching gathered for the first time in the small activity room at Calvary Covenant, chatting and laughing while waiting for him to arrive.

Half of Dylan's history class showed up, including Jim, Tilly, Betty and Susan, all wearing their Rose of Sharon blooms. Jevon came too, but he didn't wear a flower.

Scott Hutchins was parked up the street sitting in a convertible and wearing a loud print shirt. Lisa tried to conceal her wide grin as she walked by him with some other students. She avoided looking at him directly, but snuck in a finger wave behind her back as they all walked past.

Emma, Wally and Lisa greeted Dylan when he arrived. They put out their hands to shake his, but Dylan gave the three a quick embrace instead.

As the students sat down on folding chairs, Betty tapped Lisa on the shoulder. "Interesting splash design on your sleeve."

She half turned back, grinning. "It's an 'avant-garde' look, dear. Catsup, I think, but maybe salsa. Care for a taste?"

"You're so saucy."

Professor Coz and Pastor Wong stood in the front, waiting for everyone to get settled. Dylan said, "I just want you to know how deeply moved I am that you want to hear more about this radical idea called truth. Since I'm your professor in exile, from now on, you don't have to 'Mister-Coz' me. Just call me Dylan but first, for those who don't know him, here is our host, Pastor James Wong."

Following polite applause, Pastor smiled at the students. "I want you all to know that I am honored by your presence in our humble church." He gave them a nod. "So many young people have given up searching for God these days, it does my heart good to look into the faces of those who eagerly seek Him."

"I'm going to leave you in the hands of your professor in a moment, but if he doesn't mind, I'd like to say a few words to you."

Dylan was nodding yes, so he continued. "I want to give you a quick take on how I see current events from a Christian point of view. In the past generation, our schools and government have gone from just giving up on teaching God's word to militant atheism. We have gone from respecting life to treating an unborn child as an object, a possession, that can be thrown away. Our present society has gone from revering family, divinely assigned gender and marriage to—well, mocking all of it."

Pastor paused, studied the ceiling for a moment, then sighed. "Do not think for one moment that this is the result of a few people being selfish, or that modern technology has made old ways obsolete. Do not believe for one second that fine sounding things they call inclusivism and tolerance are actually motives to help people. All of this is simply Satan convincing people that man is supreme and God and His laws are old superstitions to be forgotten. The devil's goal is to rule this world through people he can control."

"I am here to proclaim that both God and Satan are real and every human being must choose between them. Our battle is not just here on Earth where, as mere humans, we would lose; but in the spiritual realm where, with faith and prayer, we can call on the mighty hosts of Heaven to fight beside us."

Pastor Wong paused again and gazed into the wide-eyed students. "The main weapons of the devil are lies, feigned altruism, deception and flattery, but his goal is death. God offers love, truth, peace and freedom and His goal is life. I'm not going to sneak in a full sermon here, but I offer you the chance to learn more about spiritual warfare in our church and our programs. Meanwhile, I'm returning you to Dylan Coz to learn about truth. It will set you free."

Dylan and the students applauded loudly as Pastor Wong walked out with a wave and a smile. "Wow. That will be quite an act to follow. Spiritual warfare—love it. I'll do my best to shed light on historical truth and reality." He pointed at a raised hand. "Tilly?"

"Are you going to start teaching history where you left off?"

"I sure can, but I want this to be informal. Any question goes." He gestured with open hands. "Wally, you look like you can't wait to say something."

"It's that big impact event..." He got up and partly turned to the others. "The one that created the moon. I'm in a Math club and we're going crazy working with it."

He looked back at Dylan. "Can I tell everyone?"

"Of course. I can't wait to hear myself."

"Yeah, well, back when the solar system was forming there were lots of little impacts as the planets swept the debris from their orbits but this was a giant one. The early earth was hit by a small planet almost half its size and angling in from the direction of the sun like the comets do today. Had to be a rare thing even then. Right, Dylan?"

"I agree."

"Okay, so here's where the probability gets really spooky. The chances that the other planet misses Earth are high. The chances that we have a relatively direct hit are much less but the chances of a glancing blow ripping off a moon sized chunk into orbit is so unlikely we're still crunching the numbers."

He saw that Dylan was nodding. "That colliding planet had to be just the right size with the right velocity and on a perfect trajectory. The impact gave us the spin and the tilted axis we have not to mention our final size and gravity. To top it all off, the chunk of rock that was torn loose formed a moon and put it in an orbit so it looks exactly the same size as the sun in our sky. Bottom line: it shouldn't have happened, but it did."

"Good job." Dylan grinned. "So, Wally, what does the Math club think explains it?"

Wally began to laugh and shake his head. "It really couldn't be by chance. We think a 'three hundred bowler' rolled the perfect shot."

Chuckling, Dylan said, "I want Him on my bowling team. One of the most common lines in the Bible is 'Then they will know I am God.' I think He likes it when we discover Him. Later, I'll tell you what He did to pull off the star of Bethlehem, really *three* things, perfectly timed. Also, I'd like to discuss why we humans are so reluctant to accept God's reality, but I think most of you came here for American History."

He opened his hands to the group. "Show of hands: how many want to learn more about America's true history before the current revisionists rewrote and spun it?"

Most hands went up. "All right, then. We were working on our Constitution. Who remembers what relationship it has to the Declaration?" Dylan tried to mask his surprise when one hand shot up. "Jevon?"

"Uh, yeah. It was a shout out for all the protests going on. We showed that king and the world what we stand for in America."

"Right, Jevon." He chuckled. "I missed the sense of that myself--street sense. We were revolutionaries after all, weren't we? We had a cause to cry out for."

"Uh huh, and we *won* that war. We stuck it to the ole king."

Still chuckling, Dylan raised a fist. "Right on, Jevon." He clicked a remote. "Now I hope this projector works."

After a bit of fiddling, a small, wavy, movie screen lit up. "And here's what one of our 'on fire' revolutionaries said:" The screen showed a portrait of Patrick Henry and the quote, "It cannot be emphasized too often or too strongly that this great nation was founded, not by religionists, but by Christians; not on religions, but on the gospel of Jesus Christ."

Betty spoke up. "And why isn't that in our texts, Dylan? It sounds fundamental."

202

"Because the God deniers want to teach the lie to all students that it never happened, but truth is truth. I think John Adams said it best in one sentence."

His picture came on screen with the quote, "The highest story of the American Revolution is this: It connected in one indissoluble bond, the principals of civil government with the principals of Christianity."

Lisa got the nod when she raised her hand. "But, I don't see the Supreme Court interpretations of the Constitution as following Christian principals."

"Ah, you're so, *so* right Lisa. We've allowed a few unelected lawyers to rewrite our laws. Here's an Old Testament quote from Jeremiah: 'The heart is deceitful above all things, and desperately wicked.' The founders were aware of this danger, you see."

"But why didn't they make the Constitution foolproof?"

"There's no defense against a judge saying, 'what they *really* meant was...' Some founders were quite worried about phrases that could be twisted, like 'general welfare' or 'for the public good'. James Madison worried that the power hungry would use them to their own advantage. Even so, they knew Congress could correct the Court if they ever got the guts."

Dylan flipped through a few slides. "Ah, here it is." Madison's portrait sat beside the quote, "The Constitution is a limited one, possessing no power not actually given, and carrying on the face of it a distrust of power."

After discussing more Christian-endorsing quotes from the founders, Jim raised his hand. "Dylan, what's your response to Thorn's accusation? She says these guys were all hypocrites because they were slave owners."

"Oh, boy. That nasty accusation really needs to be addressed, but I think we better get to that at our next meeting. Meanwhile, let's not be angry if you're persecuted as a Christian. I can see that some of you are, but it's an honor. Treat those students who are hostile to you with a dose of God's love.

"Our time is up for today, but I just want to say how proud I am to be with all of you. You should give yourself a name, maybe 'Order of the Rose' or 'The Rose Guard'? What do you think? God bless you all."

Lisa folded up her notebook, but felt her phone vibrating with an incoming text. Her message was "St1-D?" The code she knew was from Detective Ryan. It meant "Can you meet me Saturday at Denny's at one o'clock?"

JOURNALISM

A heavy fog had moved in over Oakland Saturday morning. Lisa was glad she didn't have to drive her Harley while glancing over her shoulder. No one could follow her today. It was enough of a problem to see traffic lights and street signs through the gloom.

Finally, she was in the alley leading to the Oakland Flame's parking lot. Trucks for the weekend edition were pulling out and Lisa hoped her story would be in the next one. Vera was scowling over some papers but brightened up when she knocked on the doorframe.

"Something the matter, Vera?"

"Plenty. We just lost a big advertiser. The liberal groups have been trying to shut us down, and getting advertisers to boycott us is an effective weapon."

What was your 'big sin' this time?"

"Not giving a local gay wedding a full page spread last weekend. Their wedding *was* covered but a philanthropist's daughter got first billing. This makes us homophobes and bigots in their eye. In reality, they just hate our truthful political reporting."

"But, don't the advertisers check on the accusations?"

"Most do, but some are afraid *they'll* be on the evening news with pickets outside. Never mind that. What did you bring me?"

"Oh, me." She opened her file carrier and put some papers and a flash drive on her desk. "This is one the Berkard Capers wouldn't publish. On Fridays, a few dozen students wear a flower in memory of Hayley Jones. She was murdered on a Friday and there's a flowering bush near the scene."

"That's interesting, Lisa. It's sweet, but we'd need more of an edge to get it in print."

Lisa grinned. "My article describes how the present editor labeled us a hate cult in the paper without knowing anything about us. He called for action against us and every Friday we get splashed with nasty things. Some guys got beaten up and I report three cases of tires being slashed and dorm rooms ransacked. I put some pictures in the flash drive."

"Well, that's a better story but…"

"Wait. The real human interest came when they allowed our spokesperson to speak at the student assembly on Thursday. Lately we've been calling ourselves the "Rose Guardians." Turns out they were only mildly annoyed by the idea of what they called a Christian hate cult. When they found out we were actually honoring Hayley Jones, a full riot developed."

Lisa pulled up her sleeve showing a nasty bruise. "Outside police had to come and break it up. Two of our people are still in the hospital. I documented all the details."

Vera picked up the papers with a grin. "*Now* you're on, honey, but I wish you had called us. We don't get a police bulletin like the other papers. Still, I didn't see any coverage from them in their Friday editions."

"The Chronicle gave it an inch on page eight, Tribune two inches in the middle of Local News. They said 'students rise up against hate speech once more'. No TV coverage, even though we offered some cell phone clips."

"Good, so it's really an exclusive. Did you explain the flower thing in your piece? Add anything else for color?"

"Yes, and I also added a short interview with a student in the hospital."

"Wow, Lisa, you've already got the instincts of a pro."

"Thanks, I..." Lisa bared her teeth. "I was hoping you'd let me add a scripture quote on the end."

Vera put her elbow on her desk and leaned her head on her hand. "And, that would be what?"

"If the world hates you, keep in mind it hated me first. John 15: 18"

SLAVERY SECRETS

Dylan noticed that the number of students had grown after a couple of Fridays had passed.

He welcomed them. "Sorry we didn't get to the slavery issue last time, but going over the Great Christian Revival leading up to the Revolution was so essential."

"Today, our thought police and history deniers indoctrinate you into believing that slavery was part of racism and invented by American white supremacists three hundred years ago. Actually, the mindset of slave owners is more like those who would like to convert the world to global socialism. Both regard human beings as property to be controlled by themselves. State run governments like to use nice sound bites like 'for the common good,' but in actual practice, the common people only exist to serve the power elite."

"Historically, slavery has been around since the dawn of civilization and knows no race, creed or country. For the most part, slaves were obtained from conquered or undeveloped nations, but sometimes they were simply a way of paying off a debt. How slaves were treated completely depended on the moral values of the culture. This could range from treating them like family members to the extreme Islamic method of castration and working them to death."

"I'm sure you all remember that about 400,000 Jews were kept as slaves by the Egyptian Pharaoh for many years. Read Exodus in the Bibles I gave you. Slavery was, until recent years, accepted in world culture.

"In our colonial days, the kings of England and Spain were delighted at the farm products their lands in the New World could produce, but growing cotton and tobacco was very labor intensive. There were no tractors or cotton gins, so cheap, slave labor was imported into America to serve the European market. The Kings Colonial Law forbade freeing these people."

"When America declared its independence there was a sharp division between those who would abolish slavery and those who felt their livelihood depended on it. Thomas Jefferson owned slaves, but wanted to free them despite the law. So did Stonewall Jackson. Previously, he wrote many letters to the King asking him to stop the practice, and here's a quote from Jefferson that was deleted from the Declaration of Independence."

"He (the King) has waged cruel war against human nature itself, violating the most sacred rights of life and liberty

in the persons of a distant people who never offended him,
captivating & carrying them into slavery..."

"Well," Dylan opened his hands. "Unfortunately, if we had made an issue of slavery at that time, we wouldn't have had a unified fighting force to win our independence. This issue was left to the states and by 1787 several states had ended slavery on their own. Our Constitution did, however, insert an anti-slavery line called the 3/5ths clause whereby states who continued the practice would have fewer votes."

Dylan pointed to a raised hand. "Jevon?"

"But couldn't a slave owner just let them go?"

"First, the life of any escaped slave would be difficult. They had no citizenship and anyone hiring them could be prosecuted except in a few States. Also, anyone deliberately freeing a slave in those remaining states would be jailed. Even after the Revolution, local laws remained in effect for awhile in many states. Betty?"

"But if the founders were devout Christians, why didn't they abolish slavery in the Constitution?"

"Good question. The 3/5ths clause was a start, but a vote would be needed to change things further. Early in the nineteenth century the Abolitionist Party was founded hoping to elect a president and end slavery once and for all. John Adams and his son, John Quincy, played a large role in this movement."

Betty said, "But we never had a president from a party by that name."

"Ah ha," Waving his finger, "We did. Abraham Lincoln won in 1860 but the name of his party was changed to the Republican Party. Lincoln was mentored by John Quincy when they were in the Congress at the same time and his plan for emancipation remained essentially the same. "

"Oh, no." Jevon was shaking his head. "You're not telling us the *Republicans* were the ones to free the slaves?"

Dylan and others were laughing. "Yeah, I guess *that* truth is forbidden teaching too. Here are the facts: the 13th amendment freed the slaves during the Civil War. 100% of Republicans voted for it, but only 23% of the Democrats. The 14th Amendment declared Black Americans and their children to be citizens with the right to run for Congress. 94% Republican voted yes, 0% Democrats. The 15th Amendment guaranteed the right for them to vote. 100% Republican voted yes, 0% Democrats. Question, Jim?"

"Is that cause all the Democrats were in the South?"

"No, during the war none of them could vote. These were all Northern Democrats."

There were groans all around and Jevon lowered his head, muttering to the floor.

Dylan opened his hands. "Naturally, the first Black Americans in Congress were Republicans, and in 1866,

Southern Democrats established the Ku Klux Klan to intimidate and kill Republicans. It was easier to identify Blacks as Republicans but *anyone* found working for Black rights was murdered. In their history, 3500 Blacks and 1300 Whites were murdered by the Klan."

Jevon said, "Now you're actually saying that white people died for Black rights?"

"Jevon, in the Civil War, three hundred sixty thousand Union soldiers died for the cause they believed in as Christians—giving blacks equal rights. Remember the Battle Hymn of the Republic. 'His truth is marching on.' They believed it then, Jevon, and we believe it now."

"But, I bet there's still a lot of people who would like slavery back."

"I can't say no to that, because some have the evil mindset that other people can be treated as property. That group of elitists I mentioned works to make sure the majority remain poorly educated and dependent on the state for survival. In that way they still have their 'slaves' in a way. I'd call them voting slaves."

Betty waved her hand. "So, it's a clever work-around from the guarantee of keeping all men equal."

"And all the while sounding like the opposite. They oppose most Biblical principals, but we are all equal in God's sight. The concept of abortion on demand is the same mindset as slavery: namely that unborn people are just property—property that can simply be disposed of. No emotion here: just drop it in the waste basket."

Dylan held up the Constitution. "All right folks, next week, the amendments…"

A brief shriek stopped everything. "Oh no, *no…*" Huge sobs. It was Tilly, her head collapsed onto her knees. "They said it was fine, but inside I *knew* it was wrong." Sobs.

Dylan called out "Class dismissed," and hurried to Tilly who was already surrounded by her friends. Those closest had their arms on her shoulders.

Tilly kept speaking to her knees. "Oh God, I *knew* it was wrong, but the clinic said I would be stupid to keep it. I'd lose my path to success in life.

Her friends said, "Shh, shh. It's all right, Honey."

"They told me 'Just don't think about what you're doing,' so I said yes." She looked at Betty with wet red eyes, her face twisted in agony. "I sinned big time. didn't I?"

Betty massaged her shoulder. "Oh Tilly, you've been keeping this inside, but don't you know that God forgives you when you're repentant and believe in Him?"

Tilly sat up, tears streaming down her cheeks. "Betty, you're one of the *good* girls. You wouldn't understand." With a strained voice, she croaked, "I've always tried not to think about it, but you just heard it, and Pastor Wong said it too. I killed my baby like he was *property*. I know God can't forgive *that*."

Lisa chimed in. "Oh yes he can. Right, Betty? What's that called?"

Betty seized Tilly's hands in hers. "Yes! Yes, He can. It's called sanctifying grace. It comes from God's love and is far bigger than any sin. I'm calling an emergency ladies meeting for you right now. We're going to the church cry room. "

"It's just too ugly." She shook her head. "I can't believe *anyone* could love me now."

Jim moved in behind her and put a hand on the side of her neck. "Yeah, well I still love you, Tilly." Some gasped and turned to him. His look became sheepish. "I'm not the father."

Tilly swiveled her neck to look up at him. "How could you, now that you know."

"Oh, Tilly," He picked up her hand. "A hundred times more now. Telling us was so courageous. I forgive you, and you just heard God forgives you. I've been hoping we might have a life together—you know--just me and you."

Tilly couldn't answer but she brought his hand to her lips. Her girl friends looked at each other and grinned.

Dylan pushed a tissue into her other hand. "And my lecture brought all this on?"

Lisa said, "You did good, 'Teach.'

WOMAN TRUTH

The Cry Room was intended for fussy kids during the service, but it was soundproof and had soft, comfy chairs. Emma, Betty, Lisa and Susan were the self appointed impromptu counselor/ comforters.

Tilly grabbed a tissue from a box, plunked down in a padded rocking chair and resumed sobbing.

Betty said, "The first thing I want to tell you about is Deeper Still. They do Christian retreats for women who have gone through this. You'll have a lot of company there, Tilly. You can talk with others who've been through the same thing, and I know they can help you a lot."

Lisa sat on the floor in front of her, leaned over and took her hand. "Hey, Til, our resident God experts told you that you're forgiven, and if *God* forgave you, you can do the same for yourself."

"Yeah?" Tilly blew her nose loudly. "I think I'm crying now 'cause I don't *deserve* forgiveness. I'm so ashamed."

Emma and Betty took positions on either side of the chair, Emma massaging a shoulder. "Sure you do. Look, none of us 'good girls,' as you called us, is righteous on our own. We all have our sins, but the important thing is to *call* it sin, then repent for it, change your life, and ask for forgiveness."

Betty stopped and squeezed Tilly's shoulder. "I stole something once."

They all looked at her. "Yeah, a couple of years ago—I slipped a purse into my shopping bag and thought I could just walk out."

Emma finger pointed. "The alarm went off, right?"

"Sure did. I just froze in place." She grinned and shook her head. "I'm a real dumb crook. The security guard went through everything in my bag, took down my driver's license and said he was going to file a report with juvenile authorities."

Tilly looked puzzled. She sniffed and said. "You're probably the last person I'd suspect of something like that."

"Well, Tilly, at the time I justified it in my mind since I was broke and it was a present for my mom, but the guilt ate away at me for a long time after."

"You asked forgiveness?"

"Finally, but the guilty feeling didn't go away until I repented before God. He knows what's in your heart, Til, and He can just wash away your sorrow. It's amazing."

Lisa said, "So, look, we know you like flirting and fooling around. A lot of girls do. Maybe all you need is a change of heart?"

"I can't seem to stop the flirting. It makes me feel better when I'm noticed, but it may surprise you that I've never fooled around. The guys know I'm just a tease."

"But," Lisa tilted her head and puckered. "There must have been just *one* time, right?"

Tilly scowled and shook her head. "Oh, no. I was raped."

"Whoa." All eyes widened. "And you never told anyone? Didn't you even report it?"

"Nah, I was scared, embarrassed. I thought no one would believe me anyhow. Remember, I was a cheerleader two years ago. I was tricked into going to a storage room at the gym. I thought I'd be looking at our new uniforms. I should'a ran when I saw the cot."

Betty slapped her hand to her cheek. "Oh, shoot. It wasn't Coach Williams, was it?"

Tilly smiled and shook her head. "No, no, he's a straight arrow peach." Looks of hopeful expectancy hung in the air. "When this man threw me down and started on me, he promised my F in Statistics would change to a C."

Susan grimaced. "A *teacher* nailed you?"

"No. Look, now I feel I have to say who did it, but if I tell you, you'll know something even my parents don't know. Promise you'll never tell anyone?"

Murmurs of "yes, yes," and lip sealing gestures from everyone. Tilly sighed. "You have to understand, I was afraid of him and what he might do—*still* am. It was Chancellor Stengel."

Jaws dropped. Lisa broke the silence with a whisper. "Oh—my—God."

SCHOOL CHOICE

It never is the law itself that is in the wrong, it is always some wicked interpreter of the law that has corrupted and abused it.

Jeremy Bentham, Fragment on Government (I works: 231)

NEWS BOX, HAMMER TIME (show in progress)

Charles Hammer welcomes the audience back from a commercial break. "All right, folks, as promised we have our panel here to discuss religion and our school system."

"First, on my right," The screen shot reveals a middle age man with round glasses and a tweed jacket. "We have the newly appointed chancellor of Princehaven University, Gilson Stoddard."

"Next," The camera shows a young, dark haired man wearing a pleasant smile. "Here is Reverend Roger Flint, education director at Bible Truth Seminary."

"And then," The camera pans to Dylan wearing a tight blue suit and a look of apprehension. "This is Professor Dylan Coz, recently fired from Berkard University, they claim for proselytizing students. Is that a fair statement, Mister Coz?"

"Not even close, Mister Hammer."

Charles chuckles. "Well, we're here to straighten this out for everyone. Back to you in a moment."

"Finally, let me introduce attorney, Priscilla Snark, now teaching Constitutional Law at Northern University. Before that she held the record for the most cases argued before the Ninth Circuit."

Ms Snark offered the hint of a scowl as she nodded at the camera. Charles said, "Should we call you Counselor or Professor?"

"Professor."

"All right, then," Charles rapped his gavel. "I have to admit, I love controversial subjects. It's a fact that up until a few decades ago you could talk about Jesus in any school and no one protested. My father told me they sang Gospel songs in music class and once a week he went for off campus religious teaching. It was actually an option in his public school. Things sure have changed."

Charles gestured to Dylan. "I'll start with you, Professor Coz. Tell us what got you fired."

Dylan relaxed in his chair, and smiled into the camera. "I taught courses in history and science at Berkard. The simplest explanation for my firing is that I departed from Berkard's curriculum formula and I told my students the truth."

Stoddard interrupted. "That's a lie. I read Berkard's statement. You were teaching Christianity and…"

"Proselytizing? I was not. I kept to historical quotes and only referenced the Bible when…"

"Did you or did you not subject those young minds to quotations from the Christian Bible?"

"Yes, but I…"

"Case closed. I would have fired you myself. You're lucky they didn't bring legal…"

"Okay, okay," Charles rapped his gavel. "We agreed to let each other finish. I'm going to let Professor Coz tell us his version of the firing---without interruption."

"Thank you. I'll be brief. Our United States was founded by born again Christians who…"

"Oh, *please!*" Stoddard interrupted. "They were Deists," inserted Stoddard. (more gavel rapping)

"As I was saying: Christians who wrote our Constitution. I only quoted their exact words in my course. I only put Bible quotations on screen in my astronomy course to show pertinent correlations in the creation of the universe."

"You see," Stoddard again. "He admits to quoting the Bible, and the word is *formation* of the universe, not creation."

Charles rapped his gavel again. "All right, let's get another opinion." He gestured to Ms Snark, presently lacking any facial expression. "As an attorney and Constitutional expert, tell us why this boy is in trouble."

"Of course." She released a bored sigh. "Emerson v. The Board of Education in 1947 clarified that states cannot escape the wall of separation between Church and State. Based on that landmark decision, multiple cases have further clarified that God has no place in government or institutions supported by government. Violators must be punished."

Hammer pointed at Roger Flint. "Reverend, you look like you're dying to say something."

Roger nodded and turned to the lawyer. "First, I think Professor Snark would agree that this case was a suit brought by a taxpayer who simply did not want public funds spent on a private institution. The State of New Jersey had been paying for the transportation of private students."

Snark returned a grunt and a display of shark eyes. Flint countered with a grin. "I might surprise you by agreeing with the decision that taxpayers should not be forced to give money to a private institution without voting to do so. I think it was a stretch to use the due process clause here, but if this had been the end of it, no problem."

Snark: "Your point?"

"The problem is that atheists have used this decision to foist a cascade of lawsuits in an attempt to drive religion out of schools and ultimately, America. This was not the intent of our founding fathers, the first amendment or even the judges in the 1947 court decision."

Snark: "We don't read the minds of dead people. We have informed rulings by contemporary legal minds, and stop with that pathetic, sniveling 'drive God out' thing. No one is preventing anyone from crawling into their churches on Sunday. "

Dylan: "But, those dead founders left ample writings in their own handwriting. Fisher Ames *wrote* the First Amendment and said that the Bible must never be pushed to the back of the classroom much less completely out of our schools. He felt his amendment *protected* us from government secularization. Clearly, he…"

Snark: "nonsense, we go by what he wrote into law and the Court has given us a precedent now."

Flint: "Okay, how about the precedent of Justice William Story? I'm sure you must teach your students that he is one of the 'Fathers of American Jurisprudence,' right?" Snark just shook his head and scowled. "There was a *unanimous* Supreme Court decision, and Story wrote that the purest principles of morality can be clearly learned from the New Testa…"

Stoddard: "Now, now, can't you see? They were trying to get Christianity as a government established religion—the very thing the Constitution forbids."

Snark: "Right. I teach that as an invalid precedent."

Dylan laughs. "Invalid? This same was repeatedly affirmed even up to the fifties. I can look up the exact SCOTUS ruling but I recall they said that when the State encourages religious instruction they are following our best traditions."

Stoddard: "Traditions are not law, mister."

Dylan: "But the same ruling went on to say that 'preferring those who have no religion is not in our constitution.' Despite all that, the Bible and all moral teachings were removed from public schools in 1962."

"Great," Stoddard displayed a smile with open hands. "And from then on, schools were able to concentrate on factual education, not fantasy."

"Really?" Dylan shook his head. "From the moment God was removed, our SAT scores went into free fall. They dropped a hundred points in the next decade. We no longer led the world in factual education."

Flint: "That was our nation's gruesome experiment, but it revealed the connection between morality and educ…"

"Nothing of the kind." Snark interrupted. "There were many other causes, like segregated schools and poor fund…"

Dylan: "No, look at the facts. Our Founding Fathers were entering universities in their early teens. I teach history and you teach law. Did you know that a hundred year old *fourth* grade text expects students to know what is a writ of habeas corpus, an ex post facto law and a bill of attainder?"

Hammer raps his gavel. "Whoa, and we're about out of time and you made my neck hurt from swiveling. Quick final question for each of you to answer in one sentence: What *motivated* those who removed the Bible from our schools?"

"Final word," Hammer points. "Ms Snark, you first."

"Public education has no business teaching religion, especially one favored over another. The Freedom From Religion Foundation said it best when they wrote 'it is the responsibility of school boards to keep religion from seeping into our schools.' The Boards are just the right thing."

Quick rap and a point. "Coz, go."

"Secular atheism, temporarily on the rise, led to reverse morality and the teaching of victimhood."

"Whoo, and Stoddard: your final word?"

"Sure. If our government teaches Christianity, it violates our Constitution by establishing a religion. The Bible accepts slavery. Its rules are thousands of years out of date. Its' teachings are bigoted, offensive and hated by many."

"Ten seconds. Hammer points. "Reverent Flint."

"Sinners already know their guilt and hate this reality. Consequently, they want new rules—based on an alternate truth--one made by man to mock God and reassure them that their evil ways are just fine."

SAD TRUTH

It was Saturday at one o'clock, and Sean Ryan sat at the far end of the Denny's lunch counter sipping a tall Diet Pepsi. There were two "reserved" cards on the stools next to him and Lisa took the stool closest to him. "I hope this is important, Detective. I'm supposed to be painting for my art class."

Sean chuckled and removed the reserved card in front of her. "Don't look over at me while we talk. Order any lunch you want. It's on me."

When the waitress came over Lisa grinned and said, "I'll have the lobster thermador and caviar, please." Sean had to face the wall to conceal his laughter.

After she "changed her mind" and switched to the cheeseburger, Sean stared straight ahead. "You're something else, young lady, but what I have to say to you is dead serious."

Another officer came in and sat on the stool next to Lisa. She kept looking at Sean. "Who is the dark-haired, Christopher Reeve look alike breathing down my neck?" Dark hair gave a snort-laugh.

Sean shook his head, grinning. "Okay, I give up. Turn around and greet Officer Scott Hutchins. He works with me."

She swiveled toward him. He grinned and said, "Hello, m'am—er, Ms Combes."

Lisa looked at the ceiling with a pout. "I'm *sure* we met somewhere before, didn't we? I'll bet they call you Hutch, right?"

"Why, yes they do, Lisa." He chuckled. "It's a pleasure to *formally* meet our brave, DNA-rustling journalist."

"Okay, okay, I get it." Sean stopped them. You've met before. I should have guessed, but the three of us meeting here might have been a mistake. Could I get to the serious part?"

"Sorry." She removed a writing pad from her purse. "Reporter on duty, now."

"You won't need that. First, you should know Hutch says you are being followed. Someone wants to know where you are every minute. Look out that window to the right. See the brown sedan? There are two men in front and a younger one in the back."

"Oh, shoot. Is it the FBI?"

"Nope. They're private."

Lisa gave him a quick glance. "They must be bored stiff following me. Why would they be doing that?"

"I'm sure they are looking for whomever you're talking to, your sources. Remember the bug in your computer?

These are people in high places—very influential people---who want the Berkard murder to disappear. They're not happy when anyone talks to the media."

"Really, I..." She put her half eaten cheeseburger down. "Now you're spoiling my appetite. Do you think I'm in danger?"

"I wouldn't think they'd go after a reporter who's already in print. Too obvious, and it might draw the big news people in, but just to be sure, I assigned Hutchins to keep an eye on things. I see you know that already."

"You '*wouldn't think*', huh? Makes me feel so much better. Was that all you wanted to tell me?"

"No. Do you remember Paco Gutierrez?"

"Of course. Hutch said he's our eye witness."

"Was. He was found dead in his apartment two days ago. The cause of death is listed as a drug overdose."

Lisa's fork clunked into her plate and she pushed it away. "That's *terrible*. Any sign of foul play?"

"Oh, yeah. Paco worked as a part time sanitation truck driver in Concord. I spoke with someone I know on the force there. They do spot drug testing where he works and he was clean two days earlier. No prior history of drug use either."

"Shoot, so they'll investigate more, right?"

Scott answered that one. "Nope. The FBI took over, just like here."

"I smell a huge story here. What do you think I should do, Sean?"

"If you're a fearless reporter, go with it, but no names or sources, of course. Officer Hutchins won't be far away, but keep us informed about where you're going when you leave campus."

Sean turned and made eye contact with Lisa. "But if you were *my* daughter asking that question, I'd say this would be a good time to switch your major to Art."

MIRACULOUS TRUTH

At their next Friday meeting Dylan noted Wally kept standing as the others sat down. Professor Sims was sitting next to him.

"Well, Wally, does this mean the Math Club has cracked the probability of the 'moon shot' problem?"

"We did, with Professor Sims help, but we had to take a conservative guess at the likelihood of the perfect sized planet coming at earth. Even with that, there's is a one in ten to the one hundred thirteenth power for it to happen by chance. But wait, I have something else to tell our group if I can. It's just as amazing."

Dylan sighed and grinned. "Why do I feel I've lost control here? At least you're not boring." He passed him the microphone. "Can you do it in ten minutes?"

"Sure. Actually my friend from our club is going to tell you about it." A slim man with curly black hair and round tortoiseshell glasses stood up next to him. "This is Alvin Finkelstein. He's our resident skeptic and watercolor artist extraordinaire. Alvin insisted that your one bush couldn't be making all those flowers, so what does a scientist do when he has a theory?" Wally handed him the microphone.

Alvin turned and nodded at the group. "He does an experiment. I guess you can tell from my name I'm not one of you Christians." Laughter. "But, I've been thinking a lot about God lately. I'm a real curious guy."

"So, I went over to your famous rose bush and set up my easel early last Friday morning. That was a ruse to count the flowers being removed, but I painted a picture of the pretty, little bush while I was there. I'll bring you the portrait next Friday. I'm still adding the dew drops."

"As you know, each group of your friends sends someone over early Friday morning to pick the blooms for that day. Your bush had thirty six flowers to start with."

He glanced into the bright eyes of a black woman in the front row. "Emma, I remember you were one of those flower pickers."

"As the day went on, I totaled up how many each of you picked and fifty two blooms were taken off that plant." Alvin looked up at the ceiling, his lower lip trembling. "And when I went back to the bush…" He closed his eyes. "It still had thirty six blossoms. I might have to consult a botanist, but I'm pretty sure that doesn't happen in the real world."

With that, the "Praise the Lords" broke out. Soon everyone but Alvin began to sing, "You are an Awesome God."

Alvin remained standing until they finished. "There's more, folks. Last Friday, after you flower-pickers had left, two grounds keepers pulled up in their maintenance cart. One pointed at your bush and said, 'There it is.' They got out and cut the trunk right at ground level. Then they sprayed the stump with weed killer, tossed the bush in their cart and drove away."

He studied the grim faces for a moment. "On Sunday, when I guess you were all in church, I went back to have a look. The ground was bare and you could still smell the weed poison, but a ways out from the stump, there were three green shoots coming up."

"This morning I walked back over to tell the pickers the sad news and saw Emma heading that way. When we got there, your famous rose bush had sprouted three smaller bushes from the roots. Each one had twelve blooms." He looked up, his lip trembling. "Now I believe, okay God?"

Emma called out, "The Lord reigns!"

As Alvin sat down, the students sang, "How Great Is Our God?"

Dylan enjoyed the praising and singing with the rest of them. Finally, things quieted. "So much for the ten minute idea. It may seem like an anti-climax, but in the time left, let's look at some other amendments. Who knows what a 'Star Chamber' is?"

The silence was broken when someone called out, "A planetarium?"

"No, it was a secret court created by the kings in England to persecute dissenters, or really anyone the King didn't like. The Fifth Amendment was created to prevent such an abuse. What was the main highlight in that?" He pointed. "Lover-boy, what do you think?"

Jim took his arm off of Tilly's shoulders. "Uh, it says you can't make me say I did it."

They all laughed. "Actually he's right, isn't he? You can't be made to testify against oneself. Also, it guarantees due process and prevents double jeopardy so the evil work of a Star Chamber can't happen anymore—or can it?"

"Articles one and three allow Congress to establish tribunals, that is courts, just below the Supreme Court. In 1977, with Watergate as an excuse, Ted Kennedy authored the creation of the FISA court whose mission was to issue warrants to surveil Americans suspected of dangerous foreign activity. This court keeps its proceedings secret and without records.

"Some congressmen liken it to the old British Star Chambers. While spying on citizens should be a rare event, the FISA court has okayed over *forty thousand* warrants and only denied a dozen or so. The FISA warrants may be used to create a Special Counsel and thus the comparison with Star Chambers seems justified."

Lisa raised her hand. "So, Dylan, is it unconstitutional?"

"I'd say it's a stretch. Congress could act to do away with the system or make the warrants harder to get. Right now, the privacy of innocent civilians is at risk. We have a few minutes left. Any other questions about our Constitution?"

Betty said, "The faculty here talk about liking the National Popular Vote Movement. They say we should have a pure democracy. Don't we?"

Dylan pulled out some notes from a folder. "Our founders, in their wisdom, gave us a republic with an elected representative government."

"But they say all voices are not being heard."

"Betty, let's say for instance, all laws were passed by a simple majority without restrictions." He counted the students. "There are nine women here and ten men. Someone brings in a large cake and one man proposes the law that only men get a share. It passes ten to nine. Sorry, girls, that's pure democracy."

"Stop cheering guys. Now instead, we elect a *representative* and he or she must live by the Constitution and equal protection. Bound by law, the representative recognizes the men's vote as an unconstitutional 'bill of attainder' and divides the cake equally. If the men protest, the Supreme Court will back up the representative."

"In the same way, our Founders recognized that the President would only be elected by the big cities if there was a simple popular vote. They were also afraid of the moral values tending to be lower in big cities, and they didn't want to disenfranchise the heartland."

"Benjamin Rush, one of our Founders, wrote: 'I view great cities as pestilential to the morals, health and liberty of man. They are like abscesses on the human body—reservoirs of all the impurity of a community.' Ben was a physician, can't you tell? If he wrote it today, I'm sure he would have included photos of the streets of San Francisco."

Dylan read from a paper: "John Adams said pure democracy never lasts long. It wastes and murders itself. There never was a pure democracy yet that did not commit suicide."

The students looked a bit stunned at this. "Hope that answers the question others on your faculty raise about the National Popular Vote Movement. Also, I think that's enough for you to think about over the Thanksgiving break.

We'll meet again in two weeks and then we'll get into the real motives behind the political platforms. Meanwhile, be bold and stand up for truth out there. God bless you all."

TRUTH PEEKING OUT

Lisa made her way across the copy editing floor, manuscript tucked under her arm. This time, three people she didn't even know gave her smiles and thumbs up. She returned a sheepish grin.

Once she reached her editor's open door, Vera waved and ran around her desk to meet her. Lisa opened her arms in puzzlement. "Vera, what the heck's going on?"

"You don't know?" She gave her a quick welcome hug. "Here at the Oakland Flame, we measure success by the hate mail. You just arrived. I printed out some truly choice emails and twitters for you."

Lisa shook her head, grinning. "Oh, goodie. I'm so proud."

Vera pointed to some envelopes on the edge of her desk. "There are a few pieces of snail mail for you too. Judging by the drawn-on swastikas and middle fingers, they're more of the same. We routinely run these past our sniffer and X-ray so they aren't dangerous."

"So, nobody liked what I wrote?"

"About twenty percent positive, but look: the point is a lot of people are reading it, and our paper besides. There's more good news. Your application for part time employment was approved." She grasped Lisa's shoulders and bestowed a wide grin. "You're one of us, now."

"Okay, *now* I'm feeling better, but what were most of the negative complaints about?"

"The worst?" Vera threw her head back with a laugh. "They couldn't imagine you implicating their beloved Congressman Luchow in a cover-up scandal. Then—hello. Just this morning the House Ethics Committee announced they were investigating him."

"Zing!"

"Okay, what are you clutching under your arm? It better be another article 'cause from now on, I want a weekly column from you."

Lisa handed her the manuscript with a flourish. "This piece is about the firing of another one of our professors."

"Oh, good. Sit. I'm going to read it right now."

THE PENALTY OF TRUTH

Last week, Professor Aimee West was fired by Berkard University. Chancellor Stengel issued a statement that he was acting in accordance with a petition signed by the majority of faculty members and the demand of Black Lives Matter. He said that there is no place at Berkard for anyone not committed to diversity.

Before we look at the purported "sins" of Ms West, let's review her history. She has a law degree from Duke University and continues to do pro bono representation for the poor community in Oakland. She has received commendations from local school boards for promoting tutorial programs for needy grade schoolers in poor school districts, and they have mostly black students.

At Berkard some of her students knick-named her "Fessamie," and she is beloved by many. Your reporter only took her course on statistics, but she even made that kinda fun. Professor Aimee is best known for a pre-law course on Constitutional law and I spoke with three graduating students who took her course. They told me that Fessamie's recommendations and that course were the main reason they, and so many before them, got into law school.

Then why was Berkard so upset with Ms West? Last year she did an op-ed in the LA Times advocating a return to the culture of personal responsibility. She was branded a "white supremacist" for this even though her main focus was on the antisocial habits of some working-class whites.

This year she did much "worse." She made a web video that criticized Affirmative Action, pointing out that "legislating a degree" by placing unqualified students in

239

difficult programs does them more harm than good. She called this the "mismatch effect" and gave evidence proving the beneficiaries of such preferential treatment have difficulty competing after graduation.

Then came the "killer." She said "I don't think I've ever seen a black student graduate in the top quarter of the class, and rarely in the top half. Elite schools like Berkard work hard to boast about their racial diversity and then work fanatically to conceal the gaps in academic achievement."

Her further comments dug a deeper hole for her: "I'm not saying they shouldn't go to college, but there are colleges providing a better environment for them. The fact that some would be better off in vocational training is true for all races. Improving college aptitude must start with better elementary education."

Professor West made many suggestions for improving basic education in underperforming school districts, but pointing out certain truths about Berkard was her death sentence. It was contrary to the administration narrative and they said her claims were "disparaging, false and deeply offensive." They also claimed she had violated their "policy of confidentiality," and had "subjected innocent students to her "musings about race in society."

Ms West's courses prepared students for Law School. Did she speak the truth? The Law School Admissions Council tracked the "elite" schools and found that 52% of blacks were in the bottom tenth of their class compared to 6% of whites.

The bottom line is clear. Challenging affirmative action with the truth will get you publically shamed and punished. The real scandal here is first, that colleges are not being transparent about admission policies that confound a students' success after graduation. Finally, are we going to continue to ignore what can be done to improve precollege education including school choice? Doing so will only hurt the very minorities we should be helping.

Vera looked up and dropped her jaw. "Good grief, girl, you are writing like a forty year old professional."

"So, you like it?"

"This will triple the hate mail and likely get Black Lives Matter to throw rocks through our windows."

"Shoot. You can't print it then?"

Vera laughed. "This piece is the best thing I've seen in a long while. Of *course* it's going in. By the way, the American Justice League is suing Berkard on behalf of that other professor—uh the one who sounds like a musician."

"Oh, Dylan Coz."

"Right. Maybe Professor West will be included." She gave Lisa another quick hug and gestured toward the door. "Let me show you your new desk. You even got a window by your cubicle."

THE CLUB

"Real nice country club, Bernie," Stengel said. "If I played golf, I'd join."

Bernard Luchow pointed to the edge of the terrace dining area overlooking the course. "We'll sit over there where there's some privacy. I hardly play much golf myself even though I own half this place."

A waitress followed them over, handed out bar menus and pulled the chair out for Bernard. "What can I get you gentleman?"

Luchow grinned at her. "I'll just have a Scotch and Soda—uh, some Brazil and Macadamia nuts, too." Looking at Stengel, "Have anything you want. We have a new French chef so you can't go wrong."

Stengel held the menu up toward the waitress, grasped her upper arm and pulled her toward it. "What's the second thing in this column?"

She grimaced in his grip. "Oh, that's a croissant with the chef's butter sauce. It's very good, Sir."

242

"Fine." He released her. "I'll have that and a bourbon, straight."

Stengel gave her departing figure a good leer. "Nice figure on that one, Bernie."

Luchow chuckled. "And that reminds me—I did you a big favor last month. One of those college girls you shagged a few years back decided to complain to her congressman about you. She thought I should get you fired."

"I got no calls from my lawyer. Is she gonna sue?"

"Nah, and I fixed it for you but I had to divert some funds from my charity to button her lip."

"Thanks, Bernie. I owe you one. What's this about an ethics committee?"

"Ah, it's just bad optics for my re-election. My lawyers say my connection with Reinhardt and the charity donations can't be traced. They can make guesses, but it won't matter. Besides, I have some good friends on that committee.

Luchow stared at the golfers on the eighteenth green before he squinted at Stengel. "If you want to do something useful for me, Henry, keep that fanatic journalism student of yours off my back."

"Combes? I fired her from our paper, but she's working on the outside now—not in my jurisdiction."

The waitress returned, and at arms length, placed the croissant and bourbon in front of Stengel. He smiled widely. "Why, *thank* you, darlin'."

She deftly sidestepped to avoid an anticipated butt pat. When she left, Stengel asked, "Your son is a bit of a loose cannon, huh?"

"Well," He threw up his hands. "Reggie *does* have a temper, but in the end, knocking off that bitch will do us both a favor."

Stengel nodded. "I assume you have people working to keep yourself covered, right?"

"Sure. An eye witness did show up, but we took care of him. There's no more big media coverage, so the affair should fade away. If Combes keeps poking around we'll settle with her, too."

"Good," Stengel grinned. "And I'm working on a scandal idea—should get Combes to back off."

"Nice. She's really annoying. I believe she has one source in the local police, but we're pretty sure she has others as well. We're keeping an eye on the little twit, but we may have to go lay some muscle on her."

"Excellent. I like 'muscle'." Stengel shrugged. "And, by the way, I'm hoping my planned scandal will burn a bad guy on my faculty at the same time."

"I love it." Luchow held up his glass and clicked with Stengel. "Keep me informed. Otherwise I'll have to take care of Miss 'freckle-face' the old fashioned way."

SCARY TRUTH

While she was in town, Lisa thought she better pick up something to wear for the holiday trip to her parents and she'd heard about a thrift store specializing in cycler's needs. On pulling up, she was encouraged by the presence of motorcycle parking spaces.

Lisa wandered around in the huge Goodwill store apparently looking lost when a cheerful sales-woman came up to her. "Hi, there. Can I help you find something?"

"Oh thanks. I'm going on a long trip on my bike and I'm looking for a good warm riding vest."

"Bicycle or Motorcycle?"

"Motorcycle. I'm going across the state."

"Got it." The woman raised her finger. "I used to do that. You going with the club to Sacramento this afternoon? They're starting out in that lot across the street."

"Nah, I'm all by myself."

"Really?" She looked concerned. "They sell mace in the gun shop down the street. Follow me. We have our cycle clothing in the back."

She showed her a large, rack-filled room. Lisa crinkled her nose. "I was hoping to find something in leather but with a soft lining inside."

The woman looked her over. "I don't know if we have any small woman's sizes right now. You're about a six, aren't you?"

"Uh huh."

She waved her over. "If we have any, they'd be at the end of this rack." Looking toward the last jacket, "Oh, look, maybe you're in luck. There's one left and it's a motorcycle cut, too."

Lisa quickly slipped it on and zipped it up. "Hey, this is perfect. I'll take it."

The lady turned her around studying the fit. "Uh, oh. I see why it hasn't sold."

"What?"

"It's a club cut. On the back it says 'Ride on King Jesus' around a cross."

Lisa laughed. "Well, I don't think anybody will shoot me for it. Oh, look, there's gloves in the pockets. Any charge for those?"

"Nah, it's as is."

"Great. I'm ready to go."

Back outside, Lisa sat on her motorcycle, partly unzipped the vest, and discovered a zippered inside pocket.

She pulled out a piece of paper from it and read: "Hi, slim lady. I used to fit into this cut too, but here's a warning, if you get pregnant, you'll never be able to wear it again. Course I don't regret getting married and all, but I'll miss this vest 'cause I think it helped me get married. It's been with me through lots of memories and fun times, and I wish you have the same. God bless. Mary Stearns"

Lisa folded the note with a smile and returned it to the pocket, but when she looked up she saw she was being observed from across the street. Two men, black sedan. Sunglasses. She fired up her bike and hurried back to campus.

Even though it was the day before Thanksgiving and some had morning classes, the parking lot was full of students packing up their cars. Her roommate and Emma had already left.

Lisa called Hutch. "Hi. You wanted to know when I'm leaving town. I'll be leaving soon to visit my parents."

"Lisa, you've still got bird dogs, you know."

"I've seen them. They look kinda scary. Can't you arrest them for stalking, or something?"

"Nah." (chuckles) "Look, we think they're mostly interested in finding out who you're talking to."

"Uh, huh, you say, but I have dreams of being strapped to a chair and being questioned while they're removing my fingernails."

Scott laughed. "Lisa, look, you're driving straight to a marine base. No one will bother you there."

"Alright, maybe I'm being silly. So, no special precautions, then?"

"I'd keep your cell turned off on the road and only stop for gas in a good sized town. More importantly, I'm praying for your safety, sweet lady."

"Aw, Hutch. Thanks so much. I'll check in with you when I get back, and God bless you, my dear protector."

Next, Lisa called her family. "Hi, Dad. You didn't get back to me this week. I'm still planning to find that new marine base of yours tomorrow."

"Hey, Punkin," Dad answered. "We'd love to see you, but…"

"Yeah, I thought I'd start out real early and…" Her brow furrowed as she watched two black cars on the far side of the lot filled with men looking in her direction. "Or, better yet, I could even leave this afternoon."

"Here's the thing, sweetie, the Mountain Warfare Training Center is a pretty rugged place. We only have a one bedroom and there's a light snow. Mom and I called Aunt

Miriam in Sacramento this morning. We thought we'd just wait and get together for Christmas at her place."

"Yeah, but the campus turns into a ghost town on a holiday."

"And last year you told us that was a perfect time to start your novel."

"Dad, have you read what I've been putting in the papers? Some important people know I know who killed Hayley Jones--*big* important people. I just found out they murdered the eye witness and there are four men following me. Daddy, I'm scared."

Pause. "Whoa. Okay, that changes everything, Punkin. Get on your horse right away. Evasive tactics. Remember the game we used to play? You have a navi?"

"Yes, sir--Garmin built in and tied to my headgear."

"Excellent. Should take you out on the Four, then you drop down to the 108 at Angel Camp. If you don't lose your shadow in town, power out in the mountain road. They'd need a Porsche to keep up. I'll meet you in Bridgeport. Text me when you're close."

"Sure. Sounds like you know this area."

"Always surveil your surroundings in a new location. If you still see a car in pursuit, go off road. Follow one of the the hiking trails back to the main road. See you in about six?"

"Uh, huh." Lisa chuckled. "Copy that, Sergeant."

EVASIVE TACTICS

Lisa had an idea of her own. She packed up and headed back toward the Goodwill where she found three dozen motorcycles gathering in a nearby lot. She flicked her kickstand down beside a woman about her age. "Hi, who's the man in charge here?"

Intense brown eyes looked into hers. The woman pouted. "How do you know she's not female?"

"You got me." Lisa grinned. "All right, where is she?"

"Just messin' with ya." She put out her hand. "Hi, I'm Eva. We're both singles, right?"

"Copy that. I think I'll die single." She shook her hand. "I'm Lisa. Just hoping to travel a ways with you guys."

"Oh, sure, but check in with 'big beard' over there." She pointed to a six foot man with a "beer belly," a ruddy complexion and a long, scruffy beard. "I'll come with you."

"Beardy" was in an emotional conversation with another man, but she patiently stood next to him. Finally, he smiled at her and held up his hand toward the man who kept

251

on talking about what "that cop" had done to him. "You're new. What can I do for you, little lady?"

Lisa gestured to the other man. "I can wait."

Big beard turned to the man. "Hold on one sec, okay, Sam?" Back to her. "So?"

"Uh, I'm Lisa. Is it okay if I ride with you awhile. I'm trying to avoid a guy who's been following me."

"I'm Bud. That wouldn't be a guy with a shiny helmet and a badge on his chest, would it?"

"Oh, no. Private investigator, I think. I'm no criminal."

Bud seemed amused. He stuck his neck to one side and twirled his hand indicating her to turn around. "Le'me see your cut." She twirled. "Ha. A 'Jesus girl'. Haven't seen that club for awhile. You're out of San Diego, right?"

"Me? No." Lisa thumbed toward the Goodwill. "I just bought this at the thrift store, but, yeah, you could call me a Jesus girl if you want."

"Really?" Bud's belly shook in laughter. "Well, I hope you can live by that sign you're wearing. So many can't, these days. How far are you going?"

"I'd like to ride with you up to the Four, then I'm heading east to my Dad's marine base near the border."

"Aw," Bud grinned. "Home for the holidays, but that's a bit of a run. How's your old lady running?"

"My bike? Okay. It's a fairly new Harley."

Bud looked at the man next to him. "Sam, go give her ride a quick check, okay?"

Lisa opened her hands. "Oh, that's all right, Bud."

"Lisa, give him a minute. Sam's a miracle mechanic. He can kiss a bike and make it well. We're glad to have you along, little sister, and while you're with us you'll be as safe as a babe in her mother's arms."

Lisa thanked Bud and showed Sam to her motorcycle. He spent five minutes on his knees tinkering and adjusting things as it idled, then he stood up. "She should be fine. I left your mixture a little rich since you'll be mountain climbing."

"Sam, thank you so much."

He held out a tiny black box and grinned at her. "This might upset your private investigators, but I think you might want to lose this tracker I found inside your fender."

Lisa's mouth dropped open. "Chrimeny! No *wonder* they've been everywhere."

Sam chuckled. "How about I put it on Eva here. They'll follow us all the way to Sacramento."

"Oh, brilliant," Eva said. "So maybe some goons will shoot me—not that you'd care, huh?"

"Oh," Sam laughed. "But I promise we'll bury you with *full honors*." Eva stuck her tongue out at him. "Eva, don't worry. We'll dump the little devil when we get there."

Twenty minutes later, forty motorcycles roared into life and soon they were all headed north up the 80. Lisa spotted a car with the familiar sun-glassed men following them. She wondered why, if they only wanted sources, would they follow her on vacation.

Cycle leader Bud enjoyed the challenge. Before they got to Lisa's exit, he had everyone string out in a long single file to move the following car back. Then he motioned for Lisa to slowly work her way toward the front.

When Lisa saw the turnoff for the John Muir Parkway, she sped off heading east, hiding behind a truck, and hoping real hard her pursuers didn't see her. It didn't work.

ESCAPE

Everyone had gassed up just before Stockton. Lisa kept up a fast pace, passing as many cars as she could but then she saw them--one car in her rear view mirror weaving through traffic, driving crazy fast.

She took the turn off for Angel Camp but couldn't lose them in the streets. *They could have caught me back there but they're still hanging back. They must know I can see them.*

Lisa went south on the 49 and she thought she lost them in traffic over a bridge, but there they were right behind her when she took the 108 east, a mountainous road full of tight switchbacks. *This is where I'll probably get a ticket.* She patted the pink fuel tank. *Okay, Daisy Girl, lets punch it.*

The "motor cross" was on. Lisa leaned into every hairpin, roared out of every turn and passed some cars she knew no four-wheeler could. *Catch me if you can, bad guys.*

The road leveled out where it was cut into the sides of the mountains and she eased up on her pace. She was coming up to a turn that would take her around another mountain when she glanced across the valley to the road she'd been on earlier. Her pursuers had pulled into a turn out. *Good. They're at least fifteen minutes back. Looks like they're giving up.*

The first shot whined off a rock just ahead, the second kicked up dust near her rear wheel. *Oops, not giving up.* Lisa automatically went into evasive tactics, speeding up and randomly slamming on the breaks.

Two more shots came close before Lisa came to the switch back where she could safely turn away toward the other side of the mountain, but momentarily, with her back toward the shooters, she was a stationary target. The last shot hit her bike with a loud "wang," but she wasn't hit and Daisy Girl was still humming.

The road began to wind downhill and the slopes gentled. Lisa had tamed Stanislaus National Forest and evaded the firing squad, but she realized she was almost out of gas.

Pulling off at an Exxon, she headed for some picnic tables with a view of the road and hid her bike behind them. She quickly took her helmet off and sat at a table where she could watch the cars going by and listen to her pounding heart.

It's a maroon sedan they're in, a Chevy, I think.

Ten minutes went by. No sign of the hit squad. Her head fell into her hands. *Oh, Dear Lord, I know it's You who's keeping me safe. I hope I am always in Your will, for I pray for Your protection now—in Jesus' name.*

With her breathing back to normal, it was time to fill the tank, use the restroom and down a chicken sandwich. She wiggled a finger in the hole on the edge of her rear fender. *Whoa, it just missed the tire—not to mention me. Those creeps could' a shot me earlier when they were close. Guess they got real mad when they knew I was getting away.*

Lisa was happy to leave the station at a more sedate pace and keep to the speed limit. When she hit the 395 heading down to Bridgeport, she pulled over and texted dad her ETA. He directed her to an auto repair shop in town.

Finally, she turned into Scrapy's Repair and was delighted to see her dad sitting on the hood of his Jeep in his marine fatigues. As she dismounted, he jumped down, dashed over and swung her around like a Tilt a Whirl. "Punkin! You made it. How's my combat girl? Take any enemy fire?"

She was laughing, kicking and feeling like a little girl again. "I'm fine, Dad. Nothing God and I couldn't handle."

"I never doubted." He pointed to a man working on a car under a lift. "That's Matt. We'll keep your little hog in his garage until—hey, what's this? Did you buy a motorcycle with a bullet hole in it?"

She peeked at her rear fender and wiggled her pinky in the hole. "Oh, this? What makes you think it was a bullet?"

"Sweetie, I know bullets. Come clean."

She did—and she explained that she just didn't want him to worry too much.

Dad's real stern look melted and he have his daughter a hug and a kiss on top of her head. "And I was kidding about the enemy fire. You need some combat pay, a better defense and some R & R."

After parking her bike inside, they took off in his Jeep. "All right, Lisa, tell me all about how you went from a computer tapper to combat duty. We have to know our enemy before we make a battle plan."

"Oh, Daddy," She chuckled. "You're talking like I just enlisted. What do they have you doing up here in the mountains?"

"From what you've told me so far, Lisa, these people want to harm you, or at least scare you into shutting up. On this base I teach mountain survival. So, what are you up against?"

"Well, first you should know that Berkard is really idealistic in the way they think—politically correct beyond belief, you know. I think they want the world to become one big socialistic state and anything not agreeing with their mindset has to be attacked."

"Copy that."

Lisa chuckled. "Their financial muscle comes from certain big donors and is filtered through people in political power like Congressman Luchow. His son organized the Antifa attack last spring, and he killed Hayley Jones surrounded by his people so no one could see."

"Whoa, you have proof?"

"I got the DNA proof for the police and now the FBI has it. However, I think they'll sit on it like nothing happened."

"Wait, Wait! What's this about *you* getting the DNA?"

"Oh, well the police detective I met was real burned up when the FBI took his case away so he couldn't get the DNA himself. My friend Emma and I posed as bus girls at Luchow's party and got the samples for him."

"Good grief." Dad showed his ID at the base entrance and cleared Lisa for entry. "Lisa, I don't know whether I should be really angry or just proud of you. So, what next?"

"Did I mention Detective Ryan had interviewed a witness who could identify the congressman's son and his accomplice?"

"Oh, yeah." They began to bounce up a steep, snow covered curvy road. "But it sounds like that should make it an open and shut case."

"Should be, but our contact man in the FBI says the file is secret and not being investigated."

"You have an FBI contact?"

"Emma's uncle."

"Maybe your detective should blow the case open again by showing off the eye witness to the press."

"He's the one they killed, Daddy."

Dad became silent for awhile, driving past the bumpy curves in thought. "I'm not liking this at all, Darlin." There were a few more curves and bumps. "Careful what you say to your worry-wart mom. I just told her you didn't want to be alone on Thanksgiving—and that's not a lie."

The base housing was a group of austere buildings covered in snow. The Jeep spun its wheels traveling up a short driveway.

"Here we are. Watch your step. It's slippery." Dad stopped and looked at his daughter. "Right now, you have an even bigger problem. You'll have to explain to Mom why you're not dating anyone."

Mother, Mary Combes, heard them coming and hurried out to the front porch, her arms wide open for the hug. "Oh, Lisa, I'm so glad you came all this way." Hug, hug. "But, I'm sorry you'll have to sleep in the living room on a futon."

"No problem, Ma. I'm sure it's way better than my bed in the dorm."

"Come in, come in. It's freezing out here. I thought you'd come in two cars."

Sgt. Roger Combes gave his wife a cheek kiss. "I thought it best for her to leave her wheels in Bridgeport. These curvy, slippery roads, you know."

"Oh, yes, of course." She saw Lisa quickly trying to bury her motorcycle jacket in the closet. "What a strange coat, Lisa. Is it leather?"

"Uh, yeah. I grabbed something at a thrift shop to keep warm up here." That made dad grin and look at the ceiling.

"Well, maybe I should go to town with you and get something warmer, something more feminine—perhaps a faux fur."

"That's okay, Ma. It rarely gets below fifty at the coast."

Mom pouted. "Oh, look at us just talking. You must be exhausted. Why don't you lie down in our bedroom for awhile?"

"I'm fine Mother. Is there anything I can help you with?"

"Oh, you're such a good girl." Another hug. "If you want to help, come into the kitchen. You could help me finish making the lasagna."

The counter was festooned with ingredients surrounding a partly filled lasagna pan. Mom continued, "I assume you have all the recipes I sent you. You'll probably be in an apartment next year and have your own kitchen."

She handed Lisa a tray of noodles. "Now watch. Meat sauce and cheese between each layer. This dish is a sure way to a man's heart."

Lisa went to work helping with the layers. They were quiet for awhile as Mom mulled over the right words. "Lisa?"

"Huh?"

"Can I ask you something personal?"

"You're my mother. Getting personal is in the contract." She smiled. "No need to ask. I think I know the question anyway."

"Are—are you—have you gone LBQ or something?"

Lisa shrieked with laughter and almost dropped the tray. "You got me, Mom. Not at *all* the question I guessed."

"It's okay, Dear," she whispered. "We'll still love you. I just need to know."

"Listen," she wiped her hands on a dish towel, placed them on mother's shoulders and made eye contact. "I am not les or gay, Mother, and I do like men. I even have a bit of a crush on someone, but he's totally out of reach. Besides, I don't have time right now."

"Oh, what a relief. I'm sorry to be so pushy, Lisa." She took her hands off her shoulders and made some sparkle-eyes. "Do you think that out-of-reach guy likes you?"

Lisa giggled. "You don't quit, do you? I know you're half Italian and your grandparents believed in arranged marriages by the time you're sixteen. Look, I'm not forty one. I'm twenty one and I'm sure I'll meet the right guy one day." She gave Mom's shoulders a squeeze. "Okay?"

"Oh, all right. Your mother has dreams of being a grandmother, that's all."

They finished up the pasta preparation with talk about the weather and Lisa's articles, but as they put dinner in the oven, mother added, "Just remember. A man might pass up a girl, but even a hard-to-get guy can't pass up a lasagna."

Back in the living room, Dad had a football game on. Lisa relaxed on the couch beside him. "So, Dad, I'm just gonna kick back for a few days and not worry about life back there, okay?"

Dad gave her a quick back-of-the-neck tweak. "That's perfect. I don't have to be back on duty until Friday. You survive the inquisition?"

"Yeah. Mom is just happy I might still marry a man."

"Really." He chuckled. "She's a little over the top. Say, if you want we could rent Ski Doos tomorrow and follow some mountain trails."

"Whoa. Sounds like fun. The only work I have to do is E mail an article back to my paper by Saturday, and it's almost finished."

"What's it on, Sugar?"

"Not sugar, it's on global warming."

Dad grinned. "We could use a little global warming on this freezing base. Maybe you…"

Lisa's phone text interrupted them. It was from Vera: *"First a reminder: your article is due on Saturday despite the holiday. Sorry. Second, call me on a secure line or, better yet, come by on Monday. Something really serious has come up, but don't worry for now. Have a happy Thanksgiving."*

BACK TO THE FRONT

After church and Sunday lunch, Lisa stood on the doorstep giving her mother a goodbye embrace. Her leather cut was rolled up and she was wearing a styli, form-fitting, crème colored jacket with faux fur collar and cuffs. "Mother, thank you for rescuing me from that boring dorm room and fattening me up, and thanks for the jacket, too. This was a great Thanksgiving."

"I'm praying for you, Lisa. My mother's intuition tells me you're into something dangerous and you're both hiding the secret from me. You're the most talented and brave daughter I have, but I know a secret about you too. You are blessed with a sweet, loving heart."

"Oh, Ma, thanks. Despite the fact that I'm your only daughter, I'll take the compliment."

Dad laughed and turned Lisa around toward his Jeep. At a safe distance he muttered. "Just so you know: she *will* get the story out of me." He tossed her small duffle in the back. "I don't know why we don't use women like her to get information out of captured spies."

On the way back down the mountain, Dad said he was curious to know what she had to say about global warming.

"All my articles are about bringing out the truth no matter who hates it, Dad. I've been inspired by Dylan Coz, one of my professors., and I had help on this one from a few science geeks who found out a lot of stuff for me."

"Does your article confirm that 'Inconvenient Truth' thing?"

"No, no, quite the opposite. I titled it 'The Convenient Lie.' It exposes the falsehood of man having a dramatic effect on the world climate."

Dad gave her a stern glance. "So now they'll call you, 'Lisa, the climate denier,' huh?"

"Yup, probably worse. Liars use mockery to cover their tracks."

"But, they say 97% of all climate scientists agree with them." The Jeep bounced down the exit road and Lisa waved to her mother, still standing on the porch looking mournful. "So, Lisa, what do you say to that argument?"

"That percentage is only from *government* paid or sponsored scientists. The world's non government scientists were so pissed at this becoming political that over thirty thousand of them including two thousand climate scientists in America signed a Global Warming Petition in 2015. Basically they said humans have not had significant influence on climate. They meet yearly, but as far as media coverage, they might as well be in a black hole."

"Wow. Where was the petition published?"

"Almost nowhere. The media and the government want the lie to exist, not the truth. It's part of their grand plan to gain control over corporations, and us too, of course. They like to imply that 'if we don't nationalize everything the world will end and we'll all die'."

"But you can't deny the climate is changing. Glaciers are melting."

"Oh, Daddy, the climate has *always* been changing due to solar activity and other things. We were in a mini ice age until 1860 and we've been slowly warming up until twenty years ago when temperatures leveled out."

"Wait a minute, I read that the CO2 level keeps rising so we have to pay a tax on carbon."

"Right, almost 10% in the last twenty years with no effect on temperature. In fact the non-governmental climate scientists are predicting a trend toward global cooling is likely. How about that polar vortex last winter setting records for low temperatures in Chicago?"

The road flattened out as they approached Bridgeport. Dad shook his head. "This article won't help your popularity. Hey, I know, why not propose to make everyone happy by *paying* them to emit carbon and save us from the big freeze?"

Lisa laughed. "Very funny, Dad, but my editor measures success by the volume of hate mail."

Dad chuckled as he pulled into the repair shop. "My instinct is to protect you somehow. Maybe I should send five of my marines to watch over you."

"Whoa, Daddy." She slapped him on the shoulder. "Oh, *yes!* What a great idea—cute ones about twenty five years old. Send them to me, *please*."

Sergeant Combes pulled into a parking space, doubled over with laughter. "Oh, no." He shook his hands in front of her face. "No, no, what was I *thinking*?"

"Aw, Dad, why not?"

"Cause a good sergeant..." More laughter. "doesn't send his men into a danger they can't control."

"Shucks," she said, slipping off her fancy jacket. "Could you mail this to me? It might not survive the trip if I wore it, and I've got nowhere to pack it."

"Sure."

As a man wheeled out her motorcycle, Dad said, "I had Matt fix the hole for you. Lisa, I like your Harley, but why did you pick a green helmet?"

"Cause it goes well with pink, silly. I had to spray paint it myself."

Dad embraced his daughter. "You do know how much we love you, don't you?" He held her at arms length. "I've been thinking, the more you get into print with all this stuff, the less likely the bad guys will try to harm you, at least physically."

Lisa slipped on her leather jacket. "Love you too, Dad."

"Wait, before you go..." He went back to the car and returned with a paper sack and an olive green nylon bag. "Mary packed some snacks for you and I have a present, too."

"Is that a *purse*?"

"It's called a tactical purse—CIA issue. Thought a little added protection would make you feel more secure—make me feel better, too."

"Oh, Daddy." She shook her head. "Really, I'll be fine."

Dad placed the bag on her motorcycle seat. "It has two compartments. The larger one is a regular purse, but the outer one is fully detachable. You still have the birthday present?"

"Oh, yes." She chuckled. "And I'm sure I'm the only student at Berkard with a concealed carry permit."

"You'll need it." He zipped open the outer compartment revealing an assortment of weaponry."

"What? Dad, do you think I'm deploying to Iraq?"

"Just some defensive stuff for the single girl. First, the click button is a pager alert for 911 tied to a GPS. There's no sound transmission unless you slide this button to the left."

"The revolver…"

"Good Lord, there *is* a revolver."

"It has only four shots. Not that accurate, but it's for close range." He pointed to the other things. "This is mace, and here's extra ammo and a police whistle. These are your slip on Tiger-Lady claws. If bad guys move close, you can slide your hand into the pocket and come out with whatever seems appropriate."

Lisa was laughing. She saluted. "Ready for duty, sir."

"Of course I hope you don't need any of it," he gave her a kiss on top of her head. "But its good insurance just in case. Maybe it's just so I can sleep better."

She found a spot for the snacks in the saddlebag while Dad checked and tightened the bungee cords holding her duffle. "See you for Christmas in a few weeks, Dad."

"We're counting on it. Your brother should be there too."

Lisa mounted her bike and pulled her chin strap tight. "Want me to take care of those pesky North Koreans first?"

LIBERAL LIBEL

The trip back to Berkard was uneventful. Lisa ran through her MP-3 recordings twice and tired of listening to the top ten list on radio. She felt ready for tomorrow's normal routine or even a little danger—didn't matter. Around sunset, Lisa parked her bike, grabbed her luggage, and a bag of fast food and was ready to snack and "crash" in her dorm.

She greeted her usually talkative roommate. "Hi, there. I'm back." Lisa stuffed her new purse behind the socks in her top dresser drawer with a chuckle, and dropped her backpack on the closet floor. "Crazy trip on my new bike through the mountains. Wanna hear about it?"

Her roommate didn't look up from her book. "Uh, huh."

"Hope you had a good Thanksgiving." Pause. "Well, I'm pooped and I've got to be at the paper by nine tomorrow, so I'll finish off my Carl's Junior, and hit the sack."

"Okay."

"Are you all right?"

"Yeah."

Lisa stared at the back of her roommate's book and made a face. "Don't get too excited. We'll have a nice chat tomorrow, huh?"

Early Monday morning, Lisa smiled at friends in the cafeteria but they all averted their gaze--same for her coworkers at the Oakland Flame. She marched into Vera's office without knocking. "Vera, I'm not one to be paranoid, but have I suddenly grown a skunk tail and horns?"

Vera came around her desk, concern written on her face. "You haven't seen the papers this weekend, have you?"

Lisa shook her head. Vera pointed to a chair. "I texted you we have a problem, remember? You'll need to sit."

Vera plopped the weekend editions of the Oakland and San Francisco papers in her lap. As Lisa began to read, her mouth remained open, emitting indignant chirps as she tore through the pages. She looked up at Vera who was still standing in front of her. "It's a hideous lie; a complete fabrication, Vera."

"I guessed as much."

Lisa pointed to a headline and read. "Now we know the *real* reason Professor Coz was fired. Berkard graciously chose not to reveal his extra marital affair with a student. This student, one Lisa Combes, is responsible for articles and a TV

272

appearance, not surprisingly, in his support. Combs is denying it, but we expect Coz will be arrested soon."

Lisa gave Vera a cynical smile. "I love the 'Combs is denying it' part—like someone actually talked to me."

"Let me be the reporter for a sec. Stand back and be objective. Lisa, did the professor make any friendly moves toward you?"

"Coz is like a second father to us, me included. He's a rock of morality and loves his wife like crazy."

"How would you know that?"

Lisa raised her index finger. "Ah, the reason they're doing this is the lawsuit Professors Coz and West filed to get their jobs back. If you don't have truth, then discredit those who do."

"I believe you, dear. I do, but what about those pictures?"

She got up and spread out the paper on Vera's desk. "I've only made actual physical contact with the professor on two occasions, and they're both here—at least partly here."

She pointed to the first one showing Dylan sitting beside her in the classroom, hand on her shoulder. "This was right after Stengel fired me from the school paper. I was bawling my eyes out and he was comforting me. Of course, they photo-shopped out *all the students* who were in the row right behind us."

Lisa tapped the other one. "This one's beyond outrageous. I'm at a loss for words."

The picture showed Lisa and Dylan embracing on the steps of his home. The caption read. "Student working for extra credit at her teacher's house."

Lisa was beginning to tear up. Her voice squeaked. "How *could* they, Vera? This is the most horrid thing—like ever."

"This picture has been doctored too?"

"Yuh *think*? Emma, her boyfriend Wally, and I went to his home after Coz was fired. We asked him if he would agree to continue teaching us somewhere. He agreed, and about twenty of us go to hear him at a local church once a week. Anyway, this photo was taken when Professor Coz gave the *three* of us a grateful hug when we were leaving. Not only did they remove my friends from the picture, but his wife, Sally, was standing right behind us."

"Wow. And to think these are supposed to be respected major papers. This is trashy gossip–sheet stuff."

"And now I know another reason why those men have been following me, but who would believe me if I complained about their sham?"

"You won't have to, Lisa. This is where responsible, truthful journalists take over. You have named plenty of witnesses here, and there's always evidence when pictures are digitally manipulated. We'll put our reporters on this one. The big papers will pay."

"Thanks, Vera. Uh, did you get my last article in time for today's run?"

"Sure did. It's a blockbuster, and I love your title. There will be a delay though, 'cause our Chief wants to do some fact checking. With climate change, we're tromping on a sacred cow."

"Sure, I'm happy ever everything will get independently verified. Remember our coverage on the International Symposium of Climate Scientists in Washington last July? Some of my quotes were from that meeting."

"Of course, and every year the US media pretends that climate busting meeting didn't happen."

STARTING OVER

That Friday the students were unusually quiet as they gathered in the Church meeting hall, but there were more of them than usual, plus a reporter and photographer from The Oakland Flame. Dylan walked to the podium and smiled. "I learned something important this week."

Jevon leaned toward Wally. "Think he's gonna fess up?" Wally shook his head.

"I learned I should always read the morning paper so I can find out what's really been going on in my personal life." The students laughed. "How could I not remember this?"

"Luckily, my wife, Sally, does read the news so I heard about the articles on Sunday. By 'heard' I mean I heard her scream in the next room. It was even louder than her previous record set by a tarantula on the pet door."

Dylan waited for the laughter to die down. "It was *so* loud there were two 911 calls and all the dogs in the neighborhood were barking."

"I ran to see who'd been murdered and found her doing a war dance and shaking the paper over her head."

Murmured chuckles. "Show of hands. How many of you think Sally was angry with me?"

"Looks like most of you, but you're all wrong. I hope all of you are blessed one day with a rock solid marriage like I have. No, Sally ran to me and cried on my shoulder knowing I'd been slandered." He paused for a moment and looked up. "Thank you for my wife, Lord."

"I suspect that this attack is the result of the lawsuit Professor West and I filed against Berkard to restore our positions. My lawyer has filed a libel suit against the newspapers and Berkard." He extended his hand toward the front row. "Lisa, would you like to give your point of view?"

She went to the podium to take the microphone. "Better not give me a hug, Professor." Giggles and whistles from the students.

"Sally, the Professor's wife, had one advantage. She knew she'd been photo-shopped out of the front porch photo, but with me the reaction was different. I don't have a husband. No prospects, either."

A man in the audience shouted, "I'll marry you, Lisa!"

She chuckled. "Meet me after class." The audience laughed.

"There were no barking dogs either, but The Oakland flame where I work..." She pointed to the reporter in the back and grinned. "They will investigate first and do a full story about it--a story that tells the actual truth." Applause.

"The interesting thing about being accused like this is you learn who your real friends are, and I'm happy to say a lot of them are in this room. It's annoying to know that people who don't know you well will have lingering doubts, even after reality is clearly revealed."

"I'm not going to worry about them. I believe everyone here has a genuine affection for our Professor Dylan, and I'm on top of that list. Maybe this is just a real-life lesson in searching for truth—and Dylan has spent a great deal of time and passion teaching us about it."

She extended the mike to Dylan. When he came to get it, Lisa faced the audience and said, "This is for all of us," and gave him a hug. They gave her a loud round of applause as she returned to her seat.

"Thanks, Lisa. Remember this: our ultimate judge is not man but God. And, speaking of God, tonight we need to talk about something He has done."

Dylan opened his hands to the audience. "I'm sure you were disappointed to find there were no more roses to wear today. Betty was eye witness to the reason why, so I'm going to ask her to tell you what happened."

She was a little reluctant to get up, but he coaxed her to the podium. Betty gave a few nervous brush-backs to her long, brown hair. "Uh, well, hi."

She took a deep breath. "This is going to seem strange, but it's true. On Wednesday some students asked me to join them as they put a kneeling pad in front of our rose bush." She looked to the back of the room. "Vicky, you were there."

"Anyway, putting up an altar there sounded like a good idea, so we cleared a space in front of the bush. It was really three bushes grown together. That day we put down the kneeler and planned to come back on Thursday to install a small altar."

"When we returned to the lawn, our bush was gone. Just *gone*." She gestured in the air with one hand. "We ran up to where it had been, thinking the maintenance guys had torn it up again. Nope, the old scrub bush was there instead, and the kneeler looked real silly sitting there."

She pointed at Emma and Wally. "You had pictures of the original wild bush. Anyway, it was back and the ground looked like it had never been touched."

She handed the microphone back to Dylan who said, "Why do you think God did that?"

Betty scooted back to her seat, but before she handed off the mike she said, "Maybe some miracles are only supposed to last a little while."

Dylan swept a finger over the audience. "Other ideas?"

One student said, "I think God made his point, and it was time to move on."

There being no other suggestions, Dylan said, "We can't know with certainty, but I believe it is in the Ten Commandments. God does not want us to worship an *object*, even one He put there. In time, some people would be worshiping a bush, really a false idol, as though it were divine."

"Give it some thought before next week. From now on, lets keep the memory of Hayley, and how God showed us His love for her, in our hearts."

SCOOP

The television camera slowly panned the large park, moving from a playground, past a lake and a tennis court. A woman's voice narrated: "This lovely place was renamed 'Friendship Park' by our city council last month. 'Veteran's Park' was too militaristic, don't you agree?"

The camera zoomed in toward a pretty blond woman with short hair and a microphone in hand, standing on the walkway. "This is your RNN Entertainment Reporter, Rita Fleiss, hoping for a live scoop today.

Stay with me, and perhaps we'll make some exciting discoveries together—live and uncensored." Big grin.

"Attorneys for the fired professor, Dylan Coz, continue to deny his extramarital affair with his student, Lisa Combes. Our attempts to get an interview with Combes have been turned away and student interviews have been unproductive—until now."

Close up of one finger raised and a mischievous grin. "Remember, I never repeat gossip—so listen closely the first time."

Rita turns, beckons to the audience to follow, and begins to walk down the path. The camera glides along with her so she can turn and face it when she wants. "We are strolling along toward a bench near the boat dock. One student, Jim, who asked that only his first name be used, gave Berkard Capers, the student newspaper, this fascinating tip. They asked us to investigate and here we are doing just that.

We are hoping to meet up with one, Mister Basset, a man Jim tells us is an intimate friend, and sometimes the jogging partner, of Professor Coz. Perhaps we will see them both together, but Basset is the one who is said to come here daily."

A woman jogger passes them and Rita calls out, "Excuse me, would you like to answer some questions?" The jogger shakes her head "no" as she goes by.

Rita stops and faces the camera. "Here is what we know. Basset is described as a 'ladies man,' and irresistible. He frequently gets the attention of women along this path and often runs alongside them. One can imagine that he is in a position to procure girls for his best friend, can't you?" She puts a knuckle in her mouth and gets a mischievous look. "I can hardly wait to meet him."

She waves for the camera to follow her again. "Jim says that he almost always rests on the bench around nine AM and that's where we are headed. Let's hope we are in luck today. See you back after a short break."

After the commercial break, Rita is standing beside a water fountain. Behind her, one can see a boat dock and a woman sitting on a bench with a dog beside her. "Welcome back, folks. No sign of our quarry yet, but this drinking fountain would make this a likely stopping place to, uh, strike up a conversation."

Rita looks down the path. "Here comes another jogger. I'll bet she's thirsty. Wish me luck."

A teen age girl in shorts pulls up and begins to drink. When she looks up, Rita offers her a winning smile and a hopeful look. "Hi, there, Miss. I hope I'm not bothering you, but I'm with RNN and I'd like to ask you a question if I may."

The girl glances at the man holding the camera. "On TV? Right now? Uh, sure."

"Oh, super. I'm looking for an interview with a Mister Arthur Basset. He's reported to frequent this area and he has many lady friends, who…" The girl puts her hand over her mouth and giggles.

"Ah ha, so you *do* know who I'm talking about." The teen nods her head, splashing her pony tail up and down. "And you're not eighteen yet, are you?" She shakes her head, "no." Pony tail whips side to side.

"So, look, you don't have to answer, but do you think this person has had relationships with underage girls?"

The girl gives a snort-laugh. "Oh, yeah." Giggle. "I think Arthur likes, uh, relationships with girls—young ones too. I had to pull my thirteen year old sister away from him last week."

Rita looks totally shocked. "Okay, I'm not following up on *that* comment on live TV, but can you confirm for us if Mister Basset is good friends with Dylan Coz?"

"Yup. Best buddies. I see them out here together all the time."

"Thank you, so much. I won't ask you any more questions, except if you were looking to, uh, find him right now, what would you suggest?"

"I'd suggest..." Another giggle. "I'd ask the lady sitting on the bench." She leans closer to Rita. "She knows Dylan Coz *real* well--and Arthur too." The girl jogs away but gives the woman a quick wave as she passes by.

Rita draws close to the camera lens, her eyes wide with anticipation. "And here we go, folks."

She sits beside the woman and produces another winning smile. "Hello. I'm Rita Fleiss from RNN. We've been talking to people on this beautiful day in Friendship Park. Would you mind if I ask you some questions?"

284

"Not at all." The dog began to nuzzle against Rita's leg. "Sorry, about him. What would you like to know?"

"I'm hoping to find and interview Arthur Basset. Please state your name for our viewers. I understand you know him. Is that correct?"

"Yes I do, and I heard everything Jillian just told you."

"Now, don't worry. I'm not going to force any personal information from you." She grinned. "Of course it would be fine to let it out if you *want* to. We're just looking for the truth about Basset and his friend, Dylan Coz."

"The real truth, huh?"

"Of course, Ms…"

"Yes, my name is Sally. I'm Mrs. Dylan Coz, but I see you are already interviewing Arthur. He's the dog you are petting. Careful, he's quite the ladies man, isn't he?"

PROTESTS

Emma found Lisa sitting on a campus bench, her legs curled under her. She didn't look up from the book she was reading until Emma sat down and said "Hi."

"Lisa, I happen to know you have no plans for this afternoon so I'm recruiting you for an adventure."

"Really?" She scrunched her face disrupting her nose freckles into furrows. "I'm just getting to the good part. This guy is about to be caught living the biggest lie ever."

Emma pointed her finger. "I can top that. We'll do it live, and you can report on it, too."

"There's no use arguing with you is there?" A quick poke out with her tongue. "Hope it's not a revenge adventure for what I put you through. Where are we going?"

"We're crashing two protests. The first one at Administration will be easy. Wally's there and they're protesting the admission policy."

"Emma, I hope you didn't tear me away from my novel so you can impress your boyfriend." She stuffed the book in her backpack. "But wait, isn't this about the policy that got Professor West fired?"

"Exactly. Asians are being discriminated against because their SATs are too high. Many of them are denied admission in favor of lower scoring minorities. Wally's sister couldn't get in and he's pretty upset about it."

About twenty students stood on the steps of the Administration Building with signs, occasionally calling out: "Equality," or "Justice."

Emma picked up a "Justice" sign from the ground, headed for Wally and stood behind him. She shouted, "Justice for Adel! Justice for Adel!"

Wally spun around, gave her a quick kiss and waved at Lisa. "Thanks for coming, but we're quitting at the top of the hour."

"You guys," Emma grinned. "Gotta get back to studying, huh? Did Stengel come out?"

"Not exactly, but we got more reaction from him than we expected."

"Huh? What did he do?"

"Oh, he…" Wally chuckled and pointed at the building. "He came to the window and scowled down on us."

Emma nodded. "No, that's real progress. Usually he sends an assistant to scowl at us."

The protesters began to lay their signs down in a neat pile. Wally laid his down and grinned at Emma. "Hey, I'm skipping dorm food this evening and picking up a bowl at Yashinoya. Want to come?"

"Sure, you can come get me in a couple of hours if they don't arrest us."

"What?!"

He looked at Lisa who shrugged. "She hasn't told me yet, Wally…figures, doesn't it? I'm a blind follower."

Emma opened her hands. "We're just doing an intervention for a friend. "I'm sure we'll be fine."

"Emma," he gave her a stern look. "Keep your phone on. Call if you need me, okay?"

"Not to worry." She planted a cheek kiss. "I've got a ninja warrior with me."

Wally held up a finger, but turned and walked away. Emma gestured to Lisa to follow her in the other direction. After a few paces, Lisa said, "Maybe this would be a good time to tell your ninja whom she'll be killing?"

"We're taking my car to another protest. This one's outside the Oakland office of Homeland Security. We're gonna rescue a protester from himself."

#   #   #

A good sized crowd blocked the street, half remaining in one spot and the others marching up and down the sidewalk.

Scattered police stood at a wide perimeter. Emma grasped Lisa's sleeve. "Flash your press badge to this policeman, okay?"

Lisa smiled at the officer. "Here to pick up some interviews, okay?"

"Careful," he said. "They've been splashing some officials with quick set concrete. We just made some arrests."

They drew close to the crowd who were chanting over and over: "No wall, no wall. No USA at all!"

Emma worked her way through the stationary crowd, crossing the street to the curb, but Lisa stopped her when she recognized a student.

"Excuse me, sir. "She held up her badge. "Lisa Combes, Oakland Flame. Care to tell our readers why you're protesting?"

"Can't you hear?" He glowered at her. "Walls don't make friends. They're immoral. We have to open our borders—be friends with the world—one society—equality for all."

"So no USA at all?"

"Exactly. End this place of capitalistic slave owners. Bring on a new society of peace and freedom."

"So, you want a government like, uh, what country?"

"Oh, right." He pointed a finger at her nose. "I know you and that paper. You're all about the racist police state and you won't print what I say anyway."

"No, no, you're wrong there. I promise you can read your every word you say in the next edition."

He gave her the finger and went into the crowd. Emma said, "You do have mace in that purse of yours, right?"

Lisa held up her hand and grinned. "Ninja promise. I'm starting to have fun. Say, who are we looking for?"

"I'll tell you when I spot him. Help me to stand on this hydrant."

Emma craned her neck over the crowd for a minute before she announced, "*There* he is, on the edge of the standing crowd."

"Who?"

"You'll see." She slid down. He's a friend of ours."

The two worked their way through the chanters, dodging the waving signs until Lisa exclaimed, "Jevon! What are you doing here?"

Jevon put his sign down and confronted his friends with a sheepish grin. "Protesting. What's it look like?"

Emma moved in close. "Say, brother, I know you don't believe this crap anymore. Be honest with yourself."

"But, these are my friends. This protest is a big deal for them."

"And what are we? Pond scum?"

"Course not. I love you guys, but protests are fun."

A Cheshire grin came over Emma's face. "You're right. Okay, we'll chant along with you."

She took his sign, held it upside down and began to shout in unison with the crowd: "Big wall. Big wall. No USA for y'all!"

That was too much for Jevon who couldn't help but laugh. He put his arms out and herded them away. "Okay, okay, lets get out of here before they kill us."

SINGING TRUTH

The Rose Guardians were in a cheerful mood when Dylan arrived. He grinned at the clusters of talking, laughing groups as he headed for the podium.

"Okay everyone, listen up." He waited for things to calm a bit. "If Emma didn't spill the beans already, we've organized a special field trip on our last meeting before Christmas."

Now he had their attention. "In coordination with some in Berkard's Music Department and choir members at this church, we're going Christmas caroling on campus. She has a box full of pink flowers to pass around if you want to wear one. They're not Rose of Sharon, but similar."

Amid the cheers and yeas, Jim held up his hand. "But, Professor Coz, that's strictly against the rules."

"Uh oh. They might fire me." He laughed. "But that adds to the fun, huh? With a little luck, we'll be persecuted Christians." He did a little dance while the students cheered.

"Of course this is strictly voluntary for you, but we tipped off The News Box, and they'll be covering it."

"I did a little research and campus caroling was a tradition at Berkard since its founding in 1890 until it was banned eight years ago. Time to bring Jesus back on campus, don't you think?"

The students chorused, "Jesus-Jesus-Jesus."

"Great. The Calvary Covenant choir will be here any minute and they have printouts of the songs for all of you. The volunteers from our Music Department will meet us at our first stop, outside the administration building. I want to get there before everyone leaves for the day."

Someone shouted, "Stick it to Stengel!"

Dylan shook his head. "No, we're coming with love in our hearts and hoping to turn his. I wish he'd come out and join us." He saw Jim waving his hand. "What is it, Jim?"

"I know how to get Stengel to come out and meet us— no, wait, forget it. It's too chilly to put the girls in short shorts." That got a good laugh.

The choir members filed in waving their arms and singing "Oh Come all Ye Faithful." All joined in and they passed out lyrics to everyone.

Dylan herded the students to the front door. "The church has a bus if anyone needs a ride."

When the group gathered, they totaled fifty enthusiastic carolers plus CC with a guitar. The first song brought two campus police hustling over to block the front door. Perhaps they expected an invasion, but as they sang Silent Night, several women employees came out the side door with a pot of hot chocolate and doughnuts. They were greeted with hugs and thanks.

The News Box began their interviews. They followed the group to the dorms and the outside streets where the faculty lived. Some of the faculty homes shut off their lights when the caroling began, but others came out and applauded.

The church had set up a tent lit with candles in a vacant lot off campus. When the caroling was over, they welcomed them with lots of sweets, coffee and cocoa. Tilly threw out the question, "Does anyone know who sang those high soprano notes in 'Gloria'?"

Jim replied, "Must have been someone from the Music Department. I never heard a voice that high, or loud, either."

Lisa nodded. "But when a sound is that shrill, you can't be sure where it's coming from."

Susan said, "Oh, but her voice was *so* beautiful. The resonance sounded like we were in a cathedral and yet we were outside. It gave me goose-bumps."

Betty put a hand on nearby shoulders and looked up into the starry night. "Uh, uh, guys. Those 'glorias' were a gift. I think the one who sang them was floating above us on her wings."

JOURNALISM

Lisa quickly scooted across the lobby at The Oakland Flame, but the receptionist raised a finger and stood up right away, swishing her long black hair to one side. "Hold on there, fast lady."

She slapped her hand on her mouth. "Oops, don't take that the wrong way. The Chief wants to see you." She picked up a hand set. "Just a minute."

Lisa opened her hands. "Uh, it's almost five. I wanted to catch Vera before she left."

The receptionist held up a finger and punched a button on her desk as Lisa drew close. "Harley girl's here, sir."

Laughter on the speaker, then "Send her right up."

She grinned at Lisa. "I'll tell Vera. Go right up, but just so you know; I'm a big fan of yours."

The Chief waved her in his open door. "All right, Miss. Combes, how are you doing?"

"Just fine, Sir."

"I asked Vera to wait for you, so take it easy." He gestured to a chair. "In fact, sit a moment."

"I'm working on a column for our next edition, Sir. It's a personal impression how it felt to experience Hayley's murder and the story of the miraculous Rose of Sharon that grew nearby."

"I have no doubt it will be gobbled up by our readers. Did you know that we have a large bunch of new readers who look for your article every week. We estimate about four thousand."

"Uh, oh, I hope I still get enough hate mail."

He chuckled. "Sorry, that's slacked off. You haven't read any of your mail for awhile, have you?"

"Guess not. I assumed it would only put me in a bad mood."

"Well, you should check it out." He coughed. "First, I asked you up here to tell you that our Washington insider tells us the House is expected to launch a full scale ethics investigation on our very own Congressman Bernard Luchow. It's no longer a rumor.

"Large amounts of cash are coming to his charity from a New York law firm and funneled through Reinhardt Corporation where he is a majority shareholder. Looks like the money laundering and secret operation you wrote about."

"Yes, Sir," Lisa nodded. "My FBI contact briefed me on Reinhardt, and I guess you also know Luchow's on the Board at Berkard as well."

"Really? We missed that." The Chief's eyes widened. "Your *FBI* contact?"

"Uh, huh."

"Some of us work for years to get reliable inside sources. Can you count on yours?"

"Oh, yes. Mine is in the Los Angeles district, but he's been in the San Francisco office before and knows a bunch of agents there."

"Vera told me you had a contact in the Oakland Police force too."

"I do, and that's how I know a lot about the murder and why it's being kept secret."

The Chief leaned forward, chin on hand and squinted at Lisa. "And when might we expect to see all this exploding on our front page?"

"Well," She grinned. "Still more to be learned, but if your sources can trace how the Luchow money is being used, it's time. I wouldn't be surprised if a lot of it goes into funding protests, spying on people and community organizing."

"Deal, and the committee is looking into those connections as well. Now about your global warming piece…"

"Uh, oh, you're not going to print it, are you?"

"No, of course we are. We want our hate mail to top a thousand a week." He chuckled to himself. "Look, I just need you to verify some things. You said that the glaciers have been melting at a steady rate all through the nineteenth century due to recovery from the mini ice age, and not affected by industrialization or the automobile. Also, sea ice is stable."

"Yes, the *global* area of sea ice is about the same as in 1979 but there are spots where it is receding and spots where it's growing. The paper they use that claims the ocean temperature is rising turns out to be flawed mathematically. Of course the globalists still cite it anyway.

"And you say CO_2 levels only rise *after* warming, not the other way around? We'll need some scientific references."

"It's true. I can include a graph that shows it. My sources are several publications by Zwally, Johannssen, and Giovinetto. I'll put the specific references in a footnote."

"You should. There will be an angry blowback from printing this even if you have provable facts. The left is more hysterical on the subject than Chicken Little." He handed her thumb drive back. "Add those in and we're good to go."

"Yes, sir, I'll have it back tomorrow."

"Great. Nice work, Lisa." He flicked the back of his hand toward the door. "Okay, off with you. Vera's waiting."

Vera put down the paper she was reading when Lisa arrived. "I have some news for you, sweetheart. Two of our reporters are almost finished with a report exploding that hate piece about you. Also, I sent you a completely hilarious video clip of an RNN reporter 'laying an egg' on live TV. It'll be on Box News tonight. You'll just love it.

"I don't know how the professor's libel suit is going, but I'm sure that two big papers are gonna be nursing some nasty bruises. That should make you happy, huh?"

"Aw, I'm not vindictive. Their idea was to discredit Professor Coz, not me so much."

"Wow. You sound like you almost forgive them."

"Vera, the important thing is for the truth to come out. That attack wasn't fair to Mister Coz."

"Okay, we've interviewed his wife, but who did you say was the man they sketched out in the porch picture?"

"Wally Kim. He's a student and Emma's boyfriend."

"The *original* picture, you mean."

"Right." Lisa handed her a portable drive. "This is a draft on my witnessing the Hayley murder. Could you look it over and make suggestions?"

Vera chuckled. "That *is* my job, sweetie, and one other thing. I'm guessing it was your police contact who called on our secure line. He wants to keep you informed through 'CC', whoever that is, and you're to go and see him ASAP."

IMPATIENCE

A buzzer sounded on Congressman Luchow's desk. "What's happening, Cynthia? No interruptions, remember? I have to leave for Washington tonight."

"So sorry, sir. Reggie's on the way up there. He doesn't listen to us you know."

"Me, neither." Bernard clicked off the intercom, muttered a few swear words and leaned back in his chair with a feigned look of nonchalance.

Reggie blasted in past the shouts of a distraught receptionist. "Okay, Dad, why is this thing not going away?"

"Son," Bernard studied his son's reddened face for a deliberate moment. "Son, despite you going off half cocked all on your own and killing that woman, we *are* taking care of this."

"You don't care if I go to jail, do you?"

He chuckled. "Oh, you're wrong there. Your being convicted of murder would look really bad for me."

300

Reggie stood against the desk, leaned forward on it, resting on his hands. "Always the loving father, aren't you? Just tell me why I'm still reading about *new* revelations."

"This reporter's just a college student, but one who saw your team in live action. Either she's got amazing inside connections, and that's highly unlikely, or she's making things up with lucky guesses. We need to find out if she's really talking to people in the know, so have a little patience, huh?"

"No, I will not have *patience,* Dad. Just have your Reinhardt boys take care of her so we can both forget about the whole thing."

"Well, that almost happened." He chuckled. "Reggie, go smoke a little weed and let me worry about this, okay?"

"How about I organize another Antifa action on campus when I know we can corner her."

"Reggie, look, I know how you feel, but if you go rogue again, just know I'm not covering for you a second time. I'm working on some ideas to put the brakes on this whole thing, so as you like to say, cool it."

They glowered at each other for a moment. Reggie did an about face and headed for the door. "Two weeks, Dad. Two weeks."

SCARE TACTICS

"Hi, CC? This is Lisa Combes. I'm calling on a secure line. You have something for me?"

"Sure do, but he told me not to say anything on the phone, even a secure one. I could tell you next Sunday after church."

"That long?" She chuckled. "I'd have ten different dreams by then wondering what it might be. Are you at church now?"

"Yeah, but I'm about to leave in a few minutes. I've been practicing numbers to try out at rehearsal."

"I'm only a few blocks away, CC. Be there in ten, okay?"

It was almost dark when Lisa rode down the alley between the church and an abandoned building to the empty parking lot behind. Feeling a bit uneasy, she quickly walked back to the front.

CC Jackson was leaning against the welcome counter with his banjo case. "Thanks for waiting, CC. I didn't see your car in the lot."

"Lucky me. I got the last one on the street. How're you handling the bad press?"

"No problem. All my friends know the thing with Professor Coz is a lie now, and our paper will expose it soon. So, Detective Ryan wants you to pass on his information, right?"

"Yeah, he says it's less likely the bad guys will see the connection that way."

Lisa held her hands open, her expectant eyes, bright. "And so?"

"Here's the news: Another eye witness who saw the murder has come forward and given a testimony. It's a student he says you know, but its better *no one* knows the name right now, so he's not even telling the FBI."

"That's great news. I know there were some students marching with Antifa. This one must have had a change of heart. Anything else?"

"That's it, Lisa. He said you can report it, but from an anonymous source." He picked up his case to go out front, but paused, one hand on the door knob. "Oh wait, one other thing. My son called. He said the Justice Department is going to have an announcement at five tomorrow afternoon and he thinks it's about the murder."

"Are they returning the case to Oakland?"

"Not hardly. Do you want me to walk you back to the lot?"

"That's all right, CC. I'll be fine. There's no one around."

"Okay, but go out the side door, huh? It locks automatically and you'll skip half the alley."

Lisa cautiously cracked the door open and looked both ways. The only light came from a single, flickering sulfur lamp in the parking lot. All was quiet.

She walked quickly down the alley but froze at the sight of two men leaning against her motorcycle. She spun around and sprinted back to the door. Locked. Two other men were casually walking down the alley toward her from the street.

She flattened herself against the door, put her hand in Dad's special purse and prayed. The four men took up positions only two feet in front of her. For half a minute they just stared at her while she listened to the pounding in her throat.

One man flashed a pen light beam on her face and said, "It's Lisa Combes, all right."

Another man reached out toward her. "You're coming with us."

Her hands whipped out of the purse with mace aimed at his face. "Not one step closer or you'll get it."

"Oh, look," He turned to the others and laughed. "She's got both mace *and* Tiger Lady Claws."

A taller man stood behind the other three and spoke in a commanding voice. "Okay, hold it a moment, Sammy. We'll just talk first."

He pointed at Lisa. "You do realize that you couldn't stop the four of us with any of that, and we'd just have to make you suffer for it."

"Yeah, but you'll suffer a lot, too."

That made him chuckle. "Despite the fact that we'd all have such a *good* time, little darlin', it may surprise you that we didn't come to kill you—this time."

Lisa couldn't come up with a brilliant retort, so she gave him the raspberry.

"Think of this as a warning. We can find you anytime, anywhere, so it's time you drop the murder investigation. But don't think we don't want to *encourage* your creative writing. Just stick to subjects like the school prom and the high cost of tuition, understand?"

"What if I prefer to squeeze the ugly puss out of Congress and the people grabbing for power?"

In one blinding move, Sammy knocked the mace out of her hand and with a sweep of his leg, dropped her on the ground. She groaned and rubbed her shin.

Their laughter stopped when a police car pulled into the alley and gave a short blip on its siren, but the men calmly stood their ground. They raised their hands when two policemen approached with guns drawn.

Before the police got close, one man gave Lisa a quick kick in her ribs and hissed, "You've been warned, kid." All four men stood quietly, facing the police.

Ten feet in front of them, one policeman asked. "Okay, what's going on here?"

The tall man answered, "Black Cat Security, officer. May I show ID?"

"Slowly—one hand."

The man reached into his jacket and produced a badge. The officer studied it for a moment and read the short note beside it. "Well, okay." They holstered their guns. "A note from our chief, huh? He did mention we'd run into you from time to time."

"No problem, officer. We were just here on our rounds, checking this building and breaking in some new recruits."

"Sure, but…" He gestured toward Lisa who scowled up at them as she sat blotting her scraped knee. "What's with this one?"

"Oh, too bad. She was walking the alley when we swung into it. We must have scared her, 'cause she ran and slipped." Tall man looked down at her. His voice dripped with concern. "Real sorry, miss."

Lisa stuck out her tongue at him.

The officer gestured with his arms at the men. "All right then. Carry on."

All four men hastened away while another officer came jogging down the alley toward them. He extended a hand to help Lisa sit up. It was Scott Hutchins. "Lisa, my God, are you all right?"

Lisa drank in his look of compassion. "I am now. Thanks, Hutch."

The responding officer said, "You know this woman?"

"Yes, I do."

"Looks like she just got scared. No harm done."

Scott knelt down, put his arm around her and lifted her up off the ground as he stood up. He gently lowered her to stand beside him. "Whoa," she said.

He whispered in her ear. "Really stupid of you to dart away. I had to find you with your cell phone."

Lisa gave him a scrunch face. "Gosh, I'm sorry, Hutch. Won't happen again."

She turned to the first policeman. "Could I ask you just one question?" She squinted at his name tag. "Officer Barnes?"

"Of course, Miss, but first, shut off your 911 pager." They all began walking toward the lot at back of the building.

"Is there a new policy *not* to identify the victim or ask for their deposition?"

Officer Barnes stopped and turned to her. "What? Victim?"

"Just a simple question. I'll take a yes or no."

"This was just a slip and fall, lady. No need to make a report." His brow furrowed. "So you want to make a *statement*, huh. All right then. Who are you and what happened?"

"Lisa Combes, reporter for The Oakland Flame." She grinned and displayed her badge for him. His jaw dropped."

Scott said, "I was about to tell you guys."

Lisa sighed. "Black Cat Security is the enforcement branch of Reinhardt Corporation. They're progressing toward their idea of a new world order. While they do check on properties, they also check on people targeted as a threat to their operation. Basically, they're strong arm enforcement."

"Miss Combes, our chief has *personally* vouched for them in a note they were carrying."

"Yes, and your chief was appointed by the mayor who is on the Board at Reinhardt. Truth is, my articles have been threatening to them and this was a warning for me to back off. They knocked me down and kicked me."

The look of understanding spread across his face. "I'm *really* sorry, but then, you *did* look like a scared teenager. Why didn't you say something?"

"Because you might have believed me."

"Uh, I lost you again."

"Officer, if you had tried to arrest these men, you might have been killed."

"Really?" They resumed their walk to the back lot. "You're making me think about some other things I've heard. I thought they were crazy rumors from our fellow officers."

Scott raised a finger. "We should have a private chat about this later."

Lisa nodded at Barnes. "I admit, it does sound like a conspiracy theory, but with enough facts, even the strangest of things can be true—even the resurrection of Jesus."

The other officer said, "Praise the Lord."

"Uh, just one thing," Officer Barnes pointed at her. "We're not going to read about how two officers screwed up in tomorrow's paper, are we?"

Lisa swung her leg over her cycle and fired it up. She put a finger to her mouth, looked up and pretended to be thinking. "Hmmm." She laughed. "And rat on my friends? No way." She made eye contact with Scott and mouthed the words, "Thank you."

The officers grinned and waved as she roared off down the alley.

JUSTICE?

RNN News:

The screen shot showed an empty podium outside a government building. "We interrupt our newscast for an announcement from the Justice Department. We are told that there are to be indictments forthcoming related to the Berkard Matter, and we are awaiting the arrival of the Deputy Director."

Various people began walking to and around the podium, one moving a security barrier, another adjusting the microphones. "Here he comes. The Department has been silent on this investigation and this will be the first report. Stay tuned for our analysis after."

A bespectacled, balding man came to the dais, coughed and began. "I'll be brief. We have had many requests for information regarding the incident at Berkard University, but it is against policy to discuss an ongoing investigation. The FBI has now concluded its investigation and we are handing out three indictments to those persons charged with inciting violence."

"The three in question are Russian Nationals working for their intelligence service, and..." He smirked at the camera. "I won't attempt to pronounce their names.

"Ahem. These individuals have returned to Russia, but one of them made contact with some members of a political party one might describe as right wing. We feel there was collusion involved to create violence, to discredit the University and those peacefully protesting. We will be further investigating those we suspect of Russian collusion, and I expect more indictments will be forthcoming, however, I will take no further questions at this time."

The Director turns to walk away, but a reporter shouts a question: "Sir, what about the indictments? Will there be a trial?"

He pauses a moment. "The indictments will be delivered through diplomatic channels. You should ask the State Department for follow-up."

The TV image changes to the studio, an anchor person and two Washington reporters sitting at his desk. "So, there you have it. Is this a final conclusion to this matter? Will there be a trial?"

One reporter replies, "A trial is highly unlikely since Russia will not extradite citizens to the US. We might expect any US colluders to be tried, however."

Another reporter comments, "I have been reporting on Russian-right wing collusion for some time. The colluders aim to prevent free speech and discredit peaceful, justified protests. I, for one, am happy to see this exposed. Their behavior does not represent who we are in this country."

"Yes, and it should be no surprise that anyone promoting gun ownership is also in favor of violence."

"And they love to hide behind their religion—their holier-than-thou attitude."

The host responds. "I agree, and we at RNN will continue to pursue those who collude against our country with a foreign government. We all hope justice will be done, and speaking of religion, we will return in a moment to our RNN religion contributor to answer a question raised by others." "Was there..." He chuckled. "Does anyone believe that a miracle happened on Berkard campus?"

After commercials, the scene is the host at his desk with a man in a clerical collar sitting with an exaggerated erect posture. The host: "So, reverend, before we had to cut away, you were saying your denomination represents three million followers who are upset that the rights of aliens and also women's choice in reproduction have been abandoned by those who claim to be Christian."

"Absolutely. As I explained, we demand that Christianity return to a love your neighbor policy and modernize what is meant by sin. Also, religion is required by the Constitution to not oppose the government."

"That case couldn't be made more clearly. Thanks, reverend. Look, we have just thirty seconds left. Care to comment on the You Tube buzz about the supposed miracle of the flowers?"

"Sure, that's easy." He chuckled. "God doesn't do miracles anymore. That story, as they all are, was shown to be a fraud when the perpetrator was seen buying the flowers at a local shop. The Bible advises us to be wary of those who would deceive us."

"And, that's all for today. Thanks Reverend. Tune in tomorrow when we explore the frightening relationship between those who own guns and those who voted for our current president."

TRUTH ROSES

THE NEWS BOX: "HAMMER TIME" SHOW

The host sat at a large oval glass desk, his dark, straight hair streaked with gray at the temples. He greeted his audience with a smile. "Welcome, to Hammer Time everyone. I'm Charles Hammer."

Charles rapped a small gavel on a square of mahogany. "This evening we will open with a fascinating story about what has been called a miracle by some and a hoax by others. Briefly, the claim is that a flowering bush appeared near the site of Hayley Jones's death at Berkard University, and no matter how many blooms the students removed, new ones took their place."

"Here's a photo." The screen shot shows the picture Lisa took on her phone. "So there it is. Doesn't look particularly miraculous, and RNN was quick to condemn the story, but we at the News Box love all things Hayley, so we looked deeper."

"A good journalist always interviews people with different views, but RNN did not talk to a single person who believed or even saw this phenomenon. Naughty, naughty." He rapped his gavel. "I did this interview myself."

A video begins with Hammer talking to Pastor Wong and Emma Jackson along a campus walkway. "Pastor, I'll begin with you. These "Rose Guardians," as they call themselves, meet at your church, I understand. Do you think this flower thing is a case of teenage fantasy, or what?"

"Thank you for asking, Mister Hammer." He smiles and nods. "No, this was a real Rose of Sharon bush that appeared and produced unlimited blooms for awhile. Clearly it was a manifestation of God, but the Lord took it away lest anyone worship it in place of God."

"Whoa, I didn't expect such a bold endorsement. The expert on RNN said there are no more new miracles. Why do you disagree? You actually think God did this?"

Pastor Wong laughed. "If you lived during biblical times, each of God's miracles would be something never done before. God reigns. In Isaiah 43: 19 God said 'Do not dwell in the past. See I am doing a new thing.' He can and will do new things when they suit His purpose."

"And what purpose would this be?"

"I won't speak for the mind of God, but one often repeated phrase in the Bible is 'Then you will know I am God.'"

Pastor gestured toward Emma. "I witnessed several of Emma's classmates accept the Lord as a result. That lovely bush told us that the Lord is alive and full of love for us. At the very least, this work of God brought many young men and women together in a common cause of worship."

"But what do you say to that pastor on RNN?"

"This pains me, I…" He sighed. "First understand, I will not demean a Christian brother, but it is fair to say where we disagree. Everyday, when a mind hardened against God suddenly sees truth and becomes a new person, a new believer is born again in the Spirit. In that person, who is changed forever, we witness a miraculous work of God."

"And," he held up a finger. "Our American Founders, dedicated to God, saw many miracles from the bullet holes in Washington's coat to all those battles we won against overwhelming forces."

Hammer furrowed his brow. "I don't recall miracles being mentioned in our history."

"That's because historians rewrote it. I think Professor Dylan Coz was fired for bringing this truth back."

"Wow." Hammer grinned. "Sounds to me like we could do a whole show on that subject."

Pastor Wong nodded. "I wish you would."

"But next," he held out his hand toward Emma. "This is Emma Jackson, one of the Rose Guardians and the one

317

mentioned on RNN. Did these flowers cause you to believe in God?"

Emma turned toward the camera. "I was already a Christian, but seeing a miracle first hand let me know God is present here and now. For any doubters out there, you should talk to Alvin Finkelstein. He has the scientific proof."

"Really?" Hammer nodded. "That's fine, but what do you say to your accuser about buying those flowers on Friday morning?"

Emma laughed. "Well, the part about my going into Hanson's Florist is true." She opened her purse and pulled out a piece of paper. Here's the receipt. You can read it yourself."

Hammer read aloud, "One flower basket, nine ninety five—one card of lapel pins, three seventy five."

"I bought these items were so I could gather the blooms and pin them on lapels. Hanson's does not sell Rose of Sharon flowers."

"Whoa, that settles that, at least. Thank you both for your time." He grinned at the camera. "I'll leave it to our viewers to draw their own conclusions on this being a miracle, but speaking for myself, I'm convinced. This was God doing a new thing."

SURPRISE GUESTS

That Friday afternoon the parking lot behind the church had become a bright and cheerful place, filled with cars, bikes and motorcycles. The "Rose Guardians" all knew each other, and they enjoyed waves, hugs and fist bumping whenever they gathered.

Lisa stood, leaning against her cycle seat. She was putting her phone on vibrate when she got a call. "Lisa, here."

"Oh, yes, Miss Combes, it's Sheryl from Chief Atkinson's office. Can you talk now?"

"Sure, but I'm on my way to a meeting."

"It'll just take a sec. Are you bringing in the copy for your column tomorrow morning?"

"Uh huh. I'll finish it tonight. It's been a rough week."

"Oh, sorry, but could you stop in Mister Atkinson office as *soon* as you get here—say about nine tomorrow?"

"He wants to proof my copy before Vera gets it?"

"Uh, no." (coughs) "Not that. It's something important he has to tell you."

"Should I be losing sleep worrying about this, Sheryl?"

"No," giggle. "I can't tell you, but I promise it's not a bad thing."

"You seem in a good mood. Did that vendor ask you out?"

"Shsss." She whispered. "He's sitting right over there."

Lisa laughed. "Okay, I'm getting a full report out of you tomorrow. Gotta go."

Inside the church meeting room, they were late getting started. Dylan sat tapping on his cell phone for awhile before getting up. "Hi, folks. I'll bet you are all waiting for my promised talk on everything you need to know about how this world runs. Sadly, you'll have to wait until our next meeting, but the good news is I'm about to introduce two special guest speakers. One got into a little traffic problem, but I just got a text that they'll be here in twenty minutes.

"The other is Pastor Wong and he'll be here any minute. Meanwhile…" He did a little tap dance. "I could show you a Vaudeville number…" He took another few taps. "Wait. Here's a better idea. Lisa Combes has her column coming out soon and I understand it's about Berkard this time. Lisa, how about an advance just for us?"

Lisa was shaking her head, but the students began to chant her name. She stood up before them and put her hands in the air. "Look, guys, I'm a much better writer than a speaker."

320

They kept chanting which made her laugh. "Okay, okay. Obviously, you're not going to see this in the Berkard Capers since my conservative views got me kicked off."

There was a solid round of boos. "Did any of you get into the auditorium for the Women's March Free Speech symposium?"

Susan called out, "I tried to get in but they wanted to confiscate my smart phone and my purse. No way was I gonna give those away."

"Right, Susan. I went back to the dorm and left my whole purse there except for a pad and pencil. When I got back they said the pencil could be a weapon. I said it sure could.

"When I showed my press credentials, the door guard said I'd have to wait for a statement after it was over. However, when I said my whole story for the national newspapers would be how the press was barred, they let me in but I had to promise to obey the rules.

"By the way, did you notice there were about a hundred so called antifascism and hate protesters outside? Well, inside there were only sixty eight people counting the three presenters. They apologized that Willy Smith, the conservative presenter had cancelled. I called his office later and they never even heard of the symposium.

"Inside, their main rule was 'complete silence'. All questions would be submitted in writing on 3X5 cards. I saw four others handing in cards beside me. They answered six questions, but not mine. The presenters all spoke on how America was being destroyed by capitalism, the Jews, racism and white supremacy.

Susan called out, "So, that's their idea of free speech?"

"Yup." Lisa chuckled. "And that's my idea of a story."

Betty said, "Aren't you afraid someone might go after you?"

"Nah, students just hurl profanities at me when I walk by. I'm more concerned about the four men that caught me alone in that alley outside. They threw me down and threatened me, but my bad for being alone there."

The students began to talk among themselves and Lisa moved toward her seat. Betty called, "We'll be praying for you, sister."

Pastor Wong walked in and headed for the front. "Did someone just say pray?" He gave them a grin when he reached the podium. "Thank you, Dylan, for letting me say a few words. I know who's coming next, so I'll be brief.

"First off, let me say how proud I am of you Rose Guardians--College students voluntarily meeting on a Friday night for lectures and not getting a single point of college credit. Could there be *this* many Berkard students who don't

322

buy into a Communist future for America?" There were groans and a short "USA, USA" chant. "Anyway, I'm happy we could offer our facility to help you out."

"Be sure to check out the Hammer Time show tonight. They did an interview with me and Emma Jackson. Meanwhile, I'm sure you saw me coming and going during your meetings. I enjoyed some back row college audit, but I'm also sure you've heard of the Johnson Amendment. It's a law prohibiting politics on church property and so now we'll have to close this down and you all will have to leave."

Pastor gave the open-mouthed audience a stern look. He laughed. "Only kidding. Just let them try and enforce that one, huh? The revisionists like to twist words, but remember what Dylan told you about our first congress? They used the Capitol building as a Christian church on Sundays." He chuckled. "I wish I could have those congressmen back."

"I'm assuming that most of you here are Christians. So I just want to make one point his evening—a spiritual one, but if it puzzles you, come to our Saturday morning bible study."

Pastor Wong leaned forward and looked at them intently. "We are so involved in living in the present, and in this complex world, most assume that our solutions only lie in what we do here on our own. If you are surrounded by a majority who despise and ridicule you and your views, it's understandable why you might choose to be silent. Don't be.

Jews and Christians are persecuted because Satan does not want God's word to survive."

"All of you have witnessed the never-ending Roses of Sharon. They are a manifestation of God and should remind you that God is real, ever present and ever loving."

"Let's be clear on one thing. If you believe God and His angels are real, you must also believe that Satan and his demons are real as well. No one can fight against an enemy he doesn't think exists. If you run barefoot through the jungle because you don't believe in snakes, you'll only believe when you're bitten and dying."

"Our problem is simple. Ever since the fall of Adam, Satan has contended for our minds and our hearts. He has been hard at work in America especially since our nation is dedicated to God. Satan's deceptive lies have won many battles. He shouts for hatred and death. God whispers in authority for life and for love."

He pushed back and began an animated back and forth pacing. "But, I have some good news for all of you who believe in God. We fight for righteousness side by side with a power greater than anything on Heaven and Earth, and if He is with us, who can stand against us? God has given us dominion over this earth. Execute your power with words and faith. Our covenant counter-revolution will take America back."

"In Paul's letter to the Ephesians, chapter six-twelve, he said, 'Take your stand against the devil's schemes. For our struggle is not against flesh and blood but against the rulers and the powers of this dark world, and against the spiritual forces of evil in the heavenly realms.' So, I say to you: take up your weapons of truth, righteousness, faith and your salvation. Wield the sword of the Spirit which is the word of God and you will not be defeated."

"Pray in faith and He will listen. Step out in trust and He will be with you. Do all things in love, and conquer the world." Pastor stopped and opened his arms to the audience. "And may His peace be with you."

He left through a side door with a wave while they all applauded. Dylan got up, looking at his cell phone. "Wow. Thank you, Pastor—and perfect timing too."

"I'm glad I'm not the one to follow *that* message, but our promised presenter is on the way in. She is a woman of courage…" The door opened. "and she's well known to all of you. Let me present my colleague, and co-plaintiff: *Aimee West*."

The students cheered and applauded as Aimee walked down the side aisle. Some chanted "Fess-Aimee, Fess-Aimee!"

"Thank you, thank you." She put her papers on the podium. "Course I know you're only happy because you know there's no exam after this talk." Laughter.

"Dylan asked me to summarize the reason for my firing. I'm not here to complain, but to explain what has been happening to our universities and our Country.

"Did you like the Blade Runner movie?" There were nods and "yeas." "The author was Philip K. Dick and he quipped in another book: 'Reality is that which, when you stop believing in it, doesn't go away.' In the here and now, reality still remains despite the angry indignation of those claiming to be offended, teachers being fired, and the clamor of institutional politics."

"There is a reality in every individual's potential, their education, their motivation, and the grades they earn. I am passionate about improving *all of these* for everyone, but these changes must begin in kindergarten and in the home, not in a college admissions policy.

"In this country, the majority of those poorly prepared for college are blacks, not because of intellect or racism, but because of demotivating social conditions, the dissolution of families, and poor education. For instance: in the inner city high schools, almost *no one* graduates with basic proficiencies in math and English.

"I love to work with anyone attacking those root causes, but when University policy keeps grades secret along with the key documentation about the sources of performance disparities, it only hurts the people who could otherwise be helped. The identity politics they practice is the main cause of racial divisions.

"I don't want to get preachy." She smiled and raised her hands. "That comes with my job—or the one I used to have." She chuckled. "The point is that when it comes to comparative performance in SATs, for example, it doesn't matter that revealing differences is offensive to some. The reality is still there, and the outside world hires on the basis of the reality they see. This university is more interested in pointing to their acceptance statistics than helping the disadvantaged."

"There is a terrible price to pay when people come to believe that truth will yield to power, and that political pressure should be brought to bear to bury inconvenient realities. Totalitarian regimes throughout history have used their power to overcome truth, and these regimes are responsible for untold amounts of human misery."

"We Americans have painstakingly built and defended our free society where people have a voice. Our government was designed to be the polar opposite of totalitarianism. If you wish this evil to destroy your country, you have an easy task.

Just do and say nothing and the best government this world has *ever* known will be a teardrop on the pages of history."

Aimee pounded the podium and turned her gaze to the wall, overcome by emotion.

Scattered applause increased to an ovation. Dylan came over with a tissue and put his hand on her shoulder. He declared, "I'll say amen to that."

Dylan pointed to Betty whose hand was raised. "I heard the faculty and the Board will be discussing your dismissal right after Christmas break. Is that right?"

Aimee responded. "Yes. We sent them a letter of legal warning giving them time to reconsider. They will meet in a private session January fifth at one."

Lisa jumped up. "And I say, lets show them what a *real* student demonstration is all about." She turned and raised her hands to the students. "What do you say, Rose Guardians?"

They all stood up and began shouting and jumping. "Fess-Aimee, Fess-Aimee," and "Dylan, Dylan!"

TRUTH'S OPPORTUNITY

It was a chilly ride to the Oakland Flame early next morning. A damp marine-layer fog covered the downtown, but in her excitement, Lisa hardly noticed as she pulled into cycle parking. *Whatever this good news is, I sure could use some.*

"Well, Sheryl, you look like it's Christmas morning already. So, what's the news?"

"You *know* I can't tell you, but you can go in as soon as the Chief's off the phone."

Lisa lowered her head and gave her a squinty-eyed look. "My shrewd detective instincts tell me your happiness isn't just *my* news. Right?"

Sheryl giggled. "Brad asked me out. He's an artist too, and he wanted to show me his work at his apartment."

"Uh, oh: that line."

"Right. I didn't go. I said I need to know him better, so I'll see him for lunch at Applebee's today."

"Good girl. It's not easy, but let your head do the talking. He is pretty cute, though."

Sheryl gritted her teeth and looked at the ceiling. "Oh, *God*, yes."

A light flashed on her desk. Sheryl said, "Your turn."

Lisa gave a gentle rap over the door plaque that read: "Stanley Atkinson, Editor in Chief." His deep voice responded, "It's open, Lisa."

She stood in front of his desk, a thin folder clutched to her chest. "Good morning, Sir. You sure have my curiosity up. Do you want to see the draft for my next column?"

Stanley came around his desk with a big grin. "I'll bet it's a zinger, but Vera will handle it." He gestured to a sofa chair and sat in one opposite her.

"So, here's our next story. Hayley's husband, Bill Jones, is appearing on the Sunday News Box the weekend after New Years. It's in LA. We want a reporter there to cover any back story and hopefully get an interview of our own."

"Oh. my gosh. Are you sending *me*?"

"No, Vera is covering it, and for a very good reason."

Her face relaxed into a frown. "I know, I know. I don't have that kind of experience yet, but it's good news for us. His story might lead to other things we could follow up."

Stanley was chuckling. "Look at you. Those are the instincts I like to see in a great reporter." He let out a breath.

"Now, do you want to know the *real* reason you can't cover the story?"

"Anonymous death threats?"

Stanley was laughing. He composed himself and leaned toward her. "The *reason* is because William Jones asked the producers for *you* to be there with him and they said yes. *You* are going to be on the Sunday News Box, girl!"

Her open-mouth moment lasted five seconds. "What?" she squeaked.

"Yup. They're shooting in their LA studio on the Saturday before. Vera will be there with you looking for interviews before and after the show."

"I—*wow*—they really want *me?* Guess I'll have to get an early start Saturday. What time do I have to be there?"

"Lisa," his voice dropped to serious. "Lisa, they'll send a limo for you on Friday at one and take you to the airport. News Box will assign you a personal handler and put you up for the night. The only thing you have to plan for is how to answer the questions."

Lisa shook her head grinning. "Good grief, this is real, isn't it?"

"Oh, yes, and I have to confess; we're pretty happy to have our paper's name under your picture on national television."

"Oops, the *questions*. I have some new information on the case. Do you want to print it here, first?"

"No no, whatever it is, break the heck out of it on television. The TV producers will love it and the entire nation will have to buy our paper to get your details and follow up."

CHRISTMAS BREAK

PHONE: *Hi, Hutch, I'm about to leave town. You wanted me to let you know. I'm heading out to my Aunt Miriam's near Sacramento soon. You have a great Christmas, big guy.*

Wait, Lisa, I need to see you before you go. Where are you now, Sweetheart?

I'm at Susan's house, Snuggums.

Ha, Ha. I'll be there in ten.

Scott found Lisa leaning against her motorcycle seat in Susan's driveway when he pulled up. "You really are something else," he said grinning. "Your shadows haven't been around for a few days, but after those shots they took at you, I want to take some security measures before you leave."

"Secure? If you really want to keep me secure, how about you ride with me to my Aunt Miriam's? You could drive my cycle and I'd be right behind you all the way."

Scott surprised her with, "I'd love to some other time, but my folks are expecting me." Their eyes locked for a moment. "I, ahem," He handed her a cell phone. "I want you to leave your phone behind. This is a short term rental for you to use in the meantime."

"Right, they could trace me with mine." Lisa studied the phone. "'Course it doesn't take pictures." She stood up and pointed at her motorcycle. "Last time they planted a locator under my fender."

"I remember." He unclipped a black, oval device from his belt. "And I'll bet they found a much more inventive spot for its replacement."

Scott scanned the motorcycle with his locator and, in a moment, he was holding a sending unit he found attached between the springs under her seat. "Leave this little cutie and your phone with your friend until you get back, okay?"

"Hutch, seriously, thank you so much for watching over me." She gave him a hug that lingered a bit. "You have a Merry Christmas, okay?"

"I will." Big smile. "You too, and please be careful."

"Oh, wait." Lisa pointed a finger upward. She opened the pack strapped behind her bike. "I almost forgot. I was going to wrap this and give it to you when I got back." She handed him a plastic bag. "Just pretend it was all wrapped in Christmas paper."

Scott held it against his chest and frowned. "Lisa, I don't know if I should accept this. I'm trying my best to keep things professional between us."

"Not easy, huh?" Lisa grinned. "But this is professional too, in a way. This is a more perfect disguise— uh—for your work."

Scott shook his head, pulled out a Hawaiian shirt from the bag and laughed.

"See, Hutch, this one's much more natural. It's toned down a bit, and its got palm trees and dogs. Besides, it goes better with your hair color."

"Well, okay," Still chuckling. "This is really nice. Thanks. Just promise you won't recognize me on a stake out when you walk by."

"And break your cover? Never."

"All right, you," fake scowl. "I gotta get back to the station. I put speed dials on the phone for me and the police where you're going. You take care, huh?"

"Don't worry. They'll never get me. Merry Christmas!"

"Good." As he turned to go he glanced back over his shoulder. "'Cause if they do, I'll get demoted."

She watched Scott get in his patrol car. Her gaze continued to follow him long after he was out of sight.

#　　　　　#　　　　　#

Lisa checked the house numbers on Zapata Drive in Folsom. *This is a long ways from town. Not exactly a Sacramento suburb like they said.*

Ah, that must be the place—both a jeep and a Humvee in front. Aunt Miriam's house was an eastern style, three story Victorian. She pulled in beside the cars in the driveway but out of sight from the front door. *I'll have to ease Mom into the idea of me on a motorcycle.*

She quickly took off her helmet and cut jacket then opened the box that was bungee-corded over the rear wheel. Out came the frilly short coat her mother had given her. Now she was ready to greet the family.

Lisa's brother, Nathan, answered the doorbell wearing Marine fatigues, his four year old daughter, Chrissie, clinging to his pants leg. Her niece bounded into her arms. "Auntie Lisa, Auntie Lisa! What did you bring me?"

Lisa produced a small coloring book and a lollypop from her pocket. Nathan shook his head. "See what you started, sister?"

Chrissie skipped off to show her mother while Lisa greeted Nathan with a hug. "Parents don't do enough spoiling, so it's up to the rest of us. How are things down at Pendleton?"

"Great. I'm in Nav School and I'm hoping I get to fly with the Ospreys soon." He cocked his head to one side. If you don't mind my saying, that's the *girlyiest* thing I think I've ever seen you wear."

Lisa put a finger to her lips and whispered, "Gift from mother, Nate. My cycle cut's outside."

Nathan bared his teeth and nodded. "Roger that. Not a peep from me. Say, all the women are in the kitchen getting lunch ready. Hungry?"

"Oh, yeah."

Hugs went all around from parents, aunts and uncles. Chrissie's mom, Marie, was engrossed in working hand sanitizer over her daughter's arms up to the elbows.

Sergeant Roger, otherwise known as Lisa's Dad, was selected to say grace but afterward he added, "Lisa, before you came I asked the other right wingers not to talk politics and ruin Christmas for my sister Miriam. Liberals have no defense and I'd hate to see her shot down in flames on a family holiday, okay?"

Aunt Miriam gave a harrumph. "And, for my part, I won't use the impeach word even once."

Nathan reached for the rolls. "I object. How are we going to hear about how my sister is shaking up the world of journalism before she even graduates."

Miriam said, "It's all right. I think Lisa has real talent but It's normal for someone her age not to have a fully developed mind."

Snickers all around. Lisa chuckled with them. "I understand, Aunt Miriam. Perhaps you're right. I certainly don't have some fully developed stories either, but I'm working on them."

"Well, you just keep developing, Dear. My silent husband, Carl over there, knows not to push my buttons, but I know he votes Republican and secretly listens to Patriot Radio in his car."

Carl grinned and opened his hands in a "what can I say," gesture.

Lisa clinked her water glass and stood up. "Okay, folks, I do have an announcement."

"Is it about a man?" Her mother asked.

"Oh, *Mother*." Lisa took a moment to laugh, hand on forehead. "Better than that. I'm going to be on the Hammer show second Sunday in January."

Through the applause and "ata-girls," aunt Miriam said, "I hope that show's not on that awful News Box channel." The right-wingers laughed.

Lisa coughed. "Here's another announcement—really a confession to my mother. I ride a motorcycle, Mom."

Surprisingly, Mother did not seem upset and went on buttering a roll. "I surmised as much, Dear. Your dad has been totally evasive on the subject of how you get around, and I know how much you liked motor cross." She offered a weak smile. "Could I have a look at it after lunch?"

"Of course, Mom. Thanks for understanding."

When the meal was over the women chatted during their cleanup and Nathan was assigned to use the extension ladder and clip on lights along the edge of the roof. Miriam's husband wasn't allowed to climb high ladders with his arthritis.

Lisa escorted Mom to the driveway. "Well, here are my secret wheels. I need to unpack the saddlebags and bring my stuff in."

Mother took a long look, hands on hips. "I have to admit—it's kinda cute. Did you paint the daisies on it?"

Lisa began untying the suitcase strapped to the back rack. "All of them except the big one on the front fender." She gave her mother an impish grin. "And so now you know why everyone is getting small sized presents this year."

Mom smiled. "I understand." She took a quick look around. "Listen, while we are alone—you know what I'm going to ask, right?"

"Oh, yeah." She chuckled. "And the answer is I do have a total school girl crush on the policeman assigned to watch over me. However, he's six years older and seems to want to keep our relationship professional."

Mother looked totally shocked, so Lisa added, "I know it's a big age difference, but we do get along well—you okay, Mom?"

"That's not what shocked me, Lisa. When were you going to tell me about the 'assigned to watch over me' thing?"

"Oops."

"Yes, oops. What's been going on here? Are you in some kind of danger?"

"Not really, Mom. Its just that I've got some sources that a certain congressman would like to discover so they follow me. The police keep an eye on things, that's all."

Mother Mary embraced her daughter. "Oh, Darling, you're my only daughter. Why do you have to live so *dangerously*?"

"Aw, Mom." She patted her back then released the hug. "Really, it's not that risky. I'll be fine."

Back in the house, Lisa played some games with Chrissie and was well into a vocabulary lesson when Nathan sat on the floor next to them. "Sis, I have a surprise treat planned for you this afternoon and I want to go there before dark."

He indicated they should talk in private so Lisa assigned a coloring project to Chrissie and followed him to the back yard. "Where are we going, Nate? Sacramento?"

"No. Dad told me about your situation and the guys watching you."

"Oh, I wouldn't worry. I even told Mom. They're just trying to find out my sources."

"Dad also told me you're toting a gun around that you've never fired."

"Well," Lisa chuckled. "That's true, but I don't think I'll ever need to need it."

"And I hope I'll never need my fire extinguisher either, but I know how to use it. Now, no argument. We're going to the practice range and give that little devil of yours a workout."

TRUTH SPIN

RNN NEWS:

The opening scene shows a male anchor sitting at a broad desk opposite a female guest. Close-up on the man: "Some disturbing news just came in. Two women, Alicia Wright, and Amanda Sincere are suing the Berkard Chancellor, Henry Stengel, for sexual harassment—get this: *five years* after they were students there.

Wide shot back. The woman is laughing. He continues: In a letter to Congressman Luchow, published in several newspapers these women claim to have been cornered, groped and one of them, raped.

The Chancellor has yet to be questioned but his lawyer put out this statement: "These are ridiculous charges by women, one of whom, recently answered phones at the Republican headquarters. We demand they withdraw their false allegations and publically apologize."

Anchorman turns to the woman next to him. "Miss Grosspin, you are a Democratic strategist and active in women's rights groups. What do you make of this?"

"These women are using, and trying to make a mockery of, the 'Not Alone' movement that has been empowering women to speak out against abuse all over this country."

"So, you don't believe them?"

"Not at all, and if they do not apologize to this well known and decent Chancellor, I recommend a counter suit to punish them to the fullest extent of the law."

"But, shouldn't we wait and see if there is corroborating information?"

"Look, I've been on the staff at a university too. You have to understand that faculty must discipline students and there can be angry reactions sometimes. Investigate these women and I'm sure that pattern will emerge."

Close-up on the man. "Well, there you have it." He nods with a serious, concerned expression. "We welcome the opinions of our viewers. Lets hear from you on our web site. Stay tuned for our next segment where we will have a panel discussion on how some people force their religious views on others. Be right back."

NEWS BOX TV:

We join a News Box Report in progress. A reporter is standing with the Berkard campus in the background. "And that was the statement of Stengel's attorney. The Chancellor has not made an official statement himself, and we have yet to find a student here who will comment. However we do have an open mike comment he made at a faculty meeting this morning."

A grainy, cell phone video shows Stengel standing in front of some professors. "So, this is what happens when some trailer park sluts decide to make a name for themselves. They will pay. Tell your students not to make the same mistake."

Returning to the reporter: "That's all we have on campus at the moment. Back to you in the studio."

A woman host is seated at her desk. "Thank you Sam." The camera gives her a close-up. "This is a news show and normally we don't comment here, but is anyone else wondering why no one is taking these women seri...? Hold on, my producer is jumping up and down."

A man wearing earphones dashes in from one side, puts a paper on her desk and runs back. The anchor lady holds up one finger while she reads with an open mouth. "Oh, gosh. As you can see, this *just* came in. Two more letters have come in with charges against Chancellor Stengel by former students, one with three signers and one by *six* women."

She let out a chirp and put her hand over her mouth as she continues to read. She faces the camera: "Well folks, one of these women has a three year old child and she claims it is Stengel's."

344

PRAYERS AND REVELATIONS

Betty asked to say a few words before the Rose Guardian meeting began. She cleared her throat and swept her hair back a few times. "Uh, hi everyone. I just thought with Lisa on her way to Los Angeles right now, we should send some prayers her way."

"I don't want to offend anyone." She searched the faces before her. "I don't know every one of you well, but if anyone is bothered by my mentioning Jesus, please bear with us for a moment, okay?"

The students began to chant, "Jesus, Jesus, Jesus."

Betty grinned and raised her arms. "Oh, Dear Lord, we cry out to you to protect our sister, Lisa. Grant her your favor and give her your words to say. Give her courage to face the inquisitors while she is a sheep among wolves. Amen."

Everyone was silent for a few moments, but as Betty returned to her seat, Emma yelled out, "Yeah, but Lisa's a *Ninja* sheep." The students laughed.

Dylan was smiling as he went to the podium. He rocked it forward and back. "It's hard to believe we're not that far from the end of this semester. Many of you are graduating, and I'll miss you. I will begin teaching American History at Emmanuel College in Walnut Creek soon, but I hope we can restart our Rose Guardian gatherings again this fall."

He pointed at a raised hand. "Emma?"

"Any chance of you getting back to Berkard?"

"Well…" He tilted his head side to side. "If you listen to our lawyers, yes, but Aimee and I are cautious. The University voted for our dismissal the second time around but we really appreciate that rocking protest you put on outside."

The students applauded and whistled. "News Box covered it well, didn't they, and some of you guys got to be on TV before Lisa. Of course, the networks only interviewed the students who protested your protest. They called you some truly nasty names." Boos and laughter.

"Okay, folks, as promised I'm going to delve into the truth behind the scenes of politics in America. Aimee said it best when she declared that totalitarian regimes throughout history have redefined objective reality by their political force. A dictator would put it this way: 'I control everything in this country so truth is what I say it is.'"

"Therefore, in a totalitarian regime, actual truth is forbidden and perhaps labeled 'hate speech'. This is particularly true about God's truth. I've touched on this before, but the real problem in setting up a society is not considering the very nature of mankind. Because we like to think well of ourselves, it is often said that man is fundamentally good. Unfortunately, history and reality tell us otherwise.

"The Bible tells us that 'the heart is deceitful above all things and desperately wicked.' That being the case, why would you trust a random human being, or even several, to be in complete control of you and your country. Even with the promise of free stuff, why would you allow one person or even a few to dictate your earnings, where and how you live and what you can and cannot say?"

Jim called out, "Free stuff. Gimme the free stuff." Laughter. Dylan pointed to Stephen's raised hand. "Yes, Steve?"

"Wouldn't a pure democracy take care of that problem?"

"No, because a democracy without a just set of *laws* is mob rule. Remember, we talked about that. Here's another example: 'I'm sorry, Steve, but the class has voted seven to six that they don't like your new religious views and you will be executed in the morning.'"

Stephen, laughing: "But, that's why we have laws and trials."

"Then, consider this. Hundreds of millions of people actually live under a law that would sentence you this way: 'I'm sorry, Steve, but your trial is over. Since you have converted to Christianity, you will be executed in the morning.' That's Sharia law."

Dylan studied the faces of the stunned. Jim broke the silence. "Wait, can't we torture Steve before we kill him." Tilly gave him a swat.

Dylan nodded with a smile. "Jim is always one step ahead, isn't he? The point I'm making is that we, desperately wicked humans, when left to our own devices, will devise a governmental scheme favorable to, and controlled by us, and not *them*.

"Our American system of government shook the world. For the first time all citizens would be treated equally, have unalienable rights and actually be in charge of their own government."

Jevon called out, "And you're going to say God wrote our constitution?"

"No, but God fearing men following God's Biblical principals did. It's what makes America exceptional. I think I mentioned John Adam's quote that the principals of American government and Christianity are held together in an indissoluble bond."

"Some modern democracies have been modeled after ours but, in my opinion, no one else has gotten it right. Those who want to have the old totalitarian system have had to repackage and sell it to the unsuspecting public in different, good-sounding ways. The National Socialist Party, otherwise known as the Nazi Party appealed to pride by saying 'we Germans are just better than everyone else.' The Islamic fascists seek to control the world claiming that their religion gives them that right. Communism simply claims that no individual has rights not granted by the state, but common to all these systems is the establishment an elite ruling party."

Betty raised her hand. "I thought the Nazis were the opposite of the Communists."

"Their ideology, the way they *sell* Socialism to the public, is different but the bottom line is still State control and totalitarianism. None of these man-made plans have ever worked."

"But, Socialism sounds so caring, so humanitarian."

"So biblical? God warned us with these words: 'The Devil masquerades as an angel of light. Therefore it is no surprise if his followers transform themselves into ministers of righteousness.' Second Corinthians eleven, I believe.

Jevon called out, "Yeah, well most of this university believes in socialism and taking power away from the rich, white capitalist. That's what progressivism is all about."

"Jevon, its rich white capitalists who are *financing* this socialist movement. Boros just gave eighty *billion* dollars to try and impeach our president. Their goal is to destroy our democratic republic and the rights we have as individuals. It's a *retrogressive* plan to restore totalitarianism. How did Venezuela work out?"

Jevon said, "So, what if they screwed up. At least they tried to take care of the poor and get income equality. Maybe it was just set up wrong."

"Venezuela used to have the highest standard of living in South America. On the political promises of free money and appealing to human greed, people *became* poor. Their income equality was poverty and the country quickly became a third world dictatorship. The rich elite became richer."

"Margaret Thatcher explained it this way: 'Socialism is wonderful until you run out of someone else's money to give away.' That may not be her exact words, but you get the point. Lenin gave it away when he said, 'the goal of socialism is communism.'"

"We do need to care for our poor, but those who are able to work are better off both financially and psychologically. As people enter freely into the production of goods and services and sell them for their *own* profit, our economy grows as well."

Dylan took a few steps toward Jevon and made eye contact. "Jevon, perhaps I can't convince you with a few words, but I want you to be critical in your thinking. When someone talks about a utopian scheme and their only argument is the character assassination of those with opposing views, start *thinking*. What is their motive, their ambition? Where's the money flow, the power flow, and most importantly, where's the *truth*?" Jevon nodded.

There was scattered applause. Dylan smiled. "All right, guys. You've been great. We're coming up on exam week, so this will be our last session for awhile. I can't wait to see Lisa on television this Sunday. I have it on good authority she's about to drop some bomb shells."

CRIMINAL TRUTH

Lisa was escorted from "Makeup" to the Green Room, a quiet place with sofa chairs and a private makeup counter. A man, six foot–two with his hair in a crew cut, stood up when she walked in. "Howdy, I'm Bill Jones. Hayley was my wife. You must be Lisa Combes." He offered his hand with a smile. "I'm so glad I don't have to do this interview alone."

"I'm honored to be here, sir." She shook his hand. "Let me first say how darn sorry I am about Hayley. I still can't get past it, so I know how awful it must be for you."

William's face hardened and his mouth twitched once. "Yeah, I don't like talking about it, and now I have to in front of a television audience." They sat down facing each other. "I've read everything you wrote, Lisa. You've done some research into what happened and I'm hoping you can say something to get this case open."

"Yes, Sir, I hope I can, too."

"All they keep telling me is it's still under investigation, but you were just a few feet away, huh?"

"I was. It seemed like the audience was paralyzed when Antifa did their thing. Only my friend Emma and Professor Dylan Coz were screaming for them to stop. I think the rest of us had no clue about what was going to happen."

William studied the wall and spoke softly. "I told her not to go, you know. When she insisted, I wanted to be with her but I was on duty at Pendleton."

"Oh, you're a Marine? My dad and my brother, too."

He tried to smile but his face began to contort. "If only I had been there, no *way* would those punks have gotten their paws on my Hayley. Her agent assured her Berkard had arranged for security."

Lisa shook her head. "I guess you know they only had the Campus Police on hand. Chancellor Stengel told NBC that he didn't want the event to 'look like a Police State,' so he asked the city police to stay away."

Bill's head dropped and he spoke at the floor. "I saw that interview. Stengel said the students would have been offended by—what was it? Oh, the 'White Supremacist Guard'."

Lisa reached for one of his large hands. "Did she know the Lord, sir?"

William sat up with a smile. "Oh boy, did she *ever*. Hayley was a Pentecostal—spoke in tongues and everything. I'm still a work in progress, but she had me praying every day for the causes of the world." He chuckled. "I never was gifted with tongues or prophesy."

"How about that." She patted his hand and released it. "At least we know we'll meet her again in heaven."

"Oh, yeah." William looked about the room. "I remember the last time I was in this room. I was with her. She was a regular contributor to News Box for five years."

"I know, I…" A woman opened the door and said they were ready for them on set.

"I know, I read her Op Eds and saw her on TV a couple of times. Come on, Sir." She stood up. "Let's make Hayley proud."

They were greeted graciously by the producer and the host, Charles Hammer, while they took seats opposite him at a large glass table. Hammer told them to take a deep breath and pretend they were sitting around the kitchen table just having a chat. "This is the part where I get you relaxed five minutes before we start. Mister Jones, are you okay with talking about the details of your wife's death?"

"If it helps us catch this murderer, I'm ready for hand to hand combat with a gorilla."

"Good, but as you know, the 'murder' part is disputed."

Hammer faced Lisa. "I understand you're just about to graduate from college and you've never been in front of a camera before. Think about how thrilled your parents will be to see you."

"They won't recognize me, Mister Hammer."

"What do you mean?"

"Your makeup person took all my freckles away, gave me a goofy hairdo and put me in this girly dress."

Hammer laughed heartily. "Well, you've got *me* relaxed anyway. We'll put your name on screen so they'll know. Oh, and on set we'll all use our first names, okay?"

Lisa asked, "Is it just going to be the two of us?"

"No, I have a prosecutor on line in our New York studio. He'll get some questions too. I hope you don't mind a little grilling, Lisa."

"Nah, but you should know I have mace in my purse."

"Oh, gee…" Hammer was snort laughing when the ten second warning came.

The floor manager pointed at him. "Good evening everyone and welcome to another edition of Hammer Time. Tonight we're going to probe into what's been called the Berkard Incident. Was it just a student protest and an accidental death as most of the media covered it, or was there actually a murder and a cover up? We'll try and shed some light on it tonight.

"We were going to interview Chancellor Stengel, but he just got involved in, uh, a little trouble of his own"

He grinned. "Here's who will face the Hammer tonight." He rapped a small mallet on his desk. "First, a gentle hammer for Colonel William Jones whose wife died in the incident. Then, Lisa Combes, a new reporter for the Oakland Flame who was present during the incident. She claims to have undisclosed sources pointing to murder. And finally, Mister Frank Spinelli, a prosecutor in New York City.

"I want to begin with Colonel Jones. Bill, you have all our deeply heartfelt prayers and sympathy for the loss of your wife, Hayley. We knew her well here on the Box, and we are grieved as well. Can you tell us what the authorities have been telling you?"

"More like what they haven't been telling me. Oakland police ruled it an accidental death. The FBI took the investigation over from them, allegedly because Antifa operates across state lines, and there it sits. You heard their press release indicting some Russians—a total hoax in my opinion."

"Bill, how long did it take the police to call it an accidental death?"

"Less than an hour. The media reporters talked to the Chief of Police and they were calling it that. Frankly I don't see…"

"Hold on, Bill. I heard a hammer go down in New York. What is it, Frank?"

"My God, *no one* can rule on a cause of death that quickly. A Coroner's report is required. Smells like a dead fish, Chuck. Maybe someone made that conclusion the day before, huh?"

"In fairness, the Chief used the words 'preliminary report,' Frank."

"Okay, in fairness, maybe we just have a real stupid Chief."

Charles glowered into the camera. "Can you see why this case needs a little more hammering?" He gestured toward Lisa. "All right, Miss Combes, lets let you weigh in here. Your reporter colleagues challenge the idea of a school newspaper reporter getting reliable inside sources. Are they just jealous, or do you have the real thing?"

"The real thing."

"They also point out that you were fired from your first paper and allegedly had an affair with one of your professors."

Lisa took the time to give the camera lens a winning smile. "On the second claim, the photo-shopped pictures they manufactured were so ridiculous, we didn't bother to file a libel suit. Does that give you an idea about someone wanting to shut me up?

"I *was* fired from the school paper, but the Chancellor said I could keep my job if I would just tell him my sources."

Frank in New York was pointing to the side. "Well, howdy do. Hear that? Yup, yup, listen to this girl."

Charles gave her a stern look. "But, Lisa, it is a stretch for us to believe a girl like you could suddenly have deep, reliable sources. How did you get them?"

"Telling you how would be close to telling you who. You'll know they are reliable when the facts come out and the truth comes to light."

Charles said, "Come on, Lisa, hit us with something true."

She studied his face for a moment. "Oh, all right. I'll just say what I know, but no source names."

"Oh, yeah," came from Frank.

"There is a well funded movement to take over this Country and impose a global socialist system, really an excuse for the dictatorship of an elite class. The so called 'deep state' is a consortium of well placed people eager to join that future ruling class. My pastor calls them the 'wickedness in high places.' Locally, they fund their operations which are dedicated to protests, accusations and character assassinations through Reinhardt Corporation."

Lisa paused, but no one said anything. "Reinhardt launders the money through fake charities, law firms and contributions to a congressman. The Antifa chapter is managed by the son of this Congressman and his plan was to so frighten Conservatives and Christians so they would never again voice any opposition."

Charles Hammer waved an arm and rapped the desk with his wooden hammer. "Hold it, hold it. Are you inferring that a *Congressman's* son was involved in Hayley's death? Oh, wait, we are on a hard break." He gave the camera a gleeful glint from his eyes. "Don't go away, folks."

During the break, Charles Hammer lectured Lisa on using names without proof. "Look, if you make any such claim, our station will put it right back on you to prove it. If it's your *opinion*, say so."

"Yes, Sir. I'll stick to provable facts."

Charles pushed his head forward and squinted. "My instinct tells me you're about to say something sensational, right?"

A stage hand called out, "Five seconds."

Lisa batted her eyelashes at him. "Uh huh." He returned a wide grin.

The camera indicators turned red and Hammer looked at the lens as if it had just scolded him. "All right, Miss Combes," He turned toward her. "It's no surprise that Antifa is trying to intimidate Conservative speech, but you're implying a *Congressman* is involved?"

"Yes, a Congressman with a controlling interest in Reinhardt. I also know of verifiable evidence that would indicate that this Congressman's son killed Hayley Jones."

"Oh, good Lord, girl, why not just tell the police?" In the side panel, Frank sat cross-eyed with his tongue sticking out the side of his mouth. Hammer looked at Colonel Jones."

"Lets hear what she has to say, Charles."

Hammer glowered at Lisa. "Personally, I think you're a cub reporter who's trying to be sensational and just got in over her head, but go ahead."

"First, there's this ten pound rock that was used to kill her."

"And the news report says she hit her head on it when she fell."

"That's a lie. Look at the video of the lawn. No rock. Next, she was hit at least *twice* with it as shown by the autopsy report."

"You saw the *autopsy* report? Frank, is that enough evidence to convict someone?"

"No, but don't stop her! Good Lord, I think your cub reporter is just getting started."

"All right, Lisa, you heard the man. Is that all you have?"

"Nope. There were also skin scrapings under the victim's fingernails of two men and a woman."

"And you're going to say, if someone can find a match, maybe we'll have the murderer. The police would need probable cause to get a DNA match, and there's no complete national data bank, at least not yet. You can't just start rounding up random people."

"They're not random, Mister Hammer. One of the men with matching DNA was an eye witness to the murder and he testified seeing the son and his female accomplice with their masks torn off."

There was a brief silence. Hammer tapped his hammer but spoke on a lowered voice. "An *eye witness*? Really? No reports mentioned that, but if that *were* true, that would have led to a trial where he could testify."

"It is true, but that man was murdered in his home shortly after he gave his testimony to the police."

Hammer rapping. "Ands no reports of that either. How do we know you're not making this up to grab big headlines?"

"Based on his testimony, we obtained a positive DNA match with the son and his accomplice."

Hammer glanced overhead in shock, mouth wide open. "Oops. Wait, if some congressman's son had been dragged into police headquarters for a DNA check, it would have been on every news outlet."

"Well, he wasn't. A friend of mine and I got the DNA samples ourselves. We photographed the scratches on their cheeks, too."

Frank butted in, "Way to go, *girls!*"

"All right, all right," Hammer gave a few more raps and shook his head. "We have to take another break. I think our audience would like to know how two college girls pulled that off."

With the cameras off, William put his hand on Lisa's. "Oh, *thank* you, Lisa. Maybe this will finally get the prosecutors of their butts."

Hammer squinted at them. "If this turns out to be a Sorority prank, we're all in big trouble."

Back on the air, Lisa continued. "My friend and I posed as buss girls at this socialist rally. She pulled a hair from the woman we were after and I pricked the son's finger, pretending it was an accident."

Hammer laughed. "Well even if it's not true, that's a great story and you're two brave girls if it is. Now tell us why your suspects aren't behind bars."

"Isn't that obvious? They are under Deep State protection. Our Justice Department does not prosecute the elite class. It exonerates them. The FBI took the entire file away from the police. It is being guarded by the Deputy FBI Chief and what he calls his 'Sensitive Matter Team'. My sources tell

362

me that the rank and file FBI agents are totally furious and itching to throw themselves into a congressional hearing."

"But our immediate problem is there is no way to verify your story unless your sources come forward. I'm not saying you are lying, but no reporter can touch it."

Frank added, "But the Judicial Committee in Congress can."

"And," Lisa raised her finger. "Congress is already investigating the father."

Frank chuckled. "Really? That narrows the field to just one, doesn't it?"

"And," Hammer rapped and interjected: "That's all the time we have for this segment, but I promise you we'll follow this and give our audience an update. Remember, you heard it here first." He rapped his mallet. "Thank you for joining Hammer Time."

Lisa saw she was still on the split screen. She held up two fingers and, while Charles was talking, mouthed the words, "Second eye witness."

HERO'S WELCOME

Emma, Tilly and some friends came out of the dormitory laughing, talking and trying to restrain a bunch of six balloons. Emma shushed them up at the bottom of the steps. A tall man in a lose-hanging Hawaiian shirt with dogs on it leaned against the railing looking up at them.

Emma said, "Can I help you, Mister?"

He bestowed a handsome grin on the entourage. "Just waiting for Lisa Combes to get back from the News Box. I guess you're greeting her too."

The ladies tittered, but Emma gave him a steely, suspicious gaze. "I think I know all of Lisa's friends, but I don't know you, and if that's a shoulder holster under your shirt, there's no guns on this campus."

Emma jerked back as the man made a swift move to his belt. He displayed a police badge, and a winning smile. "I'm officer Scott Hutchins, Oakland Police."

Emma bent over to study the badge. "Uh huh, okay."

That made him chuckle. "I'll bet you're Lisa's good friend, Emma?"

"Yeah, right, but why are you here in street clothes?"

"Our department has been keeping an eye on Lisa in case she might be in danger, and I've gotten to know her. I'm off duty now, so I thought I'd welcome her back after that truly sensational TV performance of hers."

Tilly wiggled up closer to them. "We're *all* her friends, Scott, so here's a welcome for you too. Are you married?"

Emma swatted her shoulder. "Tilly!"

Scott answered through the grins and titters, "I like women who speak their minds." Tilly batted her lashes. "No, I'm not married, or engaged either, Tilly."

Emma said, "Enough of this. We better get over there. Lisa could pull up any time."

Scott checked his watch. "The driver said his ETA was six o'clock. She's coming to this dorm, right?"

"No, she'll be dropped off at Susan and Betty's apartment. It's just three blocks away and we're all walking over. Why don't you come on along with us? The party's not just for women. My boyfriend, Wally, Steve and some others should be there already."

On the way they had to stop at a crosswalk for twelve students bouncing "No Damn Wall" signs. They were being led by a "Choir leader" who walked backwards, filming them. In unison they shouted: "No wall! No wall! No USA at all."

Emma rolled her eyes up at the officer. "They're back again and being rehearsed for a protest at the boarder. Someone paid for a bus to take them down right after the exams are over."

Scott chuckled. "I assume the media will be covering that, huh?"

Emma spoke into his ear to talk over the chanting. "The woman training them works for a TV producer. I've seen her before."

Soon they were all gathered in the one floor walk up apartment Susan rented. They had posted a lookout outside, cell phone in hand.

The ladies had arranged a smorgasbord dinner complete with cake and a small beer keg. Emma busied herself in setting up replays of the television show while Tilly busied herself downloading Scott's life history.

Finally, the moment came with an excited call from their lookout. Betty answered the doorbell and everyone hollered "Surprise!"

Lisa shared hugs, cheers and congratulations. Scott was the last to approach her, but Lisa put out her arms. "Hi, Hutch." His hug lasted just a tad longer than a polite one.

Tilly whispered in Betty's ear, "Hi, *Hutch*?"

After dinner they sat around the TV with their cake plates. Emma placed Scott and Lisa on the couch, blocked Tilly from squeezing in, and pointed her to a chair. She replayed the Hammer show straight through at first, then a second time, freeze-framing Hammer's amazed expressions.

When the showings were over, Emma stood in front of the TV with a second helping of cake. "So, Lisa, do you think they'll open the murder case after this?"

"You'd think they'd have to, but the politics is really strong here. I sure hope they do because Mister Jones is desperate for closure."

Tilly bestowed a huge smile on Scott. "I think we should ask *Hutch* for his opinion. He's been on the Oakland Police force for five years and got promoted twice."

Scott got up and spoke through his grin. "Personally, I don't see how they can keep this case under the rug anymore. Making up stories about Lisa and trying to frighten her didn't work. They must know that someone in the FBI will eventually leak something to the press.

"She's right about the regular agents being angry, too." He began to shake hands. "Thanks everyone. It was a great party but I've got to get going."

"Bye, Hutch. Thanks so much for coming." Lisa nodded at Emma. "He makes a good point. If they try and ignore what I've brought to light, it will look bad for the FBI's reputation."

Emma gestured with her fork. "But next, I can't wait to see those nude pictures of you, Lisa. They'll say you posted them on the internet."

As the laughter subsided, Tilly caught Scott's eye as he went out the door. She bubbled, "Maybe they could use mine and…"

"Tilly!" Emma stood in front of her. "Where the heck is Jim tonight?"

"He has a calculus final tomorrow."

"And don't we *all* have exams this week. How about you go and give your long time *boy friend* some encouragement?"

"Oh, dear." Tilly's face scrunched up and she looked at Lisa. "Sorry. I slipped up again—I wasn't thinking. I…"

Lisa got up. "That's all right, Till. Listen, everyone. I can't tell you how much this little party meant to me. Thank you all, but I don't want to be responsible for my friends flunking out. Emma's right. One more week of drudge and then we can all celebrate again."

The students began to file out, giving Lisa hugs and congratulations and thanking Betty and Susan as well. Lisa put a hand on Betty's shoulder. "I'm dying to get out of this TV dress. Can I change into that skirt and blouse I left with you?"

"They're all cleaned and pressed in my bedroom closet and hanging next to that ugly green purse of yours that feels like it's full of rocks."

When Lisa emerged, all the remaining guests had gone. Susan and Betty gave her a feigned look of surprise. "Ah, there you are. Your freckles are back."

She giggled. "That took a bit of scrubbing. Thanks again for this cool party. Such fun."

"Just remember us when you're rich and famous, huh?"

"But of course, dah-ling."

"And, don't worry," Betty's eyes twinkled. "I looked out the window and I see you won't have to risk walking back alone in the dark. Oakland's finest is out there, waiting to keep you protected."

HERO'S UNWELCOME

Scott stood opposite the entrance leaning against a tree and pecking on his phone. When Lisa came out with an overnight bag, he gave the phone a few final taps and pocketed it. "Hi, Lisa, it's getting late. I was beginning to wonder if you were going to spend the night with Susan."

"Nah, I have an American History final on Tuesday." She flashed him a big smile. "So, were you waiting for me?"

"I was. No final exams for me, of course, but my car's parked on campus, so I thought I'd walk you back to your dorm."

"Sure, but my editor thinks the bad guys won't touch me now that everything is public." She handed him her overnight bag. "Maybe you could carry this?"

"No offense, but your editor may not be an expert on these matters. You just released a flock of accusations on TV that are bound to drive the Reinhardt people crazy, not to mention Congressman Luchow. These guys have a 'hurt us, we hurt you' mentality."

He took the bag and they began to walk. "Black Cat still has you under surveillance. I saw one of them drive by a few minutes ago."

"Really? Well it's nice to have someone, as they say, to watch over me."

"My pleasure. Lisa, you really blew this case right up in their faces. Thanks. My Department thinks we'll get it back from the FBI, and we'll nail that creep."

"Oh, I hope so and so does Mister Jones. I can't imagine how horrible this has been for him and his children."

"Uh, Lisa..." He faced her, a strained grin on his face. "Could I say something personal?"

She made eye contact. "Uh, huh."

Scott stopped, his face yellow in the flickering light of a sodium lamp. "The last thing I want to do is make you feel awkward, but gosh, Lisa, I have to tell you. I've got this huge crush on you."

"Well," She giggled. "I'm glad that *one* of us had the courage to speak up."

"This surveillance should end soon and I'm just hoping we can..." He nodded and smiled as a couple going the opposite way passed them on the sidewalk. "Uh, you know, spend some time--get to know each other better."

She replied, "That's a promise, Hutch. I think you're the sweetest, nicest man I've ever met," her expression conveying much more feeling than her words. She took his hand, gave it a good squeeze, and they walked on.

"Whew. I feel a lot better, now." He returned the squeeze. "By the way, I like your looks better without all that TV makeup."

"Thanks for the compliment. I can't stand the stuff. Say, maybe we could…"

A car engine roared behind them. Scott swiveled to look and shouted, "Get down!" He grabbed her and threw her to the ground as shots were fired from the passing car.

Lisa knew he'd been hit, but Scott managed to pull out his gun and squeeze off one shot at the departing car.
She knelt over him. "Oh, Hutch, my God--*Hutch*!"

He dropped the gun and his arm began to shake. The car stopped a ways down the street, but now it backed up quickly, tires squealing. Scott rasped, "Get behind that tree— *now*!"

Lisa jumped behind it and activated the 911 button in her purse. The rear car window opened and the face of a man with a rifle appeared. He fired a shot at Scott's writhing body.

Lisa pulled out her "lady pistol," steadied it against the tree and fired two shots in return. Screams and profanity came from the car and it sped away.

She dropped to her knees beside Scott. "I'm here, Hutch."

He was semi conscious, but blood was squirting from one arm. She took off her blouse and tied it tightly above the wound, stopping the flow. Then she tore open his shirt where there was more blood on his upper chest.

Lisa applied pressure to the second wound, not noticing that the car had come back, speeding around the block. Another shot came from the car as it shot past. Lisa screamed. She slapped her hand to her side and collapsed on top of Scott.

The neighborhood fell silent. Their bodies lay still on the grass beside the sidewalk. The muffled voice of a man inside the nearby house shouted out a call for 911. Down the street, a dog began barking.

AFTER

The distant sounds of the sirens drew closer to the scene, and the dog began to howl. Police and ambulance arrived and the man who called hastened down his driveway toward them. He waved at the flashing lights and pointed toward the motionless bodies lying on the grass.

A paramedic rushed to the scene, her flashlight reflecting off Lisa's bare back. She knelt down beside them. Lisa's ear was against his chest, listening to his heart and whispering prayers to God.

"It's okay, Honey," the paramedic said. We'll take over from here. Are you all right?"

"I'm fine. I can't stop the chest wound from bleeding. Just save him, *please*."

Two other medics came, slipped Scott onto a gurney, and they all made for the ambulance. The first woman handed Lisa a short hospital gown. "Is that his blood on your side?"

"It just grazed me. Don't worry about it."

"Well, here, put this on. Bras are no longer a fashion statement. You can ride with us to the hospital."

On arrival, the trauma surgeons attached an oxygen mask to Scott to support his breathing and worked to stabilize him for surgery in the ER. They did a quick cut down and clamped the brachial artery in his arm allowing peripheral circulation to keep his arm alive. By the third pint of blood he received, Scott regained consciousness and the vascular surgeon was ready.

A nurse waved to three policemen in the waiting room where they had been debriefing Lisa. "Doctor said you can talk to him, but just for five minutes." She pointed at Lisa. "Not you, honey. He's on his way to surgery after that."

Sean Ryan and two other officers were admitted behind the curtain. He hastened to the head of the gurney, making eye contact with his deputy, Scott. "Thanks to you I'm missing my dinner, Mister 'wanna-be-a-hero'."

"Oh yeah?" Scott replied in a hoarse voice. "You're too fat anyway."

"Remember anything about the perps?"

"Brown Chevy sedan. Only got a partial plate." He coughed. "Ouch. First three were DJ7. Probably the same car our lovely Black Cat brothers used to follow Lisa. Is she okay?"

"Good catch. She's fine. You fired your weapon?"

"From the ground. One shot near the passenger window toward the muzzle flash. Don't know the result. I was losing it, but I know they came back and hit me again."

"In the arm?"

"Right, but I heard two shots next to me. She recover my pistol?"

Two orderlies came in and swept the curtain aside. "Sorry, officers, we're ready for him now."

As they began to wheel Scott out, Sean asked, "Anything else you can remember? Anything at all?"

"Last thing…" Cough. "Ow. Before I blacked out, Lisa was kneeling over me and tearing off her blouse."

RECOVERY

The officers found Lisa in a counseling room with a trauma psychologist. She sat on a steel chair, a hospital gown wrapped around her shoulders and a frown on her face. As soon as they appeared, Lisa stood up. "Just tell me if he's going to be okay."

Sean grinned at her. "I think it will take more than bullets to keep him away from you, Lisa."

"He saved my life—just so you know. He's okay, then?"

"Should be fine, but the doctors still have to take a bullet out of his chest. Can we ask you a few more questions?"

"Sure, 'course."

The psychologist standing next to her had been patting her shoulder. She looked at Lisa. "Just ask the nurse if you want to talk some more. I'm on duty until midnight. I'm so glad Hutch will be all right."

"Uh, could you ask them for my shirt back? I don't care if it has blood on it."

"Of course. I'll check back with you later."

Sean asked her, "You want to sit?"

Lisa shook her head, 'no'."

"Lisa, your tourniquet likely saved Scott's life. Did you know that?"

"Those bullets he took—they were meant for *me*. Did you know that?"

"Yeah. Did you get a look at the shooters?"

"Too dark to see much, but I'm pretty sure it was the same car that's been following me."

"Uh huh. Did anyone else beside Scott fire back at them?"

"Oh, yes." She grinned. "That was me. See, they backed up after the first pass. Must have seen me still standing. Hutch hollered for me to get behind the tree. I saw the rear window open and a rifle barrel came out."

"Could you see a face?"

"I saw a guy with a blonde mustache—he shot at Hutch on the ground. I lost it, then—made me *furious*. I fired back at him from behind the tree."

"Lisa, there was only one shot fired from officer Hutchins's pistol."

"Oh, right," She gestured with her arms. "I shot at the guy with the little lady gun my Dad gave me. I thought they'd left for good after that, but they swung by again and took another shot at me."

The officers looked at each other, amazement on their faces. "Lisa, are you telling us you were *armed?* Do you have the gun with you?"

"Oh, right, but I have a 'concealed carry' permit too. Would you like to see?"

"Uh, huh. We would, if you don't mind."

She hiked up the hospital gown and unstrapped the olive green purse from her waist. "Daddy calls this a 'tactical purse.' It was a Christmas present."

She pulled out the tiny revolver and handed it to Sean who took it with two fingers and raised eyebrows. The officers moved in to take a closer look.

Sean said, "This is a custom made ladies model, men. I believe it is German. Very well made." He held it up for them to see better, "Note the four shot chamber with two bullets fired."

"Lisa, we'll have to take this in for evidence."

"Oh, sure. I don't think I'll need it. I probably didn't hit anything but I'm glad if I scared them off."

He slipped the revolver into an evidence bag and grinned at Lisa. "A *tactical* purse?"

"Daddy's a marine. He says every girl should have one."

AN AWAKENING

Nurse Hollingsworth found Lisa in the Hospital Chapel by herself, pacing and praying. "Miss Combes?"

She froze at the sound and hastened to her. "Yes? Is everything all right? Of course I know it is, but I want to hear you say it."

"Officer Hutchins is out of recovery and should be awake soon. Doctor Adams said everything went well."

"Can I see him now?"

"Hold on. His parents have been informed, but they won't be able to be here until tomorrow. Our regulations say you'll have to wait for visiting hours tomorrow."

"Oh, M'am, that's so lame. I *need* to see him—he'll want to see me."

"I can ask Doctor Adams, but first Mrs. Hart, the psychologist, said you wanted this back." The nurse partly lifted the twisted, bloody garment out of a plastic bag. "You'd give people a heart attack if they saw you wearing it." She handed her a gray shirt with the Mercy Hospital logo on it. "Here, I picked this up from our gift shop to get you home."

"Thanks. Can you ask the doctor now?"

"In a minute, but I want to ask you something first. Lisa, there's a bullet hole in this—two actually." She held up the blood stained blouse. "The bullet went from near the second button in the front and out the back."

"Ah, must have been hit after I took it off."

"I guess so, otherwise you'd probably be dead. Mrs. Hart said you are hiding an injury under the gown. May I see?"

"Oh, it's nothing." Lisa sighed and rolled her eyes at the ceiling, but lifted the gown. "See, just a little scrape from when I fell. No bullet holes in me."

Hollingsworth let forth a "Tsk, tsk." She pouted. "Looks like a nasty gash to me. If you want me to plead your case to see your guy, I'm going to have to dress this up for you first—a nurse's duty, you know."

Lisa let out a breath, but spoke softly. "Okay, nurse, I know I'm being a pain, but I just want to see him so bad."

"I know. I know." She smiled and escorted Lisa to a treatment room where she cleaned and dressed the wound.

"No need for sutures, but change the dressing at least every other day. Your man's still asleep last I checked, but I'll ask doctor for you."

Ten minutes later, Nurse Hollingsworth was back. She found Lisa pacing and praying again. "Doctor says that if you behave yourself, you can sit with him for just a little while."

Nurse received a hug. "Oh, thank you. Thank you. I'm just all achy inside."

Nurse chuckled. "I get the picture. Come with me."

The post recovery room had six beds with curtains for each one, but Scott was the only patient. He had a huge bandage around his right shoulder and another one just below it around his arm. He was making some head jerks and groaning, not fully conscious.

Lisa sat on the bedside chair, took his left hand in hers and placed her cheek on his forearm. She sang a little song CC had sung in church. She would sit and wait, content to be beside him.

Right after she snuck in a little kiss on that forearm, she looked up, startled to see Scott watching her. "You could sing me another one, if you like," he said.

Lisa grinned and sat up sparkle-eyed. She held fast to his hand and sang him another gospel tune. "I've been praying hard for you, big guy."

"Is that why I'm feeling so good right now?"

"Scott, you—you saved my life." Her face twisted up. "You took that bullet for me."

"That was just, uh—sorry, I'm still groggy. It was duck and cover. From what they told me you saved *my* life, and twice."

"Nah, I don't think so."

"Uh, huh. First time was when you put a tourniquet on my arm. The second time was you fired back, scaring them away—and, you should have told me you had a gun, by the way."

"I, I was really *furious* at them when they hurt you, and they might have shot again."

Scott's hand slipped behind Lisa's head and he pulled her closer.

The nurse returned with Doctor Adams. She looked behind the curtain preparing to swing it open, but blocked the doctor from going in.

"Uh, let's wait a moment, Doctor."

Adams frowned. "And why is it can't I see my patient right now?"

The nurse peeked again and saw the kiss was going to last a long time. "Cause right now he's in therapy."

NEWS AND VIEWS

Officers Brad Smith and Wesley Duncan were nearing the end of their overnight stakeout shift when it happened. "Wes, wakeup. There's someone going in."

In the early dawn light a man carrying a bag and wearing a hoodie was opening the front door of the shuttered building they had been watching. Wesley said, "Let him go in and do whatever he's gonna do. Anyway, I need a minute to wake up."

Brad pulled out a pad and wrote, "4: 52 AM, Man with suitcase entered building." They watched for a minute. "Flashlight seen in second story window."

Wesley tapped his partner on the shoulder. "I'm good. Let's go. Got the warrant?"

The front door was left open so they quietly made their way up the dark stairwell with their flashlights. They found the man standing by a window, tossing out beer cans and 32 and 45 caliber shells from his bag.

The officers flicked on the lights and approached quickly with guns drawn. "Police, stop. You're under arrest."

The man turned and put his hands up. "You're making a mistake, officers. I work for the owner of this building and I got ID to prove it."

Brad took a wide angle flash photo while Wesley cuffed the man, hands behind his back. "You'll have plenty of time to explain that at the station."

"You two could be loosing you jobs doing this. You really want to tangle with Reinhardt Industries?"

Brad said, "Really? Good thing then. I always wanted to start my career as a rock star. Stand there by the window."

Wesley's next picture would show the man surrounded by the spent shells and cans. "The first eight by ten is free. After that we'll charge for the prints."

Brad tried to lift the dirt streaked window. He grunted and wiggled it. "Wesley, try the other two."

He turned toward the suspect. "None of the windows can be open by hand. Would you like to break one so the scene will look more realistic for the alleged shooters?"

"Go to h__l."

RNN NEWS:

"Good morning. This is Andrew Smyth reporting. There were two incidents of gun violence next to Berkard University last night, perhaps triggered by a party for right wing extremist, Lisa Combes.

Shortly after the party broke up, Combes was involved in a shooting incident not two blocks away. One policeman was injured by gunfire and taken to the hospital where he is expected to recover. Combes was uninjured.

Details of this incident are under investigation but we interviewed one student at Berkard who is familiar with Combes. Helen Stone is standing by. Helen?"

The scene changes to a campus shot and a reporter. Next to her is a male student with long black hair and a black sweat shirt bearing a fist and the word "resist."

"Helen Stone here with Guy Roberts, a senior student here at Berkard. Guy, what can you tell us about this shooting and the Combes woman?"

"Well, I wasn't at the scene, but near enough to hear their raging party. I sure heard the shots, too—four of them, I think."

"Do you think it's possible that Combes shot the policeman?"

"Sure it's possible. She's a little hate filled bigot and I know someone who's seen her gun. I've watched her carrying a Bible, too—right in the open."

(Camera goes to close up of Stone.)

"There you have it so far. I'll be talking with others and we'll follow this story. Back to you in studio, Andrew."

"Thank you, Helen. The second shooting incident took place within blocks of the first one, but we are still trying to determine the exact location. According to a Black Cat Security spokesperson, one of their security cars was fired upon when they were checking on an abandoned building. It is not known if the shooters were revelers from the party, but he thought it was likely that the extremists tried to break in and planned to have a second party.

"The security car did not engage the shooters further, but drove to City Lights Urgent Care where one guard in the rear seat was pronounced dead, and one was treated for a gunshot wound of the forearm. Black Cat guards only fired warning shots in the air.

The police are investigating this incident as well, but are not releasing further details at this time. Stay tuned to RNN news for further updates. Oh, this just in. Helen has more for us on site at Berkard University."

"Yes I do, Andy. I'm standing here with four students who are outraged by this gun violence near their campus." She holds the microphone toward a female student. "What do you think should be done about this?"

"They need to ban all guns on campus. Right now, those with a permit can carry them."

"And, how about in the city?"

"No guns in the city except the swat team. Sure, they can have shotguns in the country, but America needs to ban all assault rifles."

"People define them differently. How do you see them compared to hunting rifles?'

"It's when another bullet comes up when you pull the trigger. Let's stop the violence and talk peace. No one needs to shoot animals either. No more hate speech. I'd vote for blowing up the NRA and shooting their president."

Helen moves the microphone to a male student carrying a "Ban the Gun" sign. "You, Sir: looks like you're planning a protest."

"You bet we are. Gonna march from here to the Congressman's office this afternoon. You guys should be there."

"Oh. I promise we will." Helen turns back to the camera. "There you have it. This is America in action—people making things happen. Back to you in Studio."

"Thank you Helen. Student activism—love it. We should have coverage of the protest march at six PM here on the Reinhardt News Network. Stay tuned. After the break we'll have a clip from an interview with Congresswoman Moxie Watver on why thousands of women will die without Planned Parenthood."

BOX NEWS, NOON REPORT:

"Good Afternoon. This is Henry Heinz and the Noon Report. We have an update on the nighttime drive-by shooting involving yesterday's correspondent, Lisa Combes.

"Ms. Combes left a friends house with a police bodyguard about nine PM last night. They were attacked by at least three men in a car who fired on them. They were able to shoot back and the car was identified by the officer. That same vehicle is shown here at a nearby urgent care. It is owned by Black Cat Security and has been impounded by the police. We believe off duty Black Cat employees were the assassins. One was wounded and one, who was in the back seat, was killed. Names are being withheld pending notification of kin.

The scene changes to the outside of a hospital. "We are happy to report that Ms. Combes only sustained minor injuries from the incident. Her bodyguard was struck twice, but is out of surgery here at Mercy Hospital and is expected to make a full recovery."

The scene changes to Henry in the studio, leaning to one side and covering one ear. "Wait, this is just coming in. We're going to Julie Marcus at Oakland Police. Julie, what do you have for us?"

The scene changes to the outside of Police Headquarters. "Henry, I've just spoken with the desk sergeant here. He states it is too early to make an official statement, but he did tell us that a man was arrested this morning attempting to make up a false crime scene in an abandoned building owned by Reinhardt Corporation."

"Is that connected in some way to the drive-by, Julie?"

"I asked the sergeant that, Henry, but he said he couldn't give out any further public information pending investigation."

"That's interesting. Our viewers should know that both that building and Black Cat Security are owned by Reinhardt."

Julie smiled back. "And so is RNN, Henry."

FAMILY CONFESSIONS

Lisa sat at a private, shady bench on campus tapping a number on her phone. A hefty male voice answered: "Hi Punkin. Got the text you're okay. We're all proud of you. You handled that TV interview on Sunday like you did those every day."

"Thanks, Dad. The text was in case you saw the news today. You guys aren't eating dinner, are you?"

"Nah, we eat late these days. Mother is just getting things together. The security scramble chip on your phone works well—can't tell it's encrypted."

Mom's melodic voice breaks in with an echo. "But now you're on speaker phone here. Did you have any final semester exams today, dear?"

"They start tomorrow, Mom. Look, I'm calling 'cause when you see the news they'll talk about me and a drive-by shooting. Don't worry. I'm fine."

Mother screeches. "Wha-*what*? Was it close to you?"

Lisa recounted the events as gently as one can to a nervous mother. She concluded with, "Dad, your security gift sure came in handy. I thought you said the revolver wasn't accurate, but thanks."

"You think I'd give my only daughter a piece of junk? Nathan checked and calibrated it, remember? It's only a centimeter off at ten yards compared to a service revolver." He chuckled. "Don't think those punks will mess with you again. Good job, kid."

Mother said, "So—so you *shot* at someone?"

"Had to, Ma. He was gonna kill us both with a rifle, but I've been praying for forgiveness."

"Oh, Dear, but maybe that policeman was the only one to hit anyone. Is he okay?"

Lisa was glad to skirt the subject of who shot who. "I'm happy to say, Hutch is doing just fine. The doctor says he expects a full recovery."

Both parents said, "Hutch?"

She laughed. "Okay, confession time. His name is Scott Hutchins and I've gotten to know him well over the past few months. He was assigned to watch over me. Remember, I told you he's my big crush."

Mother Mary's voice took on bubbles with her words, "And I can tell by your tone that you like each other a lot."

"Oh, yes, you could say so."

Roger said, "Of course 'Sergeant Combes' will have to give any man of yours a full screening."

Lisa laughed. "I think he'll pass. Hutch looks like Christopher Reeve in the first Superman movie. He goes to church regularly, loves dogs and his dad is a marine at Camp Pendleton—an officer. I'll bet my brother Nathan knows him."

Dad chuckled. "Yo. Just passed. Mary?"

Mother was still bubbling. "Oh, Lisa, I'm just so glad you finally stopped to notice a man. How did you know he was, uh, special?"

"Well, usually when I talk to men I see them as just another person, but when I talk to Hutch, I picture him in a vision of a country house, kids and dogs in the back yard."

They all laughed, but Mother said, "Are you sure he feels the same about you, Lisa?"

"Yeah, he does. I don't know *why* he does, but yeah. I'm as plain as he is handsome, but we're going for our first real date next weekend when I finish my exams."

Dad said, "Say, that's great, Punkin. Hope you'll have time for us this summer."

Mother added: "Lisa, you are *not* plain. Boys always said you were cute. Anyway, I can hardly wait to meet this hunk of yours, but do something for me, okay?"

"What, Ma?"

"When you move into that apartment with Emma, start practicing your Lasagna recipe, okay?"

FRIENDS IN TRUTH

Sally looked at her husband. "Is the barbeque ready?"

"Yup, and Arthur's locked in the back yard." Dylan peered out a back widow. "'Course, he'll start to howl in protest soon."

"You say you only just met this Professor Sims once, and you invited him here? Fine with me, as I said, but that's rare behavior for you, my Dear."

"Yeah, I met him just before I had to leave campus." He pointed to a car driving up. "Must be him now. We really hit it off, Sally. He gave me some moral support when I needed it most. I like him and I asked him to bring his wife. They're Christians, too."

"Well, I'm delighted—but you didn't say why you invited Emma and Wally as well."

"'Cause Wally's a similar genius." He moved toward the door as the bell rang. "I thought these two should get to know each other."

Dylan met the couple with a grin. "Hey, I'm so glad you could come and visit." He gestured to his wife. "Drew, this is my wife Sally—Sally, Drew Sims; and I guess this is your wife."

Drew put his arm over his wife's shoulder. "Yes, this is Miki." He gave a furtive glance inside. "Permission to enter the rebel base?"

"Come on in, guys." Dylan shook their hands and chuckled. "No Imperial Cruisers in ten parsecs."

Miki had a round face and short black hair with a forward spike below her ear. Sally leaned her face in close to her. "You should know: Dylan slips into boyhood at unexpected moments."

Miki giggled. "Perfect. Drew never left."

Wally and Emma arrived while they were still chatting in the doorway and, after more introductions, they went through the house into the back yard. Emma volunteered to help Sally set up the lunch while everyone else got settled and had a chance to pet Arthur.

Dylan gestured toward the barbeque. "Before you get too comfortable, we're in charge of getting this fired up and making the burgers."

Miki began opening up packages of buns. "Don't ask Drew to start the fire. He'll pull out a phaser."

Drew chuckled. "Miki gets her movies confused sometimes." He turned to Wally. "I understand you're going into graduate school for a Masters. Is it in Mathematics?"

"Right. I start this fall, and I hope to take Astrophysics. Will you be teaching it?"

"I will, but not here. We'll be moving to Arizona where I'll be a research fellow at U of A in Tucson. I'm hoping to get some time in at the Kitt Peak observatory for a few projects I have in mind."

"Oh, that's so cool." He looked at Miki. "Dylan said you are a professor, too."

"I am." She held out a plate of open buns and Dylan placed burgers on them from the grill. "I teach biology subjects in graduate school."

Over lunch they discussed the progress of Dylan's law suit, the growing hostility toward Christianity in our universities and the coming Star Trek sequel. When the ice cream and cookies had disappeared, the more technical subjects came up.

Dylan gestured toward Miki. "Tell us a few details about the research project you mentioned."

"Details?" Miki chuckled. "That would take some time, but I completed two PHD research projects on the essential nature of quantum mechanics in determining biological effects. That's how I met Drew. He eats up quantum equations like you guys polish off chocolate chip cookies."

Drew opened his hands. "But, how could I *not* help her. I was becoming intrigued by Miki's hidden, uh, physical and emotional nature."

Miki laughed and zinged a napkin ball at him. "I realized early on that Drew harbored Neanderthal genes. When he looked over my work from behind, he always had to hold and massage both my shoulders."

Everyone laughed. Dylan said, "No more details needed on *that* research project. We can see the conclusion." He looked at Wally. "Perhaps you and Emma have a similar story?"

"Close." Wally nodded. "I was making some money as a tutor for students taking Calculus." He grinned at Emma. "She passed all her tests."

Dylan pointed at Wally but spoke to Drew. "Wally and his math club worked out equations for the cosmic impactor that formed our moon."

Drew gave Wally a thumbs-up grin. "Wow, good work. I'd love to look those over. I might be able to help tighten up any hypotheticals you used."

Sally and Emma cleared the plates and while they finished rinsing them in the kitchen Sally looked at Emma, a grin on her face.

"I think this discussion's going way over our heads. Anyway, it's time for Arthur's walk. Want to come with me?"

Emma chuckled. "Oh, absolutely."

As the women reached the entrance to the park and the path around the lake, Arthur became transfixed with the aroma of one tree. Emma held his leash and tried in vain to tug him away.

"What do we do now, Sally?"

"Have patience. This tree is the 'mailbox' for all the dogs. He'll leave his response in a sec—ah, there we go."

"Uh, huh." Emma giggled. "How fast can a basset hound walk?"

"For you, a good walk pace, but he rests a lot. More importantly, Emma, I notice you have an engagement ring on your finger now. Do you have a wedding date?"

"Yes, well, no date yet." she smiled. "Wally just proposed last month. He's so cute. He wore it on his pinky when we were eating at Burger King until I noticed. Then he said something like, 'Oh, thanks for reminding me. I didn't want to forget to tell you how much I love you and will you please marry me?'"

"He proposed in Burger King?"

Emma laughed. "Really, it was sweeter than it sounds. We're thinking about a date for this summer. You're invited, of course."

"That's great, but the last I remembered, Lisa said you two were being cautious about commitment."

"True. We know we're kind of a strange couple—we are, but we love each other. My real concern was marrying someone who wasn't a Christian."

"Yeah," Sally nodded. "That can cause problems."

"But I thought, he's just the sweetest guy. He always surprises me with little things I'd like. How many men would volunteer to take their date to a quilting exposition?"

They paused while Arthur and a white poodle had a nose to nose conversation. "Really? That's so thoughtful, and we all know Wally's quite the genius, too."

"I'll say. I don't think they even know how to rate a mind like his, but Wally's humble." A few quick tugs and Arthur was on his way again. "Did you know that he says he came up with equations proving there had to be a God who created the universe?"

"Really?" Sally returned a wide eyed look. "That's amazing, but I hope you don't think that makes him a Christian?"

"No, no, 'course not, but at least that got him to start going to church with me. The first two times he was interested but seemed detached."

"Did he…" Arthur collapsed into "rest mode" on a grassy patch so they stopped. "Did Wally speak to the pastor or ask any questions?"

"I tried to get him to talk but he said he wanted to read the Bible first. That genius mind of his read the *whole thing* in two weeks and, believe it or not, he's memorized every word."

"Really?" She tugged the leash to get Arthur moving. "Come on you. Okay, what did Wally do next?"

"He didn't open up until we were having dinner at Bobby's Seafood Restaurant." Emma chuckled. "He announced his conclusion that either Jesus was a crazy man, or he really *was* God, and there was nothing to support crazy."

"That's progress, but it's still all intellect, no feeling." Sally sat down on a bench. "We usually take a rest here."

Emma took a drink at a nearby fountain and sat beside her. "I remember this spot. It was in that hilarious RNN video, wasn't it?"

Sally was silently heaving with laughter. "They bleeped out the reporter's expletive when she realized the joke was on her. But tell me, when did you decide Wally was a Christian?"

"No decision necessary, Sally. One Sunday, Wally surprised me and walked up for an altar call. He was all his intellectual self, saying 'Let's see what this thing is all about.'

Then Pastor Wong put his hand on Wally's forehead and said, 'Receive the Holy Spirit.' He collapsed beside the altar."

"Slain in the Spirit."

"Oh, yeah—born again. Wally was so excited telling anyone who would listen how he could feel God's presence, how the God of the universe is actually interested in a relationship."

"Oh, Emma," She gave her a hug. "That's just beautiful. The Lord knows how to talk to each of us as individuals, doesn't He?"

"Yeah, I know. When God decides His child is ready, then 'boom-chica-boom,' it happens."

Sally laughed. "So, a wedding this summer. Your families are okay with this?"

"You mean because of the inter-racial thing?"

"Well…" She shrugged.

"Nah, no problem." Emma giggled. "We're just crazy mixed up, that's all. I might look all black, but on my mother's side, I'm a quarter Sioux Indian with a Mexican grandpa thrown in. Wally's mom is from India, married to a white man, and his Korean dad is married to a Filipino woman."

"What?" Sally grinned, "no Eskimos?"

Emma turned her gaze skyward. "I can hardly wait to see what our children will look like."

A JUDGEMENT

Lisa pecked at her keyboard, occasionally smiling at two crows on her window ledge who were clucking and cooing at each other. She had her own cubicle at the paper now and they expected her to answer letters beside producing at least one story a week.

Vera Appeared at the cubicle opening but Lisa held her hand out. "No quick moves. You'll scare the lovebirds."

She carefully slid into the chair beside her. "Oooh, I see: *real* love birds. Whatcha working on?"

"It's a piece about a friend of mine, a black woman student I met at our Rose Guardian meetings."

"Emma?"

"No, this woman's a Junior. I haven't known her that long. Name's Sylvia and she's dating a white man."

"So, what's the hook?"

"Both their families have shunned them coming from opposite ends of bigotry. She's become a born again Christian and has been challenging her colleagues in an off campus debate society."

"Starting to sound more interesting."

"Sylvia's *really* good at debating—swings the biblical sword of truth like a Centurion."

"And…" Vera chuckled. "I'll bet that's got her in a lot of trouble."

"When she got on the theme that blacks should stop acting like they're all entitled victims, some students went hysterical. Then, suddenly…"

"Wait. Surprise me when I read it. How did your exams go?"

"A 'C' in Statistics, but I should still graduate."

"And your first date with Scott?"

Lisa laughed and made a face at her. "So, how did *that* get around so soon?"

"We're investigative reporters, remember? Anyway, spill it."

Lisa turned to the crows for a moment before answering. "Vera, I figure the only way a man that wonderful could like a plain looking, bookworm like me would be if God were behind it. So, to answer your question, which is none of your business by the way, we've become like soul mates."

"A God thing, you say?"

"That, and saving each other's lives last week."

"Oh, *that?*" Vera chuckled. "Sounding a bit more than the usual 'cute-meet' story, isn't it? Look, believe it or not, I didn't come just to pry into your fascinating life. I have some good news about some professors you know."

"Really?" Her face brightened. "Did the Ninth Circuit rule in their favor?"

"Sure did, and what a surprise. Those judges sit in the left field bleachers most of the time, but with separate rulings on West and Coz, they both got by. They'll be reinstated at Berkard—unless there's an appeal, and that's most unlikely."

Lisa bounced up and clapped her hands. "Weee! That's wonderful." The crows took off.

"I'm on my way to write it up right now, Lisa, but here's the skinny. Aimee proved that her statistics on Berkard were public information. Even though they didn't want them talked about, they can't fire someone on that basis, or if they just didn't like someone."

"Sure, and upholding a firing for those reasons could burn the Progressives in a later case. What did they say about Dylan?"

"That one was close and heated, but Dylan's lawyers proved that he was recounting the actual words of the Founding Fathers. This was *history* and he was teaching history, so even if Berkard hated the references to God, they couldn't fire him for doing his job."

"Super, but I thought he was actually fired for putting scripture on screen."

"Right, but he didn't read the words or comment on them. The judges were shown a video of some his lecture. They made the case that it was presented for poetic overlay and general inspiration. While implying it, none of Dylan's words actually mentioned the creation truth."

"Really?" Lisa laughed. "So, the judges were so atheistic they missed understanding that Dylan really *was* presenting evidence that our universe was created by God."

"Sure did, but the ruling was narrow. It didn't rule out firing someone if they spoke God's word on their own." Vera grinned, "But I think it's also true they proved God didn't create the narrow little man made universe *they* live in."

NEWS?

"Good evening. I am Martin Soffit in Washington. The Inspector General has issued a report, which on the face of it, is unfavorable to Congressman Bernard Luchow of California. Merlin Weiss, our Bureau Chief has the report. Merlin?"

The view changes to a Capitol Building background. "Right, Martin, The report alleges the tired old claims of money laundering and foreign collusion leveled earlier by the partisan Ethics Committee. These claims are hotly denied by Congressman Luchow who issued a statement that he would welcome an indictment by the Justice Department since it would ultimately clear his name."

A spit screen shows Soffit as well. He asks: "Do you think there will be criminal charges?"

"More than likely, Martin. We'll have the full statement from Congressman Luchow later, but here is a clip from today when he left the DOJ."

The scene switches to the gray haired, portly congressman standing outside the Justice Department with his attorney.

He glowered at the camera, full of indignation. "I want to emphasize to the American people that this is a purely partisan witch hunt, and I expect to be completely exonerated. What is completely disgraceful is that these right wing attack dogs are now attacking my son as well. They would have you believe the lies spread by some *college student* whose only distinction is being fired by her school newspaper."

The scene returns to Martin, chuckling at his desk. "Sounds to me like Luchow's' opposition is getting desperate, Merlin.

"We followed up on that college student he referred to. Ms. Lisa Combes made those charges accusing his son on another network. She went to a college rave party afterward but is denying that the subsequent gunfire came from the party goers. She may face charges herself, Merlin. A police officer was wounded in the shooting incident."

Merlin scowled at the camera. "I'll see if we can get a statement from the Chief of Police. Sounds like Combes should have been arrested."

"They probably should arrest her, Merlin, but if you can believe it, this 'college diva' told police investigators that the shots were fired by some drive by shooter attempting to pay her back for her statements the day before. Talk about thinking you're important."

Martin began to shake his head. "So she's the *victim* now? Is it just me, or does everyone agree this ditsy, party-going student has been reading too many spy novels."

EVENING NEWS BOX

"Good evening. We have a new development in the Hayley Jones murder case. Reginald Luchow, the Congressman's son, was apprehended in San Francisco Airport attempting to leave the country. There is a warrant for his arrest on murder charges and he is being held without bail. Also arrested was Charon Madding in her penthouse suite on the charge of conspiracy to murder. Both events took place within hours after the FBI returned the Berkard case to the Oakland Police."

The scene switches to Reginald being led away in handcuffs. "A source at the Oakland City Hall reports that the mayor demanded that no arrests be made, but the Chief of Police acted anyway with the help of San Francisco authorities. We are told that a trial can be expected in a few weeks."

"Contrary to what is being reported on Reinhardt's network and others, there *was* an actual drive by shooting confirmed by witnesses and a police report. It was aimed at Lisa Combes and her police bodyguard. We have also confirmed that the car involved is owned by Black Cat Security. We are looking into a report that police interrupted an attempted cover up of these facts early next morning. They have an employee of Black Cat in custody."

"Our sources are busy checking on the web of interconnectivity between Antifa, organized protests nationwide, large money flows to Reinhardt Corporation, and the involvement of Congressman Luchow. Tune in to The Box this Friday for a special Hammer Report."

COURTROOM TRUTH

NEWS BOX, EVENING NEWS:

"Steve Rogers reporting from the Courthouse. After months of delays and seemingly endless denials of motions to dismiss, the trial of Reginald Luchow began last week. We will have a full analysis of the proceedings and today's testimony at eleven o'clock, but here's a summary of what has happened so far."

Steve turns to a woman on his right. "Monica Stable is a Box News legal analyst. Monica, do you expect yet another motion for dismissal from attorney Lucent?"

"I think you can count on that, Steve. Lucent has maintained a posture of indignant outrage ever since the arrest and has characterized the prosecution as contrived and politically motivated."

Steve raised his hands. "But, there are facts, Monica."

"Sure, but Lucent scored some points in his favor yesterday. Luchow's associate, Charon Madding, testified she saw Paco Gutierrez murder Mrs. Jones, and the scratches they all sustained were merely a result of her wild flailing about while they attempted to pull Gutierrez away."

"But, Monica, Paco's scratch was on his hand and theirs were on their cheeks."

"Not important, I guess. Charon claims Paco was an unstable drug addict and Reginald was trying to protect Mrs. Jones from him. They claim Paco's recorded testimony was a cover-up for his guilt. Prosecution's evidence of Paco's clean drug tests was countered by a sanitation worker who said how easy it was to fake clean results."

"But what about all the evidence of pre planning and co-ordination. No one would believe Paco could have arranged all that."

"True, but it doesn't prove Antifa's plan was murder, either."

"So all bets are for a quick 'not guilty', huh."

"Or dismissal of charges, but that won't happen until after the prosecution calls its last witness today."

"And who's that?"

"They've kept his name secret, allegedly for his or her protection. It's almost time for the trial to resume. We'll know soon enough who it is."

The court room was alive with murmurs and conversations when the bailiff did his "Hear ye, hear ye's" and all rose for the Judge. The prosecution remained standing until the Judge addressed them. "Unless you have more evidence or another witness, I will be asking for closing arguments."

"We do have one more witness, your Honor."

"Well then, call him."

The prosecutor spoke into his phone and two policemen entered the court room with a young black man wearing a light blue short sleeve shirt, an American flag tie and a big smile.

Reggie jumped up on his chair, pointed a finger at him and shouted, "You! You better remember your pledge."

His lawyers pulled him down but when the man passed the front tables, he made eye contact with Reggie and silently mouthed the words, "Liar."

Enraged, Reggie lunged at him, tried to climb over the table and shouted, "You're a dead man." His lawyer and two bailiffs restrained him but he continued raging. "He's a fascist plant! This trial is a *sham*."

It took four policemen to remove the screaming Reggie from the court room and place him in a room where he could hear, but not be heard. The judge asked the defense if Mister Luchow would like to make further statements or be a witness.

Lucent, his attorney, appeared to be suffering acute indigestion. "No, your Honor, but we declare this man to be a hostile witness."

The black man hopped up the steps like an athlete and took his seat in the witness chair. After he was sworn in, the Judge asked him to state his name and occupation for the record. He smiled. "My name is Jevon Patrick. I am a student at Berkard University."

Jevon gave a detailed description of the murder including Charon putting her foot on Hayley's neck and urging Reggie to hit her again. Jevon told them that after their masks were torn off, she hollered: "She's seen us now. Finish her off."

At the end of his witness, the Prosecutor asked, "Mister Patrick, you have testified that you were a member of Antifa. I assume you are no longer affiliated. Is that correct?"

"Yeah, I finally realized they were just using us and feeding us lies."

"Could you tell us why your opinion of them changed?"

"Professor Coz's class and the students I met there. It took months, but there was this sudden moment in their church when I knew what was really the truth and what wasn't."

"In church?"

"Yeah, when Berkard kicked him out. a bunch of us went to hear him teach there. It was wrong what they did to him. I ought to know discrimination when I see it. I think Professor Coz was the first white man I really respected."

"Any others?"

Jevon chuckled. "Pastor Wong gave us some zingers too, including the truth in Jesus. So yeah, now I'm hangin' with a bunch of students I wouldn't have even looked at before—and Fessamie, that's Professor Aimee West. She's cool, too."

Attorney Lucent interrupted asking where this questioning was leading. The Prosecutor said there was one last piece of evidence and Mister Patrick would explain where it came from. He turned to his witness. "Jevon?"

"Oh, yeah. After the action on campus, the cars dropped us off at some building Reinhardt owned and we took off our black clothes. They had an incinerator and Reggie handed me two pairs of gloves and told me to burn them. At the time we all thought Reggie was some kind of hero, so I kept one of his gloves with blood on it for a souvenir."

The Prosecutor pointed to his co-counsel holding a plastic bag with a black glove. "Please mark this exhibit 'C' along with a laboratory report showing Mrs. Jones blood on the outside and Mister Luchow's DNA on the inside."

The Prosecutor turned to the defense table. "Your witness."

Lucent did his best to discredit Jevon and assail his character, citing disciplinary actions he'd received in the past. His final question: "Come on, you've only convinced us of one thing. You're a loyal follower of your new friends and their Jesus cult.

"Only your friends have changed, right? You've convinced me, at least, that you would make up a story and falsify evidence on their behalf. Admit it. You don't have any higher loyalty than these friends of yours, right?"

"Sure I do. I'm thinking of three things."

"Uh huh." Lucent grinned at him. "Power? Fame? Money?"

Jevon studied the attorney for a moment. He smiled. "Nope. God, Country--truth."

AUTUMN COLORS

Dylan Coz walked into an auditorium full of students. There was some applause and scattered boos. He put down his briefcase, moved up to stand near the front row and adjusted the small microphone near his mouth.

"Mixed opinions—I like that." Dylan looked over his audience and gave them a big smile.

"I am Professor Dylan Coz, and welcome to American History. It is my hope for this class that you will look back on it as counting for more than just three credits gained. I hope you will remember it as an exciting adventure. For my part, I promise you you'll discover some totally amazing truths about our country as we embark on this voyage together."

"First, I'd like to clear the air and tell you about the changes at Berkard since last year."

He let out a deep breath. "As you all know, the Board suspended me for awhile and I won my suit to return. Yesterday the faculty met with our new chancellor, Gabrielle Weissmuller. In my opinion, she is as fair minded as she is brilliant."

"Here's what is most encouraging." Dylan began to stroll along the front row and make eye contact with some students as he talked. "She spoke about restoring civility to our life here. Disagreements are to be discussed, not reacted to by shouts, accusations and violence."

"I couldn't agree more." Dylan opened his hands and looked up toward the back row. "At my lectures, I want to hear all questions and dissents, but no screaming and shouting someone down. We will share a discussion group email address and I will respond to everyone, either here in person, or by email."

"Our Chancellor also discussed classroom guidelines. Regarding religious statements, attempting to proselytize or change a student's faith remains prohibited. However, references to religion, biblical quotes and the faith of historical figures is allowed in the context of the course material."

Dylan wiped across his forehead. "Whew." He grinned. "I'll be glad to get back to just teaching."

He walked over to the white board, wrote his name and "American History, First Settlers through the Civil War."

He faced his class. "Today, I will give you an outline of what subjects we will explore and review your course materials. To supplement that expensive text you had to purchase, I have two freebies for everyone."

"This summer I wrote excerpts from the DVD series, 'America, our Godly Heritage,' and cross referenced them to your text." He motioned to a stack of papers on a side table. "Could I have four volunteers to pass them out?"

"Secondly, you will all receive a free copy of the Bible, courtesy of The Campus Crusade." He gestured to students who stood at tables in the back of the room, waving enthusiastically. "I made them put their hand on one of those Bibles and *promise,* while they're in this room, at least, not to slip you their literature or proselytize." Scattered laughter heard around the room.

At the board Dylan wrote:

1) Early settlers: why they came and the meaning of State Established Religion.

2) Slavery: it's establishment by the King and our hard fought road to end it. Also, unsung black heroes.

3) American education: The first 240 years of teaching Bible and morality in our public schools.

4) Our Declaration of Independence and its relationship to the first Great Spiritual Awakening.

5) The Revolutionary War: a series of victories against overwhelming odds attributed to Divine Providence.

6) Our Constitution: Based on biblical teaching, the unique champion of individual liberties, and the most enduring constitution the world has ever seen.

7) The Industrial Revolution: Led by American creativity and individuals able to profit from their abilities.

8) The Civil War: Our victory for human rights and freedom for all mankind.

Dylan faced the class. "There we have it folks. This will be a course full of controversy and challenges, but I think that's the fun part.

"Dissenting opinions are welcome and they will be discussed and analyzed, not shouted out with threats of violence. Ultimately, we will seek to find truth, and knowing truth will free our minds to better cope with our turbulent world.

"One last introductory note will serve to help us understand what has made America unique in this world. I think I can say without challenge that human beings like to be in control. Until the United States came along, nations were governed by one or a few holding control.

"I think the conclusion of Lincoln's Gettysburg Address summarizes our uniqueness better than anyone else could."

A screen image came on and Dylan recited: "(We resolve) that this nation, under God, shall have a new birth of freedom—and that government of the people, by the people and for the people shall not perish from the earth."

Dylan returned to pacing along the front row. "So, as we study American greatness and uniqueness consider those who would, with selfish motives, progressively *regress* us toward a society *of* the government, *by* the government and *for* the government."

FUTURE TRUTH

Six years have past since Dylan Coz returned to Berkard as a tenured professor. A few of his colleagues still snub him and some students shout insults at him as he walks about on campus, but he has won respect and many new friends.

Dylan is patient with students who challenge the importance of Christianity in our American heritage. As the course unfolds, reality blossoms and propaganda runs from the light of truth. His students begin their life outside the university with greater knowledge, but more importantly, they begin with a measure of wisdom.

After Chancellor Stengel resigned amid the scandal and subsequent conviction, Gabrielle Weissmuller replaced him. She was more moderate and open to the expression of all viewpoints.

Aimee West, Dylan, and some others founded the "Patrick Henry Debate Challenge," an event held once each semester with Gabrielle's blessing.

The subject of the first debate was, "Governments: Republics vs. Socialist States." One student in the audience began to shout accusations and insults at the debater who was championing the Republic. Everyone expected the security team to escort the writhing, cursing student out the door, but instead the guards took him on stage to a debate podium holding him in place as he kept trying to run away. The video of his arguments collapsing before the student debater he had been cursing became a You Tube classic.

*   *   *

Now let's turn to TV. Today's broadcast of the Hammer Time show is concluding.

Charles Hammer raps his gavel and grins at the camera. "And that's all the time we have, but I saved two minutes to tell you about a change in programming starting tonight. Hammer Time will be followed by a brand new News Box show about to debut in the next time slot.

"It's safe to say we have all grown to love our sassy, freckle-faced, PC squashing, truth warrior, Lisa Combes, a reporter for the Oakland Flame. Ratings have spiked every time she rides her motorcycle over to the Box and we have had to hire someone just to handle her fan, and her hate mail.

"Lisa débuted on my show six years ago and nailed a murderer that very day. Reginald Luchow is behind bars and his father resigned from Congress in disgrace, both a result of her investigative reporting.

"Lisa has withstood withering criticism but has instinctively known how to fire back." He chuckled. "Sometimes quite *literally*. She comes from a no nonsense military family, you see. Her father and brother are still serving in the Marines. Lisa married a former Oakland police officer and lives in suburban LA with her two children.

The screen splits showing Lisa sitting at a glass desk and sporting a wide grin. Hammer continues, "My only regret about her new show is that it might knock my ratings out of the top slot."

"Never happen," she says.

"Welcome, Lisa." He chuckles. "Tell our viewers: what do you think led to your success, and I have to ask, why did you insist on wearing that outfit? I know for a fact that your producer begged you to wear something glamorous."

Lisa fluffed up the shoulder tops of a camouflage shirt and lightly touched a pink flower in her hair. "Thank you Charles, and thanks to News Box for believing in me. I also want to thank an inspiring professor, Dylan Coz, who opened my eyes to those practicing deception, and to my parents for their 'tough love'."

"My Dad *dared* me to wear this shirt, much to the horror of everyone else." She pinched the shirt at both shoulders again and wiggled it. "See, Dad, this is for all who serve. The flower is to remind me that I serve first and foremost under our loving Lord. Quite simply, if we all partnered with Him and followed His word, we would have the answer to all our world problems."

The view switches to a full screen of Lisa. "We have a busy show for you tonight, folks. I'll interview the Dean of a Christian College and we'll discuss his strategy for bringing truth and balance back into our educational system. We've also got Professor Aimee West, the brightest Constitutional lawyer I know. She will unpack those crazy Liberal lawsuits for us.

"Forgive me if I get emotional when I introduce Melody Jones, the campus crusader I've written about. She's the teenage daughter of Hayley Jones. She sports a black belt in Karate—a belt with 'truth' printed on it, a golden voice and a heart full of God's love.

"My last highlighter tonight will be my interview with a former Fabian Socialist who walked away from their promised utopia. For his protection, you will not see his face and true name. He is ready to totally uproot the longstanding scheme to destroy our American government and our way of life. Stay close, people."

On screen, the Earth appears with orange lines shooting out from one point and circling the globe. The background song plays: "What the world needs now, is love, love, love." The image fades into the cartoon of a woman sitting on top of the world and fishing. She reels in the word "truth" in the shape of a fish.

The view fades back to a close up of Lisa's smiling, freckled face. "Good evening, everyone and welcome. You're watching 'The Lisa Line'."

AUTHOR'S AFTER THOUGTS

The Democratic Party of "Ask not what your country can do for you, but what you can do for your country" died with the bullet that killed President Kennedy. Previously, Fabian Socialism progressed with only nibbling bites, but recently it consumes that party and our American republic by the mouthful. You will recall that the Fabians morphed into the Progressives, but their strategy of gradual conquest remains.

The wolf beneath the sheep's clothing on their shield logo is now revealed. Progressive Socialists truly believe that "we the people," the "deplorables," should not be allowed to continue governing ourselves, but need to be taught and ruled by the elitist few for our own "good." They demand that their flawed ideological vision must replace ours and scream out their "cause" in false outrage and unjustified virtue signaling.

The present government stemming from the American Revolution must be obliterated if the elitists are to rule. First, they plan to destroy the economy by promising everything free, causing massive debt and monetary collapse. They hope to nationalize industry and confiscate wealth with the big lie about man causing global warming that will destroy the Earth in a decade. Next, they plan to kill our precious individual human rights with a massive influx of grateful foreigners, thus transferring our rights to the collectivist whole.

Finally, they must destroy our laws founded in God's morality by demonizing these values, substituting propaganda and substituting "alternate facts" for true history. They would replace God with a humanistic pseudo morality. In short, they would have us worship man rather than his Creator.

Today's Progressives publicly embrace Socialism, including the nationalization of all corporations. The wolves no longer feel the need for their sheep costumes, yet their policies would implode our nation in the same way all pure socialist empires have in the past. Socialism is adolescent Communism and a direct path to a nation ruled by a few elitists for their own benefit.

The primary tools the elitists use in their planned treasonous overthrow of the United States are: weaponizing intelligence (FBI, CIA, NSA), appointing judges to "rewrite" laws, accusing and prosecuting others of the crimes the elitists themselves are committing, disinformation by the media, virtue-signaling, and exalting sin with feigned "righteous" outrage toward any who hold opposing views. They believe their collectivist victory must be won at all costs, and this justifies domestic terrorism like Antifa.

Massively financed for global conquest, these elitists have successfully placed sympathetic workers in our schools, universities, government and the media; so, disinformation, revised history and science are instilled in everyone, especially our youth. They hope to replace truth with their false narrative and propaganda.

The elitists teach students that the fruit of your labor belongs to the State (them) and should be redistributed to others as they see fit. They are collectivists describing the world in terms of a "victim-oppressor mentality" while concealing their plans to be the ultimate oppressor. Truth is offensive hate speech to them and must be repressed and shouted down lest it expose the lies and deception that lurk below.

For 270 years the Bible was part of our educational system, but seventy years ago it was banned by Progressive ideology and replaced by a humanist morality which rejects anything from God. Professors at secular universities are now overwhelmingly liberal. When challenged, they and their indoctrinated students, respond with hateful vilification and personal attacks. Dissenters are labeled as bigots, haters, racists, supremacists, deplorables, sexists, Nazi fascists, or just stupid. Their "debate" tactic is to shout their accusations, often laced with profanity and violence. Simply put, they have declared war on truth and the way of life America has enjoyed for over two hundred years.

Abraham Lincoln is credited with the remark: "You can fool all the people some of the time but only some of the people all the time." The cherished goal of the Progressive politicians is to get those "some of the people" up to 51%.

This story took place in a fictitious university, but it was based on current events. Many phrases are quoted from professors and the media, but the story line is fictional. The author hopes that more of us will once again proclaim truth without fear, so that those who are "fooled all the time" will become an ever decreasing fraction of American citizens.

Finally, do not lose heart in the face of persecution. To paraphrase Romans 8:31: If you stand with God and in His truth, who can stand against you?

A PRAYER FOR AMERICA

Just as it was in Ephesus, "Let this nation remember from where we have fallen. Repent and do the things you did at first." Rev. 2:5. Pray that our hearts will not be "hardened by the deceitfulness of sin." Heb. 3:13. Pray also that "our eyes be opened so we may turn from darkness to light, from Satan to God." Acts 26:18.

Pascal John Imperato began writing fiction in Junior High, became a literary editor in High School, and wrote short stories in Creative Writing classes at Johns Hopkins University. Getting a Medical Degree at Duke University, and beginning a medical practice in Pennsylvania temporarily resulted in scientific and journal writing. After a born again revelation, he resumed fiction writing, but with a messianic twist under the pen name, "John Pascal." He has published Sci-Fi, "The Revelation Trilogy" novels: "The Bee," "Domes," and "2248;" also a two book angel series: "Wingin' It," and "My Child." "Prisoner 1171" is a novel focusing on the disabled and evangelism in prison. "Fatherless" deals with street gangs and human trafficking. Details at "JOHNPASCAL.com".

Pascal writes in Fallbrook California.

www.ingramcontent.com/pod-product-compliance
Lightning Source LLC
Chambersburg PA
CBHW030540260626
47157CB00006B/2119